PRAISE FOR *THE BEAU*

T0007265

"How far will a mother go to save her son when both need a new start? To her adoring fans, Josie Nickels has the perfect life. As an Emmy winning news anchor, she peers into the lens of the camera and wows her adoring fans. However, beyond the twinkling lights and her promising career, Josie's family secrets threaten and during a moment of emotional stress, Josie can no longer juggle the life she's polished to perfection. In *The Beautiful Misfits*, Susan Reinhardt has penned a powerful novel that encapsulates how the bond of motherhood can unravel, fray to the point of breaking, yet with love, hope and hard work, be reborn into something stronger than we can imagine."

- Renea Winchester, award-winning author of *Outbound Train*

"With grace, humor, and honesty, Susan Reinhardt delivers an important novel about the tragic opioid and drug addiction gripping our country. But, at its core, *The Beautiful Misfits* is the story of a mother's unconditional love for her son and her unwillingness to give up on him. Weaving humor and heartbreak, Reinhardt reveals what it's like for a woman to walk the almost indistinguishable lines between loving and enabling and letting go and holding fast. This is a book with heart and hope. Don't miss it!"

- Tracey Buchanan, author of *Toward the Corner of Mercy and Peace*

"Susan Reinhart is a Southern treasure, and one of those rare authors who can evoke laughter and tears. *The Beautiful Misfits* also reveals her keen eye for detail and a well-turned phrase. It's a poignant tale you won't soon forget."

- Karin Gillespie, author of *Love Literary Style*

"Susan is a wonderfully gifted storyteller who combines biting wit and laugh-out-loud humor with a beautifully moving writing style. She can turn tears of laughter into the other kind in a single paragraph. You'll love The *Beautiful Misfits.*"

– Robert Tate Miller, bestselling author and movie screenwriter for CBS, NBC, Disney, and Hallmark including films such as *When Christmas was Young, Three Days,* and *A Summer Romance*

"Reinhardt writes from the heart on the serious problem of rampant drug addiction—but always with the warmth and humor her long-time readers know to expect. A wealth of finely drawn characters populate this lively look at a single mother fighting her own demons and trying with all her might to save her drug-addicted son."

– Vicki Lane. author of *And the Crows Took Their Eyes* and the *Elizabeth Goodweather Appalachian* mysteries

"In her newest novel, *The Beautiful Misfits,* Susan Reinhardt wraps all the emotions with beautiful imagery. She balances darkness and pain with the light and joyful moments of a family coping with addiction and secrets. Throughout her novel, while all her characters have their own struggles, she continues to give us signs of hope and signals that sometimes life works itself out long before we are conscious of its plans. A beautiful read where you connect with the beautiful misfits. This is one story that touched my heart."

– Lee St. John, #1 Amazon bestselling author, Georgia Author of the Year, Erma Bombeck Humor Writer

THE BEAUTIFUL MISFITS

Susan Reinhardt

Regal House Publishing

To my son, Niles

There is an endearing tenderness in the love of a mother to a son that transcends all other affections of the heart.

—Washington Irving

You were wanted. This is what you need to know.

Plans don't guarantee joy. Perfect timing isn't the only companion of contentment.

Sometimes, it's the unplanned that takes us from our own ideals. And on that one-way ride where return tickets aren't for sale.

I'm glad you're here. I wept when I knew.

A good weep. That heart-growing kind where you realize this is your chance.

I pray I will get it right.

There is nothing you will do to mute the music of love my heart forever plays.

I'm here now. I'm here tomorrow.

Please know…I'm going nowhere but on this journey with you.

THE UNRAVELING

MARCH 10, 2017

In ten minutes, Josette Nickels would go live with the day's news, just as she'd done every evening without incident for the past twenty years.

Atlanta loved her, viewers trusted her, and no matter the mayhem churning behind the closed doors of her ridiculous Victorian Gothic, she'd always separated her career from the scandals.

Such was the way of Southern women who'd grown up with duplicitous mothers keen on parceling affection. Hadn't Josie learned from the best how to live as two? As a woman who was perfect. And another who was not.

She'd not slept well the night before, her room aglow with aggressive moonlight charging through fine cracks in the blackout drapes. She'd watched the clock from the haunting pre-dawn hours, until she'd eventually given up and thrown off the covers.

By the time her dinner break rolled around, a tremor plucked at her fingertips and her silk blouse fluttered against a heart unsure of its next beat. Certainly, a couple of drinks would help, though she'd never—until then—consumed on the job.

A little tequila, two shots tops, was no worse than a pinch of Xanax. What woman wouldn't in her circumstance?

She could do this, get through tonight, then go home to reassess. That suitcase in her trunk loaded with sundresses and swimsuits meant nothing. All women need a packed bag on standby, one of the many lessons her mother had taught by example.

As she walked into the studio, minutes from going live, her

legs gave way as if boneless. She grabbed a desk and fell into the chair.

"Josie?"

"I'm okay," she lied to her producer. "Should have worn flats." She slipped on her mic and the in-ear monitoring and cueing system. The room seemed to move, like blacktop wavering under August steam. The walls rolled and the floor pulsed, but Josie managed to reach her anchor desk where she closed her eyes, willing a calm that would not come. When she opened them, she muttered her mantra: *Flip the switch.* Turn on the journalism mode and click off the personal.

One last time, she went over the shot sheet telling her which camera she'd look into for each story.

With three minutes to spare, she practiced the top story from the prompter.

And it was *that* story that shot a stream of sweat down her spine, pooling at the waistband of her granny-like Fruit of the Looms. Panties for champions. Panties for women who despise tugging out wedgies and who don't have a significant other in their lives.

"Let's roll." Her producer's deep baritone rang in her ears. "In five, four, three, two, one."

Josie cleared her throat and faced the lights, the cameras, and tens of thousands of viewers she couldn't see. But they saw her. On what would become her final evening she'd join them in living rooms and kitchens throughout a sizable chunk of Georgia.

"Good evening." Both hands trembled on the cold glass desk, mug of water to her left and laptop in the center. "I'm Josie Nickels and tonight we bring you a story of loss and laws never before enacted until now. For the first time in decades, a district attorney's office has charged a suspected drug dealer with murder following a heroin overdose." Her voice cracked and her lower belly rippled. Her entire body blazed as if she were melting from inside.

The teleprompter blurred, words fading in and out of focus.

She inhaled deeply and faced her viewers. More than ever, she wished her co-anchor were present and not home sick with the flu.

"According to arrest warrants, Adam Lamond Richardson, nineteen, of Courtside Drive in Dekalb County, reportedly killed twenty-year-old Grace Turbyfill with 'malice' caused by the unlawful distribution of heroin. Detectives believe Richardson administered the narcotic himself, causing the fatal overdose of the young woman, a sophomore studying psychology at the University of Georgia."

Her heart flipped and her throat squeezed. She reached for her water, ignoring the alarm written across her producers' faces.

She panted and sucked at the air, trying to get something into her lungs before she passed out. The station cut to a commercial, and the news crew suggested a reporter take over the anchor spot. "I'm fine," Josie said. "I just need to breathe through this little panic attack."

"You're too close to this story," one of the female producers said, placing a hand on her shoulder.

"It's okay. Really."

"Your son's still missing. Now this girl, his friend, is dead. Please, let Jessica fill in. Fucking Rob out sick again."

She thought of her children: her late-in-life daughter, Dottie, just three and born with Down syndrome. And her son, that once-beautiful little boy who'd clutched weedy flowers in his sweaty hands, pressing the blooms against her waist. A child she'd never in her darkest dreams imagined on the run, his monsters following close.

"Trust me. I'm good to go."

Back on the air, Josie paused and listened to the beeps of technology. She took in the whispers of her colleagues, aware their eyes flashed uncertainty. She exhaled with force and wiped her wet hands across her pink Calvin Klein shift, then over her mouth, smearing her matching lipstick and tasting chemicals beneath the berry flavor. She swallowed hard, the tequila sour and fiery in her chest.

Josie held up a hand and gave the camera a *one moment, please*. That's when the seams began ripping like a torn sheet and the padlock twisted and popped. Everything she'd worked for since she was eleven years old turned to shit. Straight-up shit.

That's also when she should have stepped away from the desk and let Jessica take over, because what she said next, those eighty-four seconds of spewing her business like a Baptist at altar call, went viral. And that virus snuffed out her Emmy-winning ride.

But more importantly on this day, beneath that full thieving moon, her mistake, her giant screwup, robbed her of the only man who'd ever mattered.

Her son, Finley.

And she'd do whatever it took to get him back, if only she could reach him in time.

1

ONE YEAR LATER

Maybe Miranda Lambert was on to something. She knew how to channel her pain and belt out an entire song about hiding all your crazy and acting like a lady. Keeping it together even when your life plunges from flush to flushable.

Josie heard the lyrics in her head as she wriggled eyeliner along her swollen lids and dusted her bloated cheeks with a blush that cost more than a tank of gas, gratis for joining the newest cosmetics line at Brigman's department store. Her hands shook—too much screw-cap chardonnay last night—and a cold trickle of sweat stroked her neck.

The mountain winds howled and threw branches against her kitchen window where she sat at the wobbling dinette set she'd purchased secondhand, along with most of her other furnishings, through a Craigslist divorce sale: HIS STUFF MUST GO!

One woman's heartache spread through every room of Josie's small condo in Asheville, North Carolina, a gorgeous little city in the Blue Ridge Mountains.

This place had walls so thin she could hear the ancient woman next door peeing during the middle of the night and smell her bitter coffee in the mornings. All to the tune of fifteen hundred a month in addition to the three-hundred-dollar homeowners fees just to trim the rhododendron and mow a slice of turf the size of an army cot.

She'd packed the tattered leftovers of her former life into a small, ten-foot U-Haul and thrown the last of her savings into a down payment on the patio home. She had no idea until she moved in that it was a retirement community, a final destination for octogenarians. Her eager realtor had conveniently left out that tidbit. But Josie figured she'd rather live with cane-walkers than crackheads.

It wasn't much, but the place was hers. A one-level, three-bedroom rectangle with everything, including the appliances, the color of dinner rolls. Even the kitchen floor, vinyl and patterned in fake tile, complied with the monochromatic theme. She wadded a tissue and tucked it under a metal leg, steadying the table and herself as she applied the requisite full face of makeup in a bath of natural light.

Ribbons of cool air slid through single-pane windows, and Josie shivered and tightened her bathrobe. April in the mountains was nothing like April in Atlanta weatherwise. She closed her eyes and pulled in a breath so deep her lungs ached. After counting ten beats, she puffed out the air and vowed to scoop up what she had left in her falling-down life. She'd navigate that charred and smoking wake of her public shit-show last year and suit up, show up, and slap a smile on her face.

Other women did it. They slid on their lipstick and pearls (maybe nose rings) and marched through their days *as if*. Not all *what-the-fuck*. Those women didn't give up on life until stiff arms crossed their Sunday best beneath the cold, hard dirt.

She popped a K-Cup into the Keurig and startled at the sound of rhythmic taps on her front door. Dottie toddled half-dressed into the kitchen chanting, "Ruby, Ruby here."

"Little bug, can you wait in the living room for Ruby? It's too chilly for you to be in here in nothing but a flimsy dress." The sweet child, still sing-songing her babysitter's name, returned to her cartoons.

Josie, one ankle boot on and the other in her hand, opened the door. A frenzied gale blew its way into the condo, scattering the paper plates and plastic forks across the kitchen counter and onto the floor.

"Hurry in, Ruby. Mercy, I believe God's having a tantrum out there."

The elderly babysitter burst into the kitchen, flicking away the silvery wisps of hair stuck against her road-cone-orange lipstick. "The wind is but a reminder that we are alive, dear girl," she said, pushing the door shut. "It's a hug from God. Pranayama breathing. Maybe that Lion's Roar breath where you have to stick out your tongue like a fool."

Ruby smelled of patchouli and lavender, a soothing scent that slowed Josie's heart rate. It was how Finley smelled the last time she'd felt his arms around her neck, all those months ago. "Please forgive the mess. I'm in a frenzied state trying to look halfway decent for this ridiculous test today. You'd think I was preparing for the MCAT, not cramming the eight rules for a perfect brow."

Ruby laughed, a strumming like harp chords. Even the way she walked, gliding as though her feet never touched the ground, made Josie wonder if the woman was even real or someone she had conjured during her prayers.

Ruby set her North Face backpack on the table and shucked off the hand-painted wrap that reminded Josie of Dolly Parton's *Coat of Many Colors*. The woman was eighty-five and devoted to flow and yin yoga, books by Eckhart Tolle, and living every day as if she'd been given a sudden expiration date. There was hardly a wrinkle on her, no neck folds piled up like a sharpei's skin.

"This makeup counter job may not be on par with the work you used to do, but that store is lucky to have you," she said and placed a gentle hand on Josie's arm. "Have you heard anything from your son?"

"Just that he's missing again. This time somewhere down in Florida. No one's seen or heard a word from him." Thoughts of Finley throttled Josie's pulse. A rising panic clawed at her sternum. Her once sweet and innocent baby boy, the infant she'd watch as he slept, fearing he wouldn't wake up, was now a troubled young man with jangling bones and hollowed, hunting eyes. The thought of it threatened to pull her under.

"He'll come around. Boys can take a good while to grow up. My second—no, may have been my third—husband was way too bonded to his toddler brain."

Josie managed a weak laugh, although everything in her primal, maternal mind pushed for her to race to Florida and cruise the seediest parts of town searching for her son, stun-gun and pepper spray in her glovebox. Right next to the three boxes of Narcan, a nasal spray that reverses opioid overdoses.

"Ruby, I'm done with the chasing." To say it made it real. It needed to be real. Her therapist said if she kept up this one-sided fight, she'd lose her mind. Again. "You can't imagine how many times I've driven crazed and red-eyed through three states hunting him down." Josie remembered those nights, snagging sleep in the back seat of her car or fetal-curling in a sixty-dollar motel where the unwashed bedspread reeked of sin and booze.

Ruby rubbed her palms and placed them between her breasts in what she called her hands-to-prayer pose. She hovered in the tiny kitchen and searched the ceiling as she often did when thinking. "He's what? Twenty-three years old? It's past time to let him go. Love him, of course. But until he's ready for a better life, he has to make his own decisions. You know good and well from what happened that night on TV how important self-care is, right?"

A volcano stays dormant only so long, Josie wanted to say. Everything in life has a tipping point.

"I think these mountains are helping. Everywhere I go I feel like I'm in a painting. So it's good I put a state or two between my...anyway."

"We are so blessed to live among such grandeur. The greatest works of art are born of nature. Mountains teach patience and acceptance. They are healers in disguise."

She hugged Ruby, and it was like grasping an object so fragile it might vanish. "I could listen to you all day, but this job is the only way I keep semi-sane and maintain a roof over our heads. I'd hate to waltz in late on testing day. Making women beautiful is my only marketable skill these days."

Josie moved to the sink and refilled the Keurig for Ruby. "I've got Dottie's clothes laid out. She's wearing the same Elsa costume she's had on for a week. I'm glad I got two of those dresses. Stubbornness can sometimes crop up with her diagnosis. Or it could be that she's four. Don't be surprised if she plays Adele all day. Or worse, Katy Perry."

"Everything will be fine, Josie Divine. Dottie's a delight and your son will come around, but only when he's ready. Meantime, you look like you need more rest, my dear girl. Not that you aren't a beauty. What I'd give to have your skin."

Josie pressed a palm to her face. "Wine again. And another Taco Bell dinner."

"Perhaps that's a step up from your beloved Burger King. Oh, I used to drink. Caused me nothing but problems and divorces." She spread her skinny arms upward, a silver and turquoise bracelet sliding to her elbow. "I slept with men who sure didn't deserve me and woke up one time with a fellow as fat as a swollen manatee and toothless. Rather, he may have had one or two loose and hiding in the back. Now my only highs come from endorphins. Yoga is pure tequila without the headaches."

"Tequila, huh? Never again for me," Josie said, trying to stay calm despite threadbare nerves. She threw her boots in the hall closet and slipped on flats, hoping no one would notice she'd cut out the backs. The only shoes worth wearing were those with open toes or exposed heels. Shoes that gave a woman freedom. Room for escape.

That's why she never wore Spanx. She'd bought a pair of their leggings last week and two hours into her shift she'd had enough. To hell with tummy control. Struggling to breathe, she'd reached for a box cutter, and with a quick flash of the blade, the vise-like waistband ripped and her skin expanded, the grooves in her belly not smoothing out for hours.

Ruby opened the fridge and took out a pint of strawberries. "It's been a good twenty years since I imbibed. Now, if I end up in the nursing home, I'd take it up again. Might make those fellows mumbling in the hallways strapped to their wheelchairs look more appetizing. It's just that now I've got too much real living left in me to cloud it all out with that poison. We're not here on this earth for long. Goes by in a blip."

Ruby had a way of talking that was more a run-on commentary, hands and arms joining in the action and rarely waiting for the other party's response until her monologue was complete. Others might find this annoying, but it reminded Josie of her daddy, and her heart tightened every time she thought of him. She missed the way he made her feel loved "as is." Not the fixer-upper her mother viewed her as being. She thought of that TV show, *Love It or List It*. If Josie were a home, her mother wouldn't think twice about listing it. Be done with it all.

Josie checked the time, then yanked the trash bag from the plastic can and tied the strings. Wine bottles clinked, and she cringed, wondering how many she'd emptied in the last few days.

As she brushed past Ruby and maneuvered the trash toward the door, her daughter squealed and ran into the kitchen, demanding to watch *Frozen*. Josie dropped the bag, smothered Dottie in kisses, and scooped her into the air to fly.

After she got the movie going, she fished in her purse for cash. "Here's a little extra money, Ruby. I thought if it got nicer outside you might want to take Dottie to that nature zoo down by the river."

Ruby swatted the bills. "You go on to work and don't fret over us. We might take in the new gallery that opened up in the River Arts District or visit the mineral museum. Culture and fine cuisine are everything, and I have a great-niece who also has Down syndrome, so I know precisely how to handle this cherub. And you do realize that since I began doing my Improv classes at the comedy club in West Asheville that—"

"Hold your downward dogs, Miss Ruby," Josie said, trying to keep the woman's opinions in check so she could make it to work on time. She couldn't imagine the embarrassment of being late on testing day. Not that she wasn't super grateful for the woman whose last name said everything.

My name is Ruby Necessary, she'd announced the day they met—the day this woman just *appeared* at her doorstep, as if she knew where she was needed. *As in you'll find it quite necessary to know me. Before you even ask, yes, this is my real name courtesy of my fifth and possibly final husband and not something I concocted and had legalized at the registrar's office.*

When Josie had asked Ruby where she was from, the woman had all but floated and said, *Here and there. I go wherever I'm needed.* And she most definitely was needed here. At this geriatric compound of patio homes where the streets were named for end-of-life metaphors.

Ruby puckered her lips and kissed the air. "Go, shoo, and good luck with the makeup ladies. You have a gift. I love how you made me look so deliciously sexy the other night. Heck, I might get me a new fellow one of these days, but he'd have to be in his forties, give or take, and, naturally, be a progressive. I sure wish Barack Obama wasn't married."

Josie paused in the hallway, taking in the warm scene: Dottie nestled on the couch cushions, worried about nothing more than her next snack and movie. Then an image of Finley flashed and her stomach rolled. Where was he at this moment? Was he hungry? Lonely and strung out? Maybe she should try calling again. Maybe she should phone the store and claim illness. She could drive down to Florida, promising herself this would be the last time she chased after him.

She shook her head at the thought. What good what it do?

Ruby followed Josie to the door. "Remember," the elderly woman said, "that if perfection eludes us, what we have in the moment is enough." She opened her palms as if to receive a blessing. "May peace be with you. May. You. Be. Peace."

"Today, I shall give peace a chance," Josie said, knowing this was unlikely, and stepped outside into a blinding morning sun and tempestuous wind that belonged to March instead of late April. After she set out the garbage, she flicked her key fob to unlock the car, jumping back as if shot. Something hard had slammed into her side.

Below her feet, a fat newspaper lay heavy and damp. She didn't take the local paper. She received her news through digital subscriptions to the *New York Times* and the *Washington Post*.

Josie studied the gray lump and decided it must have been meant for the widow next door. Older people enjoyed the solidity of newspapers, and at least ninety percent of this complex packed their refrigerators with Ensure and milk of magnesia. Sunset Villas was no more than a final pit stop before Glory, a little tidbit her realtor left out as she raved over the amenities. *There's a lap pool, state-of-the-art gym, and two defibrillators right on site.*

Nothing like going to a bank or paying bills and writing her address: 34 Could Be Worse Court. At least she didn't live on DNR Drive.

Defibrillators. Mercy.

She held the wet paper between her thumb and forefinger. Where had it come from? Surely it didn't just drop out of the sky. She got in the car and tossed the newspaper onto the floorboard, then looked up and saw movement from the corner of her eye. The café curtains in the kitchen window fluttered. And just before they closed, she glimpsed Ruby, a half-smile on her lips.

As Josie started the car, she grimaced at her reflection in the rearview mirror, the wind's handiwork making her hair look as if she'd been on her back all night. Doing what? Fornicating? It had been so long since the last time, she'd probably need an instruction manual: *The Born-Again Virgin's Guide to the Mattress Mambo.*

During the ten-minute commute to work, her tankish car was no match for this spring typhoon and jerked like a dog against its leash. The sudden slap of brutal air chilled the leather beneath her leggings. She didn't think she'd ever get used to this mountain weather, fickle as a preteen girl and just as unpredictable. One day cold. The next like gulping steam. Raining at her condo. Sunny and clear less than a mile down the road.

She rolled down the windows, hoping to blow away her hangover, but as she inhaled, her eyes watered and her hair whipped her cheeks. She mumbled, in random order, a litany of daily affirmations and prayers. Anything to keep her tethered. "Be strong, be brave. Live in the moment. Count all blessings.

You are a good mother. You are not afraid. You are happy as a size 16, even though a year ago while on television you once squeezed into sixes, even if it was just for a few weeks. Embrace this day with grace and gratitude. Lord, make me an instrument of thy peace. Please give me another chance with Finley. Keep him safe and send him back home.

"Keep me, O Father and/or Mother, from the wine and drive-throughs. Instill in my body the desire to exercise and let go of things I can't control. Don't let me be led astray by another man. One-and-a-half was enough. I say 'half' because I woke up with that one man I hardly remember after my TV breakdown and I'm still not sure if I slept with him in the biblical sense. Please forgive me for my wrongs, Jesus, Lord, Buddha, dear Gandhi, and Mother Teresa.

"All of you know, I need to stay away from starting a relationship. I mean, not that I have any takers, but just in case, tinfoil my heart in resistance. Go ahead and just duct-tape it, and please, lead me to that second chance with Finley. Help me figure out a way to reach him without enabling him. And also allow me, please, to get to him before you do, if you catch my drift.

"PS Thank you! For Ruby. I know you all had a hand in this."

2

Strange to think that if she failed her certification test this morning, she'd have to *unjoin* the cosmetic artistry team. She'd probably end up banished to the dreaded shoe department, where for twelve bucks an hour she'd spend her days cramming corned and callused feet into stiff leather and coaxing hammertoes into Skechers.

Josie was likely the only woman with a pulse who hated shoes, loathing the way they constricted her feet even when going up a size.

She inhaled sharply. She hadn't felt *this* much pressure facing a camera every evening at her old job. She went over everything she'd be tested on one last time: the creams and serums and which did what. She wondered, smiling, if learning such drivel—*rubbish*, her Anglophile mother had called it—would calcify her brain.

"Oh, Mrs. Jacobs," she said to the rearview mirror, "that bronze lip looks terrific with your auburn highlights."

She glanced at her phone. Only eight minutes. Her pulse tapped against her left temple, never a good sign. She wanted to leave, join Frank, her ex, in the search for Finley. But it was long overdue that she turn on her Wise Brain, suck it up, and move forward with her life.

Another caterwauling blast of wind cut through the mountains and blew into the open parking garage at Brigman's department store, nudging her car as if to assert its dominance. Josie lugged herself against the car door, preparing to make her way toward the gallows. *No, don't think such thoughts. Remember the Emmys. You still have it in you to succeed.*

She certainly wasn't about to let scant and unscrupulous Pauline make a fool of her today. That woman was as lovable as a horsefly. The coworker from hell who'd recruited her to the store for some suspicious reason.

Josie parked and heard a deafening sound. When she stepped from the once-luxurious, now falling-apart BMW 640i Gran Coupe that once belonged to her late father, she saw the source of the noise. Another wheel cap had sprung from the tire and lay defeated on the concrete. She couldn't believe a car that cost more than a decent doublewide had decided to shed its parts. Muffler last Monday, left front wheel cap a week prior, and now the back right wheel cap cracked like an oyster.

Note to self: Check the warranty on the Beemer during lunch today. Second note to self: Sell the car; it's far too pretentious for her taste. She'd buy that Subaru favored by the hippies here in Asheville and pad the extra money in her dwindling checking account. Maybe she'd finally splurge on a new cell phone since hers was half-shattered and the size of a deck of cards.

Josie scooped up the wheel cap and threw it in the back seat where it landed on an empty Arby's bag. Her eyes rested on the unread newspaper on the floorboard. She picked it up, thinking she'd chuck it into the trash, but changed her mind and left it in the car.

Once inside the store, the escalator lowered her into center court where the sounds of associates counting coins and opening cash registers signaled the start of a new day. Hanging LED lights looped from the top of her bay and across the counters. A champagne station bled into part of the shoe department where La Belleza, the new line, had borrowed plush chairs and a sofa for the women to lounge while enjoying nibbles and mimosas. It was La Belleza's procedure to set up all fancy, pop-up-spa style, while an associate underwent certification. What better way to judge and score them as they worked with actual clients between rounds of verbal testing. More like verbal abuse, from all Josie'd been told.

And what better way to lure clients than offering nibbles and bargain-basement sparkling wine, a chance to drink before noon without the guilt.

Josie spotted Pauline prancing, dressed in what looked like children's size 6x black leather pants and a lace cami. Her double-D implants surged beneath a long sheer top. Josie guessed her to be around her age, mid-forties, and saw that she'd already pinned a client to the chair, reminding Josie of those dried insects staked to Styrofoam.

She looked up when she saw Josie and offered a snide smile. "Excuse me a minute, sugar doll," she said to the flawless Hispanic beauty in the chair. "I'll be right back, little lovely, and I promise to bring you that miracle cream called El Milagro our adorable Sergio was selling on QVC last night. We got a shipment in stock."

"Home shopping is for drunks, pillheads, and losers sitting on their sofas and taking government handouts," the woman said, leaving Pauline speechless.

"Fabiana is waiting for you in the back office," Pauline said, pulling Josie aside. "I hope you're prepared for what we have in store for you today." She grinned, revealing oversized veneers her lips didn't cover. Even in repose, she had a mouth that could make a baby cry. "As you're aware, you'll be doing makeovers, so any that result in sales, you be sure and ring them for me."

"Most certainly not," Josie mumbled as she walked past ladies' clothing, the plus-size department, and to the windowless offices where she found Fabiana, La Belleza's account coordinator, seated with a sheaf of papers in the conference room, its long table scattered with Chick-fil-A bags and crumbs from the previous evening.

She stood and extended a hand. "So good to see you again, Josette. I want you to relax and enjoy our little exercise." Josie shook her soft hand. Fabiana, a second-generation Brazilian American, wore a smart black suit edged in white piping, a double-strand of pearls, and a set of spidery false eyelashes. She was a beautiful woman for her age, which was indeterminate, her face a glossed haze of cosmetics and fillers. "Too many girls get uptight and try to overthink it," she said. "Remember, it's just makeup and skincare. We're not curing cancer."

Josie curled her lips into a tight smile and nodded. Her nerves began a slow tap-tapping. Even as she rubbed her arms for warmth, sweat beaded along her hairline. She tried to remember all the products jumbled in her head, but thoughts of Finley pushed at her heart.

"Well, now," Fabiana said, tossing her empty coffee cup into an overfilled wastebasket. "Let's start with the basics and then flow into the demos. Pauline has lined up appointments for you. One on the hour starting at eleven, with a lunch break at two. I'll grade your skills, but it won't be obvious. I'll simply shadow you as if I'm the one trying to learn."

"Sounds good," Josie said, voice emitting an embarrassing squeak. "I'm excited to start." Excited to start? Who says such? She was about as excited as a dog scheduled for neutering.

Josie followed Fabiana into an office. Fabiana closed the door and took a seat behind one of the manager's desks. "Before we begin, you do realize that we brought you from Atlanta because one of our best associates, Pauline, said you would be a valuable asset. With your former public career and such."

She bristled. Fabiana had likely seen the video of her on-air meltdown—the tape Josie couldn't bring herself to watch in its entirety. Those eighty-four seconds that stole her son, her precious little boy turned addict turned missing. But aren't most women, even decent and caring women, allowed one teensy nervous breakdown? At least that's how Josie justified the not-so-Lilliputian stunt she pulled that night on television.

"Asheville is our biggest door," Fabiana said, referring to Brigman's. "We must do everything we can to bring in higher year-end numbers than any other line in this store. And as you know, this means upselling." She folded her hands and paused. "When a woman comes in to buy a mascara, we don't simply pull one from the drawer and ring it up. We suggest…what do we suggest, Josette?" Fabiana stopped, waiting for an answer.

Josie almost raised her hand as if she were in second grade. "We suggest her lashes would be much longer and thicker and in better condition if she paired the mascara with our lash primer." And with that, her IQ plummeted from 140 to 110.

"Perfect. Anything else?"

Josie wiped her palms on her skirt and swallowed. "We ask if she has time for a little service to pamper her."

Fabiana inhaled and closed her eyes. When she opened them, she said, "That's the idea, but here's how we say it: 'Allow me to treat you to a new eye look, perhaps one that will lift the lids without the need for surgery.'"

Josie pushed the chair back to uncross her legs. Her left foot had fallen asleep, and she wanted to hop up and down to wake it up.

"After you give her the eye look of her choice," Fabiana continued, "then it's time to address issues such as crow's feet, puffiness, bags, and dark circles. I always tell my BAs, my beauty advisers, to tap in our Ojos Firmes eye cream because it has an immediate effect. Eight times out of ten it leads to a purchase."

Josie nodded, her head like a flashing strobe. All she wanted to do was check her phone to see if Frank had any news related to Finley. He was her only connection to her son and he'd blocked her after the on-air incident. It was a crazy dance, and Frank called only when it suited him or when he wanted money. Few things were more panic inducing than not being able to reach your children.

"So, how would you close this sale?" Fabiana asked and placed a fist under her chin.

Josie knew what Fabiana wanted to hear. "Shall I put all this on your Brigman's card today and give you the chart on how to use these wonderful products at home?" *Be kind. Be nice. Get through this bullshit because it's a job that pays enough to keep a roof and essentials.*

Fabiana twisted her dark-red mouth. "Okay, not bad. But you must always try to work into the consultation how using our line can prevent facelifts and such down the road. You could add something like, 'Prevention is the key to avoiding expensive surgeries.'"

Oh god. Josie wanted to go home. She endured another

half hour of such ludicrous scenarios before Fabiana scribbled the last of her notes and directed Josie to the counter where Pauline's client sipped a mimosa as she awaited her La Belleza experience. Josie figured she'd already blown the big Q&A with Fabiana, so she had to shine during the live consults and makeovers.

She exchanged a look with her friend Monica, who mouthed, "Bathroom. Now."

"I need to freshen up a little if that's okay," Josie said to Fabiana. "I'll be quick. A jiffy." Oh, Lord. Why was her speech so juvenile when nervous?

"Two minutes," Fabiana said.

She found Monica at the mirror brushing a pink color onto her white cheeks.

"I don't think I can do this," Josie said, peering under stalls for feet. Seeing no one, she continued, "You should have seen Pauline seethe when we walked up. There's something up with her…I don't know."

Monica flipped her head to fluff her straight black hair, which had no intention of showing signs of body. But with a figure like hers, hair shouldn't be a concern. Josie would love to have a shape like Monica's. Not too thin, curved where it counts, long legs, Hilary Swank arms, and full pouting lips, not filler inflated. "She was dead set on them hiring you," Monica said. "She's a hard one to figure out, but don't feel bad. She steals all our sales too. Except for Philly's. She's scared of that one."

Josie rearranged her hair, hoping the hair spray from this morning would keep its hold in the back. "I'm going to do my best to ignore most of her comments."

"Hey, listen, Philly's coming back from her little sabbatical today." Monica grinned like a child expecting Santa. "You've got to meet this crazy-ass ex-supermodel working over in Lancôme. She comes in at noon and I'll bet she'll do her announcements. That ought to make Pauline lose her cool."

Josie had no idea what she meant but was ready for anything

to distract Pauline. "I'd better head back," she said, giving Monica a quick hug. As soon as she rounded the corner, she heard a rip. Her skirt had caught on a clothing bar and a six-inch gash gaped, her underwear now in full view of the Lord and everybody. Thankfully, the counter had a stapler.

When she returned, Pauline was boring her client to death, still yammering about Sergio and what he peddles on QVC. "He can simply transform a woman to her supremeness," she said, while Fabiana beamed, reminding Josie of a proud dance mom hanging on to every word. "He gives us all the chance to be Venezuelan-caliber beauties."

"And to avoid costly surgeries down the road," Fabiana chimed in while the client reached her limit and made a call, scowling and speaking rapid Spanish into her phone.

"Okay, Josette," Fabiana said, nodding toward a woman waiting on the sofa. "Please seat Mrs. Whitson. And offer her another mimosa." Then, quietly, she added, "Booze opens those Prada bags."

The cheapo knockoffs, too, Josie wanted to say, her hand grasping the giant hole in her skirt she'd meant to staple together. She smiled at the middle-aged woman dressed in tailored, lawyer-ish clothes. Clothes like those Josie's mother favored. "Hola, Mrs. Whitson," she said loudly so that Fabiana could hear she was using the official greeting. "Buenos dias and welcome to La Belleza."

Mrs. Whitson winked, olive eyes shining with conspiracy. Josie realized with alarm the woman must have recognized her from the news. "I'll take these for you," Josie said, throwing the client's empty cup and plastic plate into the trash, then stashing her vintage Fendi in a cabinet. Quickly she found some tape and slapped it onto her torn skirt.

As she prepared for the woman's makeover, Fabiana's eyes burned hot on her back. Josie locked eyes with Mrs. Whitson, who winked again. "Would you care for another mimosa before we...we..." God, she was tongue-tied. What was the line they'd learned? "Before we..."

Fabiana interrupted. "Before we get started on the most amazing, skin-glowing, and youth-activating experience you've ever imagined."

Mrs. Whitson focused only on Josie. "Great. I'm all yours," she said with excitement before turning to Fabiana. "Could you please give us a moment?"

Fabiana, pouting, stepped aside to watch her star beauty adviser, Pauline Succop (a.k.a. Suck Up), in action while spouting every cliché La Belleza had ever invented.

Mrs. Whitson reached for Josie's hand. "I want you to know that you saved my son's life." Her eyes swam with tears. "He watched that four-part series you did—*The Heroin Highway: A Millennial Apocalypse*. Watched it over and over and came to me one night and let everything out. I had no idea he was hooked on opiates." Josie handed her a tissue. "He's been clean two years."

Josie's throat knotted. "Thank you. I'm so glad he's doing well." Hearing of other mothers whose kids got clean brought conflicting emotions. She was happy for them. And sad that sobriety eluded her son.

"Not just well," Mrs. Whitson said, still holding Josie's hand. "He lived for a year at that halfway house you helped fund. He's married. Has a job."

She thought of Finley. Was he sleeping in a Florida crack house, feeding his monsters in a filthy den of spent needles and burned soda cans? The gorgeous blue ocean and powdered beaches on the other side of his misery? If he'd been jailed, Frank would have called asking for money as usual. If he'd been in the hospital, both would have been notified.

She could all but smell her son's Dior, witness in horror his ever-diminishing body as the demons fed from him like parasites. He believed that poison would plug holes in his empty places and make love to his mind, forgetting how it fucked his brains.

Not much left she could do. She was numb and had exhausted all avenues. He invited these beasts. Threw out the welcome mat and served them his soul. It was up to him to send eviction notices.

Here she was, able to save other people's children with her words, her works. Just not her own. "That's wonderful he got his life back," Josie said to Mrs. Whitson, a weak spark of hope crackling when hearing of an addict's recovery. "You're overdue a bit of luxury. I know you must have gone through so much."

Fabiana walked up and eavesdropped. Josie'd better tamp down the personal talk and get straight to business. The woman ignored her and continued speaking. "How is your son? Is he doing better?" She had likely read about him in the papers.

Josie noticed Fabiana staring at her with an expression that seemed to say, *Get back on track—the money track.*

"He's...well...I'm not sure." Her voice broke and tears pricked.

"As long as they're breathing, there's hope," Mrs. Whitson said, giving Josie's hand a final grip before letting go.

Fabiana cleared her throat. "Josie, let's start with cleansing her skin." And so the routine and testing began.

"Tell me about your skin and your concerns," Josie said, widening her eyes so Mrs. Whitson knew she was doing as advised.

"Oh, well," she said, playing along. "It's just horrendous. I can't seem to get rid of these dark spots and deep wrinkles. I look like a potholed road in need of a good fill."

Fabiana jumped in, as excited as a kitten lapping up a tin of Fancy Feast. "We've got so many products and serums that can address and cure all that."

"Fabulous," Mrs. Whitson said. "Do you mind stepping back for a while and letting me work with this delightful creature." She tipped her head toward Josie. "No offense. We need a bit of space."

Fabiana's nostrils flared as she spun toward Pauline's client. For the next forty or so minutes, Josie cleansed, toned, moisturized, and applied cosmetics to this woman who spoke her language. A woman who knew how it felt to watch a child turn against his teachings and make choices that could—*would*—kill him. When she finished the makeover, she led Mrs. Whitson to a large mirror facing the entrance where the lighting was perfect.

"Who *is* that woman?" she said, viewing her face from multiple angles. "I want every single thing you've put on my old face."

Josie ran a mental tally. This would come to well over a thousand dollars. "You don't have to buy all this," she whispered.

"I saved more than ten times this when your work gave my son life instead of a funeral," she said, and then addressed Fabiana. "She's a keeper. I'm not sure who you are, but I'd guess from your hovering you're the ringleader. Let me say this. You're a lucky lady to have this one."

Josie flushed as she rang up the massive sale and threw in all sorts of treats and samples.

"We certainly are fortunate," Fabiana said curtly, joining Josie by the register and casting a warning look over the number of samples she was giving away. An hour after Mrs. Whitson left, a second client had also spent a small fortune and loved the look Josie had created.

Then at five past one, all hell broke loose. A third woman, the last before lunch, took her mimosa and a place in Josie's hot seat. This client, nose scrunched as if smelling something unpleasant, wore silk and sneers.

Nothing, absolutely nothing Josie did, suited her. The lip color was tawdry, the brow groomer stained her skin a pinky red, and the serum felt like rancid honey. The perfumes made her sneeze. And the creams, so she said, caused itching and instant inflammation.

Without a second thought, Josie knew the woman was a plant. She saw Pauline watching with a creeping smile. Flustered and weak from hunger, Josie moved to the back side of the counter, out of view, to collect herself.

Monica, from the Clinique counter, rushed over. "I've got your back," she said. "You wait and see." She snickered as she walked back to her bay.

Josie popped a mint into her mouth and returned to the hard-to-please customer. "Shall we try another color palette?" she suggested. "We want to do our best to make sure you—"

The woman wriggled in her chair. She slammed her mimosa on the table and stood as Fabiana lingered next to Josie like lint. "I've decided this line is not for me. I am going back to Estée Lauder immediately to have one of their more skilled girls reverse this facial travesty."

Josie heated with embarrassment. "I'm sorry. We can always—"

"ATTENTION, BRIGMAN'S BEAUTIES!" a woman shouted from the store's intercom system. "Are you hearing me loud and clear, ladies? If you have a hankering for *free* samples of our five-star products, you need to STOP, DROP, AND ROLL ON OVER TO THE LANCÔME COUNTER IMMEDIATELY! No, it's not a fire drill, but we've got a few surprises over here at LANCÔME that might light a fire in your heart. OR…put OUT the fire that Brigman's card is burning in your pocket. And, ladies, don't forget my motto. Say it with me. One, two, three…BETTER LATE THAN UGLY!"

The booming voice, with its slight Jamaican accent, broke apart in laughter. Fabiana clutched her heart as if she were about to meet her maker. The crotchety lady who was waddling to Lauder quickly redirected toward Lancôme.

This must be Philly. Josie adored her already. Pauline's face blazed rose, then red, and peaked at puce.

"ONCE AGAIN, LADIES, STOP AND DROP EVERY-THING AND ROLL ON OVER TO LANCÔME. We'll give you free foundation, or if you prefer, we'll wipe you down, then grease you back up and start from scratch."

Josie peeled off a bark of laughter and clutched her stomach. *Do not laugh, not in front of Fabiana. As soon as you get a break, make a point to meet this woman who seems to enjoy a good gag as much as you do.* Well, used to, before Finley found salvation in substances.

The store grew silent, except for a few laughs from customers and associates. Philly seemed to have finished.

Pauline abandoned her client and beelined around the corner. "Somebody get Philly off the PA right now. Now with a capital *N*! If that woman makes any more announcements during our certification event I'll go—"

"To Mr. Hoven," said a woman as tall as a professional basketball player and with another foot of upswept hair. She pushed her chest right into Pauline's bird face. "Run. Find Mr. Hoven, you little windbag."

"This is our event, Philly, and you've been warned not to make those announcements when other lines are having certification training. Do it again. I dare you."

"Oh, you wait. I've got an entire script for today's menu of glory," Philly said as Pauline turned and stomped off. Fabiana monitored the drama as she sipped a frappuccino.

Finally, she spoke. "You. I need you over here, please." She all but shoved Josie behind a towering shoe display for privacy. "I've seen all I need to see today, so I'm heading back to Charlotte. I'll let you know in a few days my thoughts on an official certification." She exhaled sharply. "And also, whether you're a true fit for this line. Don't think I didn't see that tape running up and down your skirt."

Josie's hand flew to the tear. She'd meant to tie a sweater around her waist but forgot. Maybe she should go ahead and let Fabiana know Pauline had set her up.

Then again, best to just let this all go. She certainly had deeper concerns than cream-to-powder blushes.

Once in her car, after the long, exhausting day, she remembered the newspaper still damp on the seat. She had a peculiar urge to open it, and when she snapped the rubber band, her eyes widened at the headline below the fold. South of the latest Trump news, and a piece on a woman stabbed downtown, someone had circled an article in black Sharpie and included exclamation marks around its borders. *Read this!* Words in the left margin. And words to the right: *It's the only way to save your son!*

She clutched her throat where a fast pulse thrashed. Her breathing turned shallow.

The headline—*Experimental Rehab and Resort Shows Signs of Hope*—stretched across the top photo of two young adults sitting in front of a tiny aqua camper shaped like a canned ham. Three chickens pecked at their feet, and behind the youth, dozens more campers in pink, red, and canary yellow filled the frame. She read the article.

A well-respected and former Atlanta psychologist is gaining attention for his experimental and highly unconventional rebab and resort combination located in Burnsville, forty miles west of Asheville. On a sprawling organic farm surrounded by the Cane River, Vintage Crazy Resort and Rehab is showing promise in recovery rates, an area in which traditional rehabs have too often failed. Paul Gavins has opened what he calls a "cafeteria approach" to treating addiction, meaning the traditional Twelve Steps aren't the only option for addicts. At Vintage Crazy…

Josie shook her head as she read further. This sounded nuts. What kind of rehab gives a person such options as moderation and harm reduction? Medicines to ease cravings? She tossed the paper in the plastic grocery bag she used for trash.

Ridiculous. Another crackpot cashing in on people's fragilities. Whoever meant for Josie to see this had to be deranged. And she was determined to figure it out. Someone knew exactly where she lived. And she'd never told anyone. Not even her mother.

3

Before she became one of them, Josie used to avoid women like herself. She would cast her eyes in another direction as she passed their glass counters, that place where youth is promised for a price.

Many a woman spent idle time prowling these glittering department stores, buying handbags and shoes on credit to ease the brunt of sour marriages and unmet dreams. Buying half-empty promises and believing that something as simple as the perfect cream could restore fire in the cold, darkened places in their lives.

In her previous, pre-meltdown life, Josie had experienced their magazine-ad eyes in smoky hues, matte lips as startling as Anne Hathaway's. They were young and luscious, anxious to succeed. Or they were middle-aged women beautiful in that way of roses two days gone. Outer petals dry and crumbling and those within still vibrant and velvet soft.

They wouldn't give up until they took a final breath, continuing the tillage of their faces, fertilizing the skin with thousands of dollars' worth of products claiming to restore what time had plundered. A second harvest from land once fallow.

They hypnotized potential buyers with three-dimensional displays, banners, and backlit posters of celebrities and models, creating an illusion that anyone, if properly tended, could resemble Natalie Portman, Lupita Nyong'o, and Julia Roberts.

Maybe a potential customer strolled in to buy sheets or towels on sale in the home department. Perhaps something as practical as a Vitamix or a Cuisinart. She might be on her way out the door with a grocery list in her wallet next to her credit cards and yellowing family photos.

But when she passed the counters strategically placed in center court near the exits, if she so much as paused, so much as peeked in their direction or lifted a bottle of perfume for a quick smell, the drawbridge opened. Soon she was submerged, treading floodwaters and knowing only a new Elizabeth Arden lipstick or Lancôme's gel-to-oil night cream would bring her to safety.

Now they had her as they fawned and oozed charm. Their attire was sleek and black. Hair dyed raven or oxidized impossibly platinum. Those beautiful misfits looked so perfect but had personal lives as colorful as any Flannery O'Connor created. Their lives ranged from dramatically heartbreaking to fall-on-the-floor hilarious. Lives salted with the type of absurdity that made them all the more endearing.

The regulars often bonded with those behind the glass. How could they not love a woman with the power to dole out free packets of the latest dark-spot corrector, maybe slip them a leftover mascara or cheek stain from last month's gift-with-purchase?

What choice did those beauty advisers have but to sneak peeks at the logos on a woman's handbag, the size of the diamond flashing against the left finger? Michael Kors? Common and not pricey enough. Louis Vuitton? Maybe, but could be a fake. Chanel or Christian Louboutin? Perfection.

An excellent beauty worker knew that once a woman experienced her warm, rose-and-spun-sugar-scented fingers, working in the creams and serums and touching their faces as no man had in years, the fine lines dissolved. And so did resistance.

Purses opened, credit cards smacked the counter, and a certain type whispered: "Can I just put it all in my pocketbook so my husband won't see the Brigman's bag?"

She would leave the store with at least half a grand or more on her card and a bag stuffed with potions and promises. She'd possess the latest colors, the perfect foundation, and delicate powders illuminating the skin. Her once-sagging eyelids would now rise with strokes of a blending brush, hues that seduced the face north where gravity tap-danced south.

Once a beauty adviser invited a woman to have a seat in her

chair, it was like rolling out the flypaper. That chair, her will-
ingness to enjoy a "free" half-hour service, well…that's when
self-restraint became skin deep.

Now Josie was one of them, a beauty worker in matte lipstick
rolling out the flypaper. As she sat alone in the darkened booth,
waiting for her lunch, tears fell in silence, the way dew beads
before dawn. She thought only of Finley: how she hadn't felt
the stubble of his cheek against her own in more than a year
or smelled the Dior Sauvage cologne on his Polos, the properly
dressed addict that he was.

The last time they'd embraced on a rare sober day told a
story of beginnings; hazel and amber eyes reflecting light with
easy smiles. And middles: the sharp blades of shoulders and the
push of ribs through skin gone gaunt.

As for endings, she begged God for a happy one.

She knew this wasn't his fault. People thought addiction was
a choice. A weakness of character. Josie had interviewed dozens
of addicts for her Emmy-winning news reports and knew that
most people grappling with this disease fell on the sensitive,
whip-smart spectrum. They were Black and white and every
color in between. They were rich. And poor. Gay and straight.
They came from families intact. And families severed.

She thought of Dottie and how she wore her heart in her
wide-open smiles and generous hugs. Her disability gave her
an advantage in that she would never suffer the intensities that
capsized Finley. He, who seemed skinless as he faced the world,
all life's hurts and injustices worming through bone and blood
and sending missives to self-medicate.

As Josie sipped her hot tea and contemplated ordering a
glass of white wine, the memories vanished when her phone
dinged with a text. She jumped, nearly knocking it off the table,
and her heart seemed to stop when she saw the message from
Finley.

"I need money NOW! You know my PayPal link, so fucking

USE it!!!" Instead of feeling crushed by his abusive words, Josie clasped her hands in prayer. *Thank you, God. My boy is alive.*

Her quaking thumbs flew across the keys. "You're safe? Where are you?" She hit send, then realized her mistake. Blocked. One-way communication was all she could hope for unless she found phones he wouldn't recognize. That had worked for a while, and she would leave him a trail of encouraging words, like Hansel scattering breadcrumbs. *Find your way home, son.*

He'd caught on and stopped taking calls from unknown numbers. Josie had become an expert in extracting meaning from every word he wrote. All caps told one story. Sloppy spellings told another. Punctuation revealed the hidden context.

This message told her unequivocally that Finley was back on drugs. He'd never talk to her this way when sober. Ever. It also told her he was super-pissed, typical after coming off a bender and needing cash for the next fix.

The phone pinged again. "THIS IS ALL YOUR FAULT! I CAN'T LIVE WITH DAD ANYMORE. SEND MONEY NOW OR YOU'LL NEVER HEAR FROM ME AGAIN."

Anxiety scratched at her ribcage, and she summoned the server for a glass of wine, the guilt of her liquid crutch a penance she'd pay. Josie's former moneyed friends had a hard time wrapping their heads around what had become of her boy. Here was a child of privilege and talent, a son of successful parents who had loved and, at times, probably coddled him as he'd been an only kid for nineteen years. Here was a young man who easily could have been a tennis pro or a doctor like his father, but instead wasted his days smoking dope and ingesting poison in a dark basement, baked eyes on a flat-screen TV and fingers hammering game controls.

Josie had witnessed Finley's failures twist the faces of those high-achieving family-values types who grew uncomfortable just hearing his name. No one ever asked, "How's your son doing?" They didn't want an answer because to acknowledge him would rattle their armor of high-performing stocks and upscale addresses—such fragile walls they falsely believed protected their progeny. *If Emmy-winning and much-beloved Josie Nickels had a kid on the skids, then no one was safe.*

Those friends were gone and, with their departure, all that judgment. She thought about them while picking at her chicken curry, those women whose sons had snagged college scholarships and girlfriends looking as though they'd spent their lives exfoliating and toning and never drinking anything stronger than a Starbucks latte, coconut milk, no whip. Those please-and-thank-you girls destined for do-gooding and Junior Leagues.

She thought of Finley's last girlfriend and tensed. That dead-eyed girl with the pinpoint pupils, the serpent tattoo crawling from her frayed tank and winding around half of her neck. She remembered the girl's hands, fingernails chewed to pulp and blood, and dirty forearms inked in cultish emblems.

She wondered, as she sipped the glass of Riesling she had no business drinking, if they'd have another chance. She and her boy. She wondered, as she paid the check and boxed three egg rolls for her coworkers, if he'd live long enough for such a day.

Josie unwrapped a peppermint, slipped it under her tongue, and trudged back to her job hawking skincare and brow groomers. "A mall job at your age," her mother had squawked. "With your education and all those Emmys you never even bothered to display." It irked Josie when people flaunted their honors, lining trophies on mantels or hanging frames to walls so others could see and touch their self-esteem.

Her job didn't define her. Success didn't rest upon the golden statuettes she'd jammed in a Rubbermaid tub. Success meant getting it right with her son. Reaching his heart before it rotted, or stopped from a malignancy of his own making.

For now, she had her little girl to consider and this new job in cosmetics so unlike anything she'd ever done. Her mother had all but coded when Josie plunged from celebrity to service work in a matter of months, spiraling from prime-time news anchor in a huge metro market to slinging lipstick at Brigman's. There were certainly worse jobs, such as sitting in an office eight hours straight.

At least she'd put some miles between this life and that one. Asheville was a good four hours and two states from her career detonation. Not many people from around here watched WSTA in Atlanta, Georgia.

Josie pushed away distressing thoughts as she entered the store through sliding glass doors, rubbing her arms as the cold air hit her. She made a note to "borrow" a sweater from the women's department. She'd have to be extra cautious and rein in her clumsiness. No sense wasting what money she had on an ugly sweater doing nothing for her plus-size hips.

As she stowed her purse behind the counter, Monica shouted, "I smell Asian Dragon. Get your fanny over here now." Her eyes zoomed in on the egg rolls, and she peeled off the standard white lab coat as if she were a dermatologist and not a makeup artist for Clinique. Josie held the food like a waitress serving haute cuisine. "Ooh, you're spoiling us with all your treats," Monica said.

"Well, you skinny thirty-somethings need them much more than I do." Josie patted her plump belly, this extra weight like a new kid in town she'd have to get used to. Or rid of. But honestly, it didn't trouble her and felt almost comforting. All those years in television of forcing her large bones into submission, whittling and carving her body into a shape God hadn't intended. Every woman needed a vacation from self-scrutinizing. Life was too unreliable to spend it beating oneself down even if her past all but shouted for a *Jerry Springer* show.

Monica, whose mother is Asian and her father Scandinavian, personified Goth, her skin white and whipped as a wedding cake and made more so by lips stained the color of old blood. She dipped her egg roll in hot mustard and held it like a torch. "You look fabulous, honey," she said. "Remember this every time you see a luscious dessert: 'Nobody, and I mean *nobody*, wants a bone but a dog.' It's all about gobbling without guilt."

Josie smiled. "I'll have to remember that one. Burger King and Taco Bell have been my lovers of late."

"Well, I understand. After what you went through back in

Atlanta. I don't know how you survived those vultures playing that video of your…your…anyway." She reddened and ducked behind the counter for a bite of the egg roll. When she surfaced, soy sauce on her face, she nodded toward Josie's counter to indicate a customer had walked up.

"You mean my giant hissy fit," Josie finished for Monica. "That's why women shouldn't hold stuff in for too long. It's like a girdle begging to explode." She checked out the client at her counter, helping herself to the foundation testers. "Speaking of fits, I better get her before Pauline does."

She would give this job her best, no matter what her uppity mother thought about it, and enjoy the women either chasing or delivering beauty. She would think of Finley tonight, after dark, after more wine. Nights were the worst with their inked skies like black drapes conjuring the sinister, suffocating her with all those what-ifs her therapist kept saying would kill her. *Let it go, let it go, let it go*, she'd chanted. All those clichés slapped up on walls for those who couldn't deal with their truths.

The La Belleza client had taken a seat in one of the makeup chairs, flinging her Brigman's shopping bags across the floor. Josie put on her professional I-am-stable-and-here-to-make-you-beautiful face. She approached the woman, reading her cues in the tapping foot and downturned mouth.

"Hola. How are you doing today?" The lady's eyes shot skyward, not a full roll, but still. "I'm Josette or Josie. Either one. And you are?"

"In a hurry."

"How about I treat you to a quick, ten-minute luxury service?" Josie's sales were down, and La Belleza stressed that pampering led to upselling. And upselling kept shareholders in yachts and young women.

The woman grimaced and crossed her arms over a Bvlgari that cost more than Josie's condo payment. "How about you match me in two minutes instead? And don't let that other woman who works here near me. She always tries to sell me everything but my own dental work."

Josie forced a laugh and reached into her velvet bag for her makeup brushes, trying to decide which foundation shade the washed-out woman in her chair might buy at fifty dollars a pop.

She glimpsed the fine May afternoon buttering the main entrance in sunlight. She longed to step into the rays, feel them against her face. The warm days had a way of infusing hope, and for a moment she could almost forget everything destroyed. How death rattled its keys, wanting her boy. How she'd better find a way to change the locks.

She marveled at the blooms escaping the Bradford pear trees, swirling in plain view as if snowing. Nearly eighty degrees and low humidity, perfect for a hike with her little girl had she forgone the wine like a proper mother.

"I don't have all day," said the woman in hot-pink leggings and an unforgiving Lululemon tank top, open in the back and revealing a spine resembling garlic knots and arms that looked like beef jerky. "I have Zumba in thirty minutes and a hot stone massage right afterward. All I want is a sample so don't go and try to slap on powder and blush or the whole shebang."

"I won't," Josie said, trying not to stare at those arms as she chose three testers from the unit. "I'd rather sample the goods myself before I buy." She wasn't going to push it with this lady who looked slightly embalmed in a yellow-based foundation with no blush or lipstick, a common problem she'd seen on older women going for the trendy nude lip only the Under-Twenty-Ones could pull off. "Let me sterilize this brush and then we can—"

"For God's sake, just squirt on hand sanitizer and use your fingers. I'm not about to buy your overpriced brushes. I got my set at Target for twelve dollars."

Josie continued fake smiling, reminiscent of a Miss Georgia contestant crowned first runner-up.

"Let's get on with this," the client said. "I came here one time and that skeletal woman working here—you know the one I mean—all but strapped me to this chair. For over an hour, mind you."

The woman's eyes traveled up and down Josie's body, making her self-conscious. Josie took a brush and striped the woman twice below her jawbone, blending the foundation into her skin. "I think the cool tone works best," she said. "Here, take a look."

The lady swatted her hand at the mirror Josie held. "I can't tell anything from this harsh lighting. I'm going to stand in front of the entrance and check in the natural light. Just go back to whatever it is you all do over here, and if I decide to buy it, I'll find you."

Josie's smile faded as the woman race-walked, pumping those Slim Jim arms, to the entrance. She felt a charge in the air. A typical Saturday rush formed like a Category 1 hurricane with conditions ideal for intensifying.

The moon, waxing gibbous and a day away from its full expression, spiked the atmosphere with portent. She didn't need charts or visuals to know exactly when a moon swelled. She saw it in faces—in tight smiles and manic eyes—and in moods that swung, tongues that turned sharper, voices that pitched higher. It was under such a moon she'd had her breakdown. Under such a moon both her babies came squealing into the world.

The Lululemon woman returned shaking her head. "I want something a little lighter. Dark shades age a woman. Your skin's nice. All heavy-set women seem to have good skin."

Here we go. Josie arranged her face with an understanding smile.

She tried to think of pleasantries, but her mind had suddenly gone fuzzy from the Riesling wearing off. "Everyone's skin has something beautiful about it," she said. "Now, let's shape those brows after we get a good foundation match. I once read that a woman is never fully dressed without her brows." The client's mouth opened as if she was on the verge of a choir solo. Josie knew this was a lost cause and that her little bon mots weren't effective. "Okay, let's just tone your face and use…" She lost her thought. What was the point of trying to make this grump pot happy?

The woman continued scanning Josie from head to toe, assessing. She frowned and bit her lacquered thumbnail. "Aren't you that woman from the news? Down in Atlanta who—" She stopped and pointed. "Well, I knew you looked familiar when I saw you. I can't believe a woman of your caliber could up and lose control on television and embarrass her family like that!"

So she'd seen the viral video of her cataclysm. Josie's cheeks warmed as she cleared her throat and rubbed her neck, knowing the red splotches were a giveaway. "I…well…I wish I could take all that back. I'm working on repairing things."

The client fiddled with her hair and nodded. "That's how strong women move forward and don't wallow in the past. Quite a few may not understand how a broken woman can pop out of bed and carry on with her day. I lost a baby to pneumonia and four days later I pushed a grocery cart through Publix choosing a pork roast for what was left of my family. I remember I had on my grandmother's cameo brooch and lipstick. Imagine!"

Josie felt the tension loosen. "I'm so sorry about your baby."

"It was twenty years ago. Not a day goes by I don't think about her. I listen to happy songs to take my mind off it."

"When I get down and out," Josie said, searching for a way to relate to this woman, "I listen to Miranda Lambert. Dixie Chicks or whatever they call themselves these days. Anything country and sad to put things in perspective."

"That Miranda looks good since trimming up a bit. I see so many young women just let themselves go. You'd be a knockout if you'd sweat a little, maybe take a dance class or kickboxing. Get a better haircut and a deep conditioning."

Her comment stung, but Josie had long ago realized that the rudest women were often the saddest, the most in pain. At least she'd called her young. That was something. She turned to the woman in her chair, considering how to respond, though her personal life wasn't any of the client's business. Just because a woman may spend more on foundation than a cable bill doesn't mean she's given carte blanche to insult. "I've been doing yoga here and there," Josie said, touching a snarl in the back of her hair. Well, if she couldn't see it, it wasn't worth worrying over.

"Yoga is for all the liberals in this hippie town who'd rather lay around moaning on a mat than put forth any effort."

Josie thought of all those years in television and the excruciating daily workouts, an unspoken requirement for her job. That's one thing she didn't miss.

"Are you weighing yourself daily? I find that's a must in keeping firm control of the weight witch. Too many girls today are just sitting around on their phones letting the pounds pile up."

The nerve of this woman. Josie had quit stepping on the scales the day after her little (okay, huge) on-air catastrophe. "I used to weigh every day," she said. "I didn't realize how such a single act had all that power. Setting the tone for the day. I gave my scales to charity, along with my ironing board. Getting rid of those two menaces has been liberating."

Just as the woman started to reply, something heavy hit the counter, followed by huffing and grunting. Pauline had flown in on her broom and dropped a box of stock.

"I can take over from here," she said, her voice raising the hair on Josie's neck. Pauline clutched her saline-maxed chest and panted as she pulled Josie to the side. "You have an emergency call. Did you not hear the store paging you?"

"No, I—I've been busy matching up this—" She froze, wondering who could be calling her.

"It's probably a cop. No doubt your son again. I left the number at the register. And by the way, you have a nasty hole in your leggings."

Josie felt as if she'd been punched. "How do you know anything about my son?"

"It's not like nobody knows who you are around this place. We all know about Josette Nickels and her sordid little past. Why do you think you were hired?" Pauline cast her eyes from Josie and focused on the woman in the chair squirting all kinds of shades onto her forearms. "D-grade former celebs are good for business. Lancôme hired that Philly freak years ago and their sales are through the roof. Chanel, too. They have their own personal train wreck."

Josie took a deep breath and willed her heart to stop flitting. This *emergency* call didn't floor her as it would have years ago before collect calls from jails, hospitals, and even psych wards seemed the norm. Before her ex had posed as the emergency on the other line to extort more money from her. Still, her nerves kicked up as there was always the chance the call was related to Finley. But he'd *just* texted her half an hour ago.

She pushed a fist into her diaphragm to avert a panic attack. If you own your breath, no one can steal your peace, Ruby was fond of saying. Everything's fine, and this is another of Frank's crying-wolf schemes to con her out of the remaining fumes of her savings and the carcass of her 401(k).

"I'll finish up with the client, then return the call," she said.

Pauline slammed a fist on the counter. "This sounds serious. Just another day in Josie's House O' Drama." She tried to frown but the Botox proved fatal. "I'll handle this client. She's mine anyway. Technically you aren't supposed to give full makeovers until you're certified. If you don't pass…well, I guess you won't have a job."

Josie clenched her jaw and narrowed her eyes. She started to speak, then decided she'd deal with Pauline another day. Instead, she thought of all the previous phone calls—some from Frank but others from cops—concerning Finley and his eight years of run-ins with the law, little crimes that started slowly before rapidly accelerating and giving Josie emotional whiplash. One minute he was acing his serve on the tennis courts and the next he was stealing a neighbor's washing machine to buy dope. A washing machine, of all things. Ruining his future on a front-loading Maytag.

Pauline circled Josie as if sizing up her prey. "Go. This is my client, remember?" Her eyes flew to the woman who had made a huge mess. "I've warned you plenty of times not to take my best customers. Nobody wants a woman half put together working on them, and until you're officially certified—"

"I heard you."

Pauline continued her tirade. "Every day there's a major flaw with your appearance. Yesterday it was the sole of one shoe flopping out like you pulled them from the Goodwill bins. Last week it was blobs of foundation all over your shirt. I don't know how you ever made it on television. Big-shot news anchor with runs in your pantyhose."

Josie saw something strangely familiar in Pauline's face, and she straightened as if a metal rod had fused her spine. She felt a fleeting déjà vu spread like smoke.

She gathered her banged-up Kate Spade and entered the vacant store manager's office where the sickly smell of cologne and defeat overpowered her. She lifted the receiver, and with a trembling finger, punched in a number she didn't recognize.

On the third ring, Frank answered, his voice pitched high and his words coming fast.

"You need to send your son money," he said. "He got busted last week in Florida and I had to make bail to get him out. How come it's me always paying bail?"

"Because after I paid it once, I told you I wasn't going to do it again." She was relieved Frank had found him, and that even though he had been arrested, he was at least safe. For now.

"So, you wanted him to die there with all those hardcores?"

"I wanted him to learn in there. Learn not to keep making the same mistakes."

"He's never going to let you back in his life if you don't support him."

Josie's head throbbed. "He's never going to let me in as long as you keep telling him I abandoned him."

"Well, you did."

"You gave me no other choice. When you said you couldn't handle raising Dottie and that I needed to put her in a home, I saw the face of a stranger. Not the man I married."

"You're horrible. PayPal him some money now!"

"I was told this was an emergency call?"

"I had to call the store because you weren't answering your cell. You haven't sent Finn money in over a month."

Here we go again. "Every time I've sent money, he relapses. I'm done buying his drugs. I told you *and* him I would pay every cent of rehab, but neither of you seems to think he needs it."

"He's broke and trying to get a job, but no one will hire him with these bogus charges."

"What was he charged with this time?" Josie asked. Frank always covered for Finley. On rare sober days, Finley confessed to Josie as if she were a priest. That's when she'd hear all the *I love yous* and *Mom, I never blamed you for any of this.* And even, "I miss you and my sister and want us to be a family again."

"They said he stole a truck."

"And? Last I heard that is a felony."

"It was a guy he knows. The dude said he could borrow it, then called the cops on him."

"Let me speak to him," Josie said, tears stinging. "Please, Frank. You can't keep doing this to me. He's my son. You could at least have him unblock me from his phone."

"You have my number and I expect you to PayPal me a couple of thousand today. We owe a lawyer at least a grand and this Florida nightmare wasn't free."

Josie shook her head, floored by his requests. She gazed at the ceiling as if searching the heavens for wisdom. "I don't have that kind of money, Frank, and you—" Before she could say, *You can give up the free-loading life and use your damned doctorate of dental surgery degree,* the phone went dead.

It wasn't Josie's fault he threw it away to create and schlep sculpture when the mood struck. He'd spent more than ten years making good money on bad mouths and then decided dentistry was beneath his God-given talents. Josie's career had provided more than enough for an excellent standard of living back then. Key word: then.

She wiped her teary eyes with her sleeve. This man had been her world at one time, but people are always changing. And marriages often slide through phases just like moons.

Her cell buzzed again. She saw Frank's number and eased her thumb over the red decline button.

4

Josie had been at work half an hour, ringing up the odd eyeliner and a couple of mascaras, when Pauline arrived wearing a rubberish skirt that nearly showed her religion *and* denomination.

"I have several clients coming to see me today for their pre–Mother's Day makeovers," she said, eyeing the towering cart packed with perfume and skincare sets for the moms or clueless husbands searching for last-minute gifts. "Why have you not set these out?"

Mother's Day. Josie's chest tightened. She wondered if she'd hear from Finley on Sunday, if he'd be mad she sent self-help books instead of PayPal dollars when he'd surfaced from his Florida "vacation" with a brand-new charge on his ever-lengthening record. She thought of the clay handprint he made for her in kindergarten, how he'd picked flowering weeds, squeezed limp and damp in his little hand, and had given them to her while shyly looking at his feet. Last year the day had passed without a word—the first Mother's Day he hadn't acknowledged her.

"Did you not hear me?" Pauline asked, scowling. "I'm going to prepare for my appointments, and you need to have all these sets out immediately."

Josie started to speak and stopped, figuring she'd pick her battles. For the next hour, she arranged the front, side, and back counters with the gift sets, wrapping them in lapis-blue bows, La Belleza's official color. As she was finishing, an over-accessorized elderly woman tapped her arm. "Do you mind helping me?" she asked, her glassy eyes reminding Josie of jellyfish.

La Belleza had two areas for consultations—a couple of chairs up front and two more on the back side where Pauline wouldn't see her working. "Of course. Have a seat," Josie said. "Have you used our products before?"

"No, I've always used Noxzema and Ivory soap," she said, trying to get settled in the chair which was too high for her petite frame. "I've been wanting to try this stuff after seeing Sergio on QVC. What a fine ass he has!"

Josie cracked up. Sergio, jazz-hand waving, rainbow hottie that he was, certainly got the older women fired up and eager to try this line. This type of bawdy lady is exactly what she needed today to take her mind off Finley. "I'll just gather up my weapons of choice and we'll get started," she said.

At the station where Pauline worked, she asked to borrow cotton rounds and cleanser.

"Excuse me, Chelsea," Pauline said to her client who couldn't have been more than sixteen. "This will only take a moment." She turned to Josie. "Until you're certified, I don't want to see you touch another face. Is that understood?"

"You're busy and La Belleza stresses that we shouldn't make our clients wait." Josie looked over her shoulder to make sure her customer hadn't left.

"Stall her until I'm done here. These teenagers," she whispered, "are nothing but a waste of time. They never buy. Start off with a hand massage and when I finish with Chelsea, I'll do the consult and makeover." She was like a teacher barking orders, but Josie wasn't wasting what energy she had on Pauline today. She'd start with the hand massage and go from there.

The client's eyes were closed when she returned, and snores puttered from her lips. "Ma'am?" Josie tapped her shoulder. The woman startled. "Sorry. Hope it was a good dream."

"Oh yes," she moaned. "I was laying on the beach without a stitch of clothing, and along comes this glorious naked man who—I better shut my mouth."

"Maybe I ought to let you go back to sleep," Josie said, smiling as she set the cotton pads, cleanser, and face chart on the small island counter. "Do you mind giving me your name? We can go over this how-to guide once we have you looking young as a coed."

"Wilma. Mrs. Wilma Youngblood, widowed and ready for

romance." She popped open her mouth as if shocked by her own words. "I'm almost ninety and let me tell you, a woman's needs don't disappear. Ye Olde Thatched Cottage doesn't seal its roof if you know what I'm saying." She slapped her thigh and laughed.

Josie fell in love with Wilma Youngblood on the spot. "If you're going to start trolling for men, let's get those hands soft as kittens. I'm going to give you a heavenly hand massage."

"I'd rather be giving a handsome fellow a heavenly hand job," she said. Josie heard a honk of laughter. Monica had returned from lunch and decided Mrs. Youngblood was far more entertaining than trying to sell Moisture Surge. They exchanged a wide-eyed glance, the kind that says, *Stick around. We're about to get a show here.*

Josie needed to steer Wilma down another lane before a lower-level manager called security on the woman. "That's a wonderful handbag," she said of Wilma's vintage crocodile purse, which she clutched as if protecting a baby. "I'll need to put it somewhere safe before we start."

After storing the bag, Josie mixed Manos Suaves with a spritz of the En Flor perfume, heavy and cloying with the scent of gardenias. "The hands have lots of nerves and pleasure points. I'm going to treat you today before we start on your face."

She held out her ancient arm clanking with bracelets and waved her gnarled fingers strangled in diamonds. "It's like that church I used to go to where they always wanted to wash my feet. I'd just as soon show people my little cottage as my goat hooves."

Josie heard Monica laughing nearby, as she squeezed the lotion bottle so hard a glob shot out, pale pink cream landing on Wilma's silk scarf. "Gosh, I'm so sorry. Let me blot that for you or you can take it off and I'll have it laundered for you."

"You think I'm going to yank this off and show you my traffic stoppers? I wear scarves so the men don't stare at my offerings." She shimmied her chest like an adult dancer.

Josie unleashed a bemused snort but didn't respond, not

wanting to encourage this. She dabbed the woman's ruined scarf, took her hand, and massaged the arthritic knots. Mrs. Youngblood tipped her head and closed her eyes, probably imagining Sergio had swept her up and forgotten for a moment his gayness or that she was older than the automobile.

This was why Josie preferred working weekdays. It was quieter, or at least more entertaining. Women shopping during business hours had such charming, no-nonsense demeanors. Maybe because they weren't trapped at a desk nine-to-five, racing home during rush hour to get a meat and two sides on the table. Then there were these older women who either loved what she'd done to their faces or were too many cataracts away from caring.

When Josie reached for Mrs. Youngblood's other hand, she stopped her. "I don't see a ring on that finger," she said, pointing at Josie's left hand. "Pretty thing like you ought'n be single."

"I was married for almost twenty years," Josie said. Gosh, that was almost half her life with Frank. "I promised myself no more men until I got a few things straight with myself first."

"Was it the sex?" Wilma asked and Josie colored. No, she wanted to say. That was the only part that worked. "You young people need to realize exactly how we oldies made even the impossible work in our day. Let me tell you this in case you happen upon another fellow." She reached for Josie's arm and drew her closer. "Never turn your husband away. I don't care how tired you are or how many dishes are gathering flies in the sink. I don't care if the cat box is full or if the baby's diaper weighs more than the television. You all need to realize that men are simple and need only three things."

"And what are those, Mrs. Youngblood?" Josie figured she'd say something along the lines of "The good Lord, a good woman, and the need to be right."

"The three essential things a real man needs," she said, her voice building, "are food, fucks, and a TV turned to ballgames." Her face lit up and she seemed to enjoy the anything-goes speech that's afforded the elderly.

Josie held a hand over her mouth to suppress laughter. A customer stopped in her tracks, looking appalled. When Josie saw Monica's astonished face in her peripheral vision, she lost control and laughed so hard a trickle warmed her Lane Bryants.

She thought about the types of laughs: polite and restrained, genuine but not mind-blowing, and her favorite, the kind so deep it brought tears. She wiped her eyes as Pauline hot-footed over and led her toward the escalator.

"Get a friggin' grip," she said. "She is one of our biggest spenders, you idiot. Did you see her handbag? That's real alligator. I'll take over now with Mrs. Palmer."

"Her name is Mrs. Youngblood and you can't possibly know her. She's never been to this counter in her life."

Pauline sashayed up to Mrs. Youngblood and placed a territorial hand on the woman's shoulder.

"Take your hands off me," Wilma shouted. "I'm having the time of my life with that other woman there." She flicked her hand at Pauline. "Shoo, fly, shoo. Go on now, ya hear me?"

"Josie isn't certified. I'll be taking over now."

Wilma leapt with surprising agility from the chair. "I don't care if she doesn't know shit from Shinola. This is my business I'm bringing to this department store and I'll—"

"It's fine, Mrs. Youngblood. Pauline has lots more experience than I do. Be sure and come say bye before leaving. I want to see that makeover Pauline does on you."

"Well, for shit's sake. I hope I don't leave this store looking like she does. You know how every time you go to the beautician, you come out with the same haircut she has? All these beauty sorts do is turn you into a version of themselves. I can already tell by looking at her she's a wet rag. Looks like a scrawny crow, I'd say. Like if she can't find a hamburger soon, she won't live another day."

Pauline, hands on hips, stupid grin on her face, seemed unshaken by these comments. Probably because she wasn't half listening.

Wilma's eyes twinkled as she faced me. "Now don't you

forget my advice about the menfolk. I had a sister whose seventy-nine-year-old husband shot her in the ass for refusing sex. These men take it seriously, honey, wrong as that rascal was."

"For God's sake," Pauline said. "This isn't a friggin' brothel. And you!" She swiveled to see Monica still watching. "Get back over to your counter. I'm tired of seeing you here. Tired with a capital *T*."

The way Pauline talked about words with capital letters, the way her chin seemed to be missing a key bone, which gave her a boomerang profile, sent prickles up Josie's scalp. It was all too familiar. But from where? From what? She observed for a few minutes, studying Pauline winding her hair in her fingers and working it into a loose bun with a cheap clip.

Josie touched her own hair, the ends so dry she wouldn't be surprised if a chunk broke off in her curling wand one morning. A person could tell a lot about a woman, not by her handbag but by the condition and color of her hair. And at the moment, Josie's looked as if she was heading to the Pump and Munch for a forty-ouncer and a box of six-dollar ColorSilk. She'd made an unfortunate blunder adding those DIY brassy highlights.

She fixed her eyes on Pauline's spackled face, the liner too heavy, the lipstick three shades darker than necessary. She tried to imagine her cleansed of all that foundation. Not a pleasant picture, but from a distance, she's the type one might call striking. Up close her pores were too large, and her eyes had that crinkled smoker's texture, her skin tone screaming, *I'm on a permanent master cleanse* and *my hobbies are smoking Misty menthols and drinking vodka under a broiling Florida sun.*

"What are you staring at?" she asked, greasing Mrs. Youngblood's face like a rotisserie chicken. "Go back up front and if someone buys anything, be sure and ring it in my number. I want printouts of every transaction."

It's okay. You've got this. It's not the life-altering stories you once covered. It's just makeup.

As Josie scanned the sales sheet taped beside the cash register, she heard a tiny voice. "Ma'am? Can you help me? That other lady ran off." It was the teenaged client, Chelsea, with half a face of makeup and the other half forgotten.

Josie couldn't believe Pauline would leave her in such a state. "Sure, sweetheart. Do you mind, though, if I remove that heavy eyeliner? You're too pretty to look like a hungover Cleopatra." Chelsea grinned and took a seat.

When Josie finished, Chelsea admired her delicately made-up face. "I'll take the foundation and that blush you used. Oh, and this mascara, the ivy liner, and the lipstick."

"Let me gather these for you," Josie said. "It'll only take a minute or two."

"Wait," Chelsea said. "I also want the foundation brush and the fluffy one for powder. And the powder too."

Josie rang up the sale. Nearly three hundred dollars from this sweet teenager Pauline had abandoned, thinking she wouldn't buy. A wave of rebellion hit. Josie reprinted the receipt with her name and number at the bottom. She taped it to the register for all the world (and Pauline) to see.

When Josie finally took a bathroom break, she searched her phone in the privacy of the back stall. Two messages.

Finley: "MOM! I can't live with Dad any longer. I need you to pay for a deposit on an apartment right now before I relapse again. You owe me this for leaving me with him and all that private personal shit you said on TV!"

Frank: "We need money. Finn's lawyer is getting the charge reduced to a misdemeanor and you need to PayPal me so I can cover his bills. I know you squirreled away a fortune somewhere. I'm paying all his expenses. You can PayPal me right now!!!"

If Josie had access to their phones, she'd tell Finley her love was permanent and going nowhere. That she would do anything (but give him money) and everything (within healthy boundaries) to help him get clean. That she knew he was using and that his destructive lifestyle had escalated. Then she would tap in Frank's number and tell him to fuck off and start filling teeth again.

When Josie returned to the counter, Mrs. Youngblood was

slumped in the chair, surrounded by Brigman's bags. She did not look happy. She did, however, resemble a pole-dancing corpse.

"Did you buy all this?"

"I plan to bring it all back too," she said, smacking her lips. "That other lady was as much fun as a round of rabies shots. I bought this manure just to shut her up. You know what that praying mantis of a she-devil had the nerve to say to me?"

"I wouldn't be surprised by anything Pauline says."

"Here, first take these bags and be so kind as to help me to my car." Josie loaded them in a cart and held the woman's elbow as they walked to the parking lot, the sun warm on her face.

They paused at Mrs. Youngblood's long Cadillac DeVille, one of those burgundy eighties numbers. "That harlot Pauline woman said this malarkey here in these bags would do wonders for my face but that my neck was too far gone. Said I'd be a knockout if I had a neck lift. Here I am on the verge of turning ninety and she's saying all this horseshit."

"Your neck is fine and you're beautiful." The nerve of Pauline. Anyone else would be fired for those comments.

Josie opened the car door and loaded the bags while Mrs. Youngblood took forever getting behind the wheel. At this rate, it would take her a good twenty minutes to even get out of the parking lot. "I'll be back to see you," she said, accidentally flicking on her wipers. "Remember what I said about the menfolk. These women today think everything's all about them. Service your man and the world shall open forth."

Good Lord.

Instead of easing the burgundy behemoth from her spot, Mrs. Youngblood yanked the car in reverse, gunned it, and tore ass out of the space, her tires crushing a Bud Light can and leaving a streak of rubber. So much for thinking she'd be a dawdler.

When Josie came back to the store, Pauline was primping at the mirror, blending more concealer under her eyes, purpled from the likelihood of bulimia. "Where have you been?" she asked in an accusatory manner. "I'm going to have my hummus, but if my next client comes in, don't even bother getting started. Page me." She held a Ziploc baggie with a few pathetic carrots. "I want you to soak cotton balls in our perfumes and hand them out. We've got to sell these sets before Monday. If not, it's doom, Josie. Doom with a capital *D*."

She caught her breath, suddenly remembering. Only one other person she knew did the capital this and that routine— her father. The sole man on earth who loved her with no conditions, no expectations, no hidden agenda, and no second and flawed personality lurking beneath the one shown to others.

"Hello? Earth to Josie," Pauline said. "Try to act like you're having fun and put a smile on that moon pie. It's a good thing we have at least one hefty gal at the counter to raise the self-esteem of our less fortunate clients."

Leave already. Josie ignored her and fastened ribbons around cotton balls she'd drenched in fragrance. She sneezed three times into the crook of her arm.

"Jesus Christ. I'm leaving this to you so don't screw up. Take a damned Zyrtec." Pauline rubbed her forehead as if suffering a migraine. "Oh, and before you clock out, you'll need to clean up this entire center court and sanitize each and every station."

Fantastic. All this abuse for around thirty-five grand a year. Less if Pauline continued taking all the sales for herself. Josie had agreed to move here for fifteen dollars an hour plus commission because the only other skills she possessed were: 1) marrying a former dentist-turned-sculptor who enjoyed bong hits, playing mind games, and Minecraft; 2) perfectly delivering the daily news; 3) flying limber and gracefully (in her heyday) from the trapeze bars in that fairly fabulous college circus act.

No one was beating down her door to rejoin the ranks of on-air personalities after what had happened, not unless you count the Atlanta-based reality show called *Ex-Wives of Hotlanta*, wanting to bank on her misfortunes. The latest was a call from a producer wanting her to appear on a rehab reality show.

"You have to start somewhere and rebuild your life," her therapist had said when Josie mentioned the cosmetics offer in

Asheville. "Asheville is a city where many come to heal. Back in the day, it was the place for people to recover from tuberculosis, and there was a mental hospital where Zelda Fitzgerald lived until she burned in the fire on the grounds. I did residency work there before they shut down. One of the most beautiful cities I've ever visited."

Her counselor was right. Asheville, with 360 degrees of spectacular mountains, was like living in a comforting embrace. She knew she couldn't have repaired her life in Atlanta with its stressors at every turn. All that traffic and everyone trying to one-up and outdo each other. In this town people seemed embarrassed by possessions and good fortune.

When Josie finished her job foisting cotton-ball allergy attacks on poor souls, she found Pauline, both hands on her bony hips. "What might I ask is this?" She held a sales slip by the corner as if it would burn her.

"It's a receipt," Josie said with a rictus grin. "What a sweet young woman that Chelsea is."

"I'm calling Fabiana later today. You were told not to touch a single face until certification."

"You walked off and left her. She wasn't very happy about—"

The counter phone rang and Pauline lunged to answer it, always thinking it might be a senile woman wanting another couple jars of Piel Radiente Joven at three hundred a pop. "Yes, Fabiana. She's right here."

Pauline smirked and pushed the phone to Josie.

"Hello?"

"Josette? It's about your certification results. I'll be coming in next week to go over everything with you. As of now, please follow Pauline's protocol."

"Yes, ma'am…okay…well, bye."

Pauline's chest seemed to swell if that was possible. "I guess she told you I'm in charge?"

"When were you not?"

"I'm leaving in a few and this place is a wreck. Also, the cleaning service canceled, so before you go, I need you to empty the trash and vacuum the floors. If you have time, you can alphabetize the foundation drawers and dust the tester units."

"Yes, Lady Tremaine," Josie said, thinking of the wicked stepmother in *Cinderella*. "Shall I wash the windows and scrub the terrace and sweep the halls and clean the chimney while I'm at it?"

"You're on thin ice."

"Good thing I can swim," Josie said as Pauline clacked off to eat her thirty-calorie feast.

5

"Happy Mother's Day," Josie droned into the phone, wondering if her voice sounded as flat as she felt when leaving Katherine Nickels a voice mail. Naturally, her mother would screen all calls. She'd rather avoid Josie on Mother's Day. And most other days. "Just wanted to wish you well and hope you're enjoying a relaxing afternoon."

Well, that wasn't so bad. Josie was relieved her mother hadn't answered, knowing Katherine, recently retired from law, would launch into another round of closing arguments to sum up Josie's imploding life. Their last exchange had come the week before she moved to Asheville.

"Go ahead and throw your life in the bin!" she'd said. "Here you are, summa cum laude graduate of FSU and lowering yourself to work in retail. Retail! Ringing up the odd pair of Dearfoams and God-knows-what. I can hear you now saying, 'Y'all come back now' all day long."

"It's actually a new opportunity for me. Asheville's wonderful, and when I get settled, I'm going to see if Finley wants to—"

"That chap will do nothing but fester in that fuggy basement teeming with radon."

Josie's stomach had churned. "This would be a great place for him with so much to do outdoors, and the mountains, they make you feel...I don't know. Cradled."

"I don't have time for this," Katherine had said. "You spent your entire career in television and it's bloody time you went back. Don't call me until you've signed a contract at another station."

They hadn't spoken since. Katherine had not even asked about Dottie, her only granddaughter. Josie forced these thoughts aside and decided to enjoy this windless and obscene-

ly gorgeous afternoon. The distant mountains, layered like blue
pyramids, were too beautiful to seem real. And those in close
range stood as lush and green as a tropical forest. Everywhere
she turned, the views left her stunned.

It was now a little past one and she and Dottie had eaten at
McDonald's (because Dottie screamed for a Happy Meal with
the My Little Pony toy inside). Josie smiled, picturing her mother's face had she seen her "brunching" at Mickie D's. Single
mom in stretchy leggings and a bag-lady 2x top, hole under the
right arm, and dipping fries in ketchup while the more stable
mothers opened their sentimental cards and poured water in
crystal vases, set their flowers on a dining room table where
their beautifully dressed children and doting husbands had prepared a lunch fit for Kate Middleton.

When she and Dottie returned to the condo, the deathly
quiet neighborhood closed in on Josie. Sitting at her kitchen
table, clutching a sweating paper cup of Diet Coke, she made
a short mental gratitude list. She had her beautiful daughter, a
place to live, a job—still without formal certification because
Fabiana had said she needed time to sort out whether Josie
had passed or failed. She had a son who was alive even though
he hadn't called or texted since his last demands. She felt the
anxiety nettling her nerves, that thinned-out feeling that left her
slightly deboned.

Josie stood from the table, threw the cup in the trash, and
checked her phone again for incoming texts. Nothing. It was a
beautiful day, with a sky so blue it looked washed and waxed.
She'd been meaning to take Dottie to Carrier Park by the French
Broad, a long river flowing north instead of south, more than
two hundred miles of it snaking into Tennessee. It was a perfect
day to spend outside. She packed a canvas bag with snacks and
sunscreen, along with Mary-Mary, Dottie's once-plush mermaid, in case she grew irritable.

An outing would do them both good, and Josie loved rivers,
their intoxicating scent of both life and death, that subtle smell
of living fish and dying leaves. She could kick back and relax

hearing it rush with such purpose, watch the breaking rapids and the occasional turtle raising its head.

Rivers were confident. They knew exactly where to go. What to do. She used to sit by the Chattahoochee that wound through Atlanta's suburbs while Finley tiptoed in the cool water, net in his hand as he hunted crawdads, joy spread across his face. Such a happy child.

Traffic was light as they drove across Tunnel Road and took I-240 onto Patton Avenue, turning off at Amboy Road. "We're here," Josie said, unbuckling her daughter. She shielded her eyes, wishing she'd remembered her sunglasses to block the glare bouncing off this sapphire sky. Hand in hand, they followed a paved trail along the river's scenic shores where the sounds of urgent water, birds making plans, and dogs barking joyfully were almost as soothing as lying on the cotton-white beaches of her beloved St. John, the most gorgeous island she'd ever seen.

As they walked, Dottie spotted the playground, which sprang from the grassy center of the former Asheville Motor Speedway, closed in the late nineties. City officials repurposed the track for bicycling and skating.

"Castle, Mama! Castle," Dottie squealed, eyes on the wooden wonderland with swings and tunneled slides, all sorts of bridges and turrets. It was a long walk and Josie carried her a good distance, though her back ached from Dottie's weight. She saw a small crowd convening, groups picnicking on blankets. Moms and dads. Sisters and brothers. Little nuclear families. Josie twinged with what? Regret? Envy?

She slathered a protesting Dottie in sunscreen and sat on an empty bench, watching her child shoot off to play, her mouth open, cheeks pink with the wonder of it all. She soon found a group of children who welcomed her. Dottie never had trouble making friends, a trait they shared.

A few minutes later, the phone in Josie's pocket vibrated. She braced herself and stepped into a patch of shade to read the message.

"Happy Mother's Day!!!!! I love you. Your sober FOR GOOD son." Every muscle in her body relaxed and tears pooled. Maybe she and Dottie could arrange a trip to see Finley. If she knew where he was. Maybe, if he really *was* clean, he'd release the lock on his heart for a day or two. Give her that opening to return to his life. This was a wonderful first step, she thought, wondering how long it had been since he'd said I love you.

Josie could survive without her mother's love. But not her son's. Her post-meltdown counselors harped about her loving him too much, going against every belief she'd held as a mother. The women of MAC (Mothers of Addicted Children), her online support group, commended the merits of tough love, but often their proclamations rolled off Josie's radar, statements such as "Just take away their homes and cars and money," and "Throw them out on the street, and problem solved," and "If they don't suffer enough to hit bottom, they'll keep on using."

In the beginning, Josie scoffed at such suggestions, believing this flipped the innate nurturing switch, one of the most primal instincts God gives a mother. And while she didn't do a lot of tough-loving in those early years when rescues seemed his birthright, the later years had changed her and she oscillated between despair and numbness. Giving in and pulling back. And finally, the breaking point leading to the meltdown.

It didn't make sense that a child, who once cried every time he volunteered at the homeless shelter, the tenderhearted boy who'd zip down the car window and thrust crumpled dollar bills into the hands of downtrodden people working the street corners, had become someone she didn't recognize.

Josie's thoughts broke when she heard a piercing scream. Dottie flailed at the bottom of the slide, face planted in the wood chips. She rushed over. "Let's go, sweetie," she said, picking her up and checking for injuries, kissing her daughter's fat wet cheeks. "You have a tiny scratch on your chin. Mary-Mary wants to doctor it up."

Dottie settled but continued whimpering. "I want river. River, Mama."

"Next time, precious. Not today."

Josie toted her for what felt like a mile to the car, opening the door to a blast of heat and silently cursing the black interior. She powered down the windows and cranked up the air-conditioning. No sooner had she buckled Dottie into her booster seat did the red check-engine light flash. "I need to sell this car," she said, more to herself than anyone as Dottie clutched Mary-Mary and sniffled, head against the window, a piece of mulch on her forehead.

Josie ignored the warning light and drove home. She'd skim the car's manual later this evening. She thought about what she might make for dinner, her mood upbeat, not wanting a power struggle over broccoli. "Want to make doggie boats and do crafts tonight?"

Dottie perked up and wiped her runny nose. Doggie boats were the only meat she'd eat, and Josie bought the organic, un-cured frankfurters and whole wheat buns. She always stuck a black olive at the top to give the wiener dog a head, and it was strange how Dottie went nuts over those pitted kalamata olives and gobbled them up like her Fruit Loops.

"Mary-Mary wants doggie boat," she said. "She wants three, Mama."

After supper and the better part of two hours making unicorn dream catchers from a kit, Josie opened the BMW manual while Dottie watched *Princess Lillifee and the Little Unicorn*. As she flipped through the thick book and wondered what sort of person reads a car manual, an envelope fell out and landed in her lap.

She picked it up, tracing the coffee ring staining the faded pink paper. The recipient's name had bled, but Josie could see an R, an O, and what resembled a T.

Robert. Her father. She lifted the torn flap and pulled out a photograph no bigger than a business card. A newborn baby stared at her, an infant girl lying in a clear hospital bassinet and wrapped in the standard hospital receiving blanket—white with pink and blue candy stripes on the edges. She turned the photo over, hoping for a clue and getting nothing.

She slipped on her reading glasses and studied the baby's angry, birth-battered face. It was an old picture. If it was Josie, why wasn't there also a photograph of Juliette, the twin sister who died not long after they were born? She'd seen only two pictures of her and Juliette. In one, they faced each other as if embracing. In the other, they were on a bed, again facing each other and covered by a blanket with yellow daisies, Juliette with her head turned and Josie staring straight into the camera.

She reached for her cell to call her mother and changed her mind. What if this baby wasn't her *or* Juliette? She tucked the photo into its envelope and placed it in the drawer beneath all her granny panties. Her imagination was racing again, like a horse after gunfire, and tried to conjure a soothing memory, wondering when in the world it had become this hard to do so.

Even while in bed, Dottie sleeping next to her, Josie tossed and punched her pillows trying to get comfortable and shake this unsettling feeling. Her mother hadn't returned her call from earlier today, hadn't even used her old trick of phoning when she knew Josie wouldn't be around so she could leave a message. That way she'd have the first and last word on matters, same as when she was Queen of the Courtroom.

They say a woman marries her father, but Josie married her mother. Katherine disappeared, usually to England to see her aunt, when Robert wasn't meeting her exorbitant needs. Frank had done the same with his unexpected packing and bolting, suitcase thudding as it landed in the trunk, engine firing, tires crunching. This soundtrack of desertion. And here was Finley, following old patterns. "I just need to get away for a bit," Katherine would say on the way out the door, wearing one of her Thierry Mugler suits, passport in her purse. "I know it's not your father's fault, but I've endured as much as I possibly can of this family's dysfunction."

Katherine fully believed her husband carried the faulty genes that snake-bit each generation, never having the altruism to at least skip one. She claimed the Nickels blood was nothing but disastrous chromosomal combinations, producing a pool of progenitors ranging from simple-brained to brilliant and soaked in eccentricities.

"I'm telling you, your dad's side of this family hasn't seen a normal human being since Columbus dashed over here," she said. "Probably not even then. I'm the only mother I know with a child in the circus. A circus, for God's sake!"

Josie had read that at least eight percent of human genetic material comes from viruses and that all of us have at least one hundred broken genes. Her mother had a point. The Nickels line most assuredly racked up the mother lode.

Addictions, mental illness, poorly functioning organs, and the unbridled parade of verifiable kooks and freaks, characters beyond what one might label "colorful," blighted (or illuminated, depending upon whom one asked) her family tree.

From birth, Josie bore her mark of physical defect and chose clothing concealing the long, zippered scar running from her sternum to her lower abdomen—the ten inches of fibrous tissue always a reminder of her mother's deep-seated resentment.

Four months and four days. That's how long her twin had lived, a death her mother still grieved daily, adding another serving of guilt to Josie's plate for surviving a surgery her sister had not.

Juliette Faith Nickels: Born on Friday, April 16, 1971. Died on Friday, August 20, 1971, six days after surgery both had undergone for congenital liver issues. Another reason Josie should avoid alcohol, though doctors said her liver had repaired itself years ago.

Only Josie's mother, who was fascinated and obsessed with the aunt who forever shunned the States and lived in London, claimed the sole beneficiary of sanity in the family. This woman who plugged through life pierced with a pebble for a heart and her put-on British accent.

If *she* defined normal then Josie much preferred dining at the buffet of bad genes and unfortunate maladies rather than walk the earth in prudish pretense, void of even an ounce of joy.

"You commandeered the placenta and left her with a bum liver," her mother often said. "Doctors said Juliette might have survived had she gotten proper nutrients."

Josie opened a bottle of Barefoot pinot grigio, hoping to banish thoughts of her mother, the photo of that baby, and the obsessions about whether or not her son was sober. Two hours later, she fell into a light sleep. She dreamed of St. John as if her subconscious knew she needed the respite. There, on her beloved Virgin Island, the aquamarine water shimmered against the reefs in Salt Pond Bay where she spent wondrous hours facedown on the surface, snorkeling until she could no longer bear the sun's sting against her flesh.

There, the fish came to her: tangs and parrots and the solitary queen angel with its electrifying blue body and incandescent yellow tail, the most breathtaking of reef fish. So alone and regal, shy as they swam, fins streaming like ribbons on a gift. She swam in water clear enough to reveal God's secrets in the gentle waves, heard the voice of reason in a tender tide, and tasted solace in the salty breeze.

In her dream, Finley rushed to her sobbing, asking that she find him a rehab—treatment he'd refused for years. "Did you know," Josie said to him in the dream, "that ninety percent of the world's creatures live below the surface? Did you realize that if you get clean and have a year under your belt, I'm going to take you to St. John? You'll get to see firsthand how the world beneath us is so much more serene than what's above us."

Josie awakened the next day to a text on her phone. Dottie, refusing to sleep in her own room, stirred when Josie sat up. She felt woozy from the bottle of wine she'd downed last night after stewing over that photo and wondering who exactly that baby was. She reached for her readers, one of many pairs she'd collected from dollar stores, and read the text.

"Do you NOT think that I need money? That addicts can live off NO food? So, Dad is the more broke parent but he gives me twenty times more than you! You can delete me out of your life. You have ruined mine. You really DID cause all my abandonment issues and addictions. My therapist told me so!"

As she read the last words another message flashed. "If you don't give me any money to live on, I promise to God I will never talk to you another day in your life and I WILL NOT come to your funeral. I'm starving!!!!! I haven't eaten in three days!"

Josie's heart jackknifed and her hands shook as she searched Google for a number. Two hours later, as soon as Mellow Mushroom opened, she called.

"Yes, I'll have two large pizzas, extra cheese, please. One ground beef and the second pepperoni." She gave them her old address in Atlanta. No one would accuse her of child cruelty by starvation. No one would accuse her of enabling for sending over food. Would they?

She knew he'd relapsed. He wasn't hungry for pizza. He was hungry for drugs. Sending him cash was all but putting a down payment on his coffin.

Josie's intuition blazed. There had to be *something* she could do besides sit around and wait for him to die. A mother's instinct has always been to protect at all costs. Her time to save him—and by God she would—was running out.

She checked her son's Facebook account for clues but found she was blocked. No surprise. She clicked on Frank's page and searched his photos. When she came upon one of her and Frank shortly after their marriage, a sadness enveloped her. They had once been so happy. He'd been a wonderful husband in those early years.

Was there anything she hadn't tried to save their marriage? Counseling those four sessions until Frank called it BS. A trial separation. A marriage retreat. Going back to church.

Nothing had worked in the long-term.

6

Like a lot of women who looked back on failed marriages, wondering what went wrong, which parts were theirs to own, Josie tried to remember the good years with her husband and found herself thinking of their wedding day. It had been a splendid warm Saturday afternoon, May 21, 1994.

That was the day she felt the baby's kicks, tickling like popping bubbles. Josie thought it interesting that the first time she'd felt her child quickening was the very day she was marrying his father. Was that a sign? Was her baby saying, "Go for it, Mom," or something altogether different? Something like, "Walk out, Mom. This is a big mistake."

Two hours from that first kick, she waltzed down the aisle and married the love of her life and the father of her child. She wasn't a hundred percent sure how she felt at the time. She also wasn't a hundred percent sure how *he* felt either. Would they have ever married if she hadn't found herself knocked up? Yes, surely. She'd loved that man like crazy.

She'd confirmed the pregnancy one evening after she purchased a test and slid into the ladies' room at Kmart. She'd had a crampy feeling, as if she'd start her period any minute, but after a few minutes, a pink plus sign appeared in the little window. It was unmistakable.

Not fully believing her eyes, Josie had bolted from the stall and found a woman washing her hands at the sink. "Does this look like a plus sign to you?" she asked.

The poor woman had looked shocked, as if she'd walked in on something too private for her liking. "Yeah, I guess so," she said before quickly scramming.

Josie had carried that urine-soaked tray around all day and would pull it from her purse and stare at the pink sign that seemed to grow bolder and more distinct every minute. She'd cried and thanked God over and over. She remembered the evening she told Frank about the baby. She'd missed a period and immediately knew. Six pregnancy tests later she faced him with the news.

They had met for dinner at the Pinch Me Crab Shack near the Florida State campus. Josie had stared at her deep-fried shrimp, the smell inspiring waves of nausea. She sipped a Diet Coke while Frank, who'd come over from the University of Florida where he was in dental school, ordered a twenty-ounce Miller Lite.

He had been her one and only. And she'd held off losing her virginity until she turned twenty-one, finally making love with Frank, her boyfriend of a year, on her birthday. A week later she visited the university health services to get birth control pills. Two years later she was here, two months pregnant at a crab shack.

Frank cracked his crab legs and pulled out long, unbroken strings of white meat, dangling them. "This," he said, "is how it's done." He sank the crab into warm melted butter, then slid it into his mouth. He dipped another piece and held it for her. She'd never loved him more, knowing he was the type to always be present. To offer emotional support.

"Remember when we met," she said, trying to find a way to break the news. "I was doing my last show for the Florida State Circus?"

He raised his glass. "You," he said, "captured my heart the moment you swung from that trapeze. I knew when I saw you flip and catch the other bar that you were the only woman for me."

It was an odd sort of talent but pretty fitting for a Southern girl. Some loved cheerleading. Others twirled batons. The freakier girls seemed destined for the circus. "You were pretty persistent," Josie said. "Following me around until we'd packed up for the night."

He reached over and held her hand, the warmth of his touch bringing her courage. "How many men can say their girlfriends are trapeze artists? A star of the FSU Flying High Circus?"

She looked down at the napkin in her lap and saw it shaking against her legs. She had to tell him. She'd chosen a public place because even though Frank was kind and typically calm, she'd glimpsed his poutier side, where he'd disappear and resurface as if nothing happened. His flare-ups she couldn't always predict.

"Frank," she began, her heart rate kicking up, "I know this isn't good timing and that we weren't planning to get engaged until next year—" She stopped. His face had gone white.

"Tell me this is not what I think it is," he said, voice rising.

"What do you think this is?"

"Are you about to Dear John me? Here in public?"

She searched his eyes. "No. Frank, I'm...we're...it's just that...well, I might be a wee bit pregnant." *Wee bit?* She sounded like her mother.

His face froze and he said nothing. Then he stood, opened his wallet, and tossed sixty dollars on the table. "For dinner." He left the restaurant, and she didn't hear from him for two weeks, ignoring the red flag warning her of what may come.

One late morning as she dressed for her afternoon job at the station, she heard a knock on her apartment door. A delivery boy held a glass vase brimming with what seemed like a dozen sunflowers, her favorites. She tipped him three dollars and rushed to the kitchen to place the enormous flowers on the dinette table. She snatched the tiny card from the floral pick. *Josie, my love. Marry me. PS I'm not a fool and know what I have in you. XXOO Frank.* Tears welled but she wasn't ready to call him, an inner voice whispering for her to wait.

Three hours later the phone rang at her desk in the newsroom where she was working up a story exposing frat hazing on campus. "Whaddaya think?" he said, and she could hear the smile in his voice. Two weeks later he presented her with a deep-green emerald engagement ring he'd designed and had custom-made. Two months later she was about to be married.

She'd smoothed the tambour-embroidered lace of her gown, the same dress her mother had worn, belonging to that great-aunt who'd moved to London as a young woman and never left. She'd felt the bump of her lower abs, firm with life as she stood from the vanity and twirled in the fitted, beautifully cut gown, its swishy A-line skirt floating beneath her waist.

In the mirror, the iridescent beads shimmered against the sun drifting through her bedroom window. Her parents' fifteen-room Beaux Arts mansion spoke Southern elegance at its uppity best.

As she admired the gown, she heard staccato raps at the door. Without invitation, her mother burst into her pink-and-cream bedroom with its billowing canopy bed that made Josie feel protected. "You look beautiful," she said, scanning her in her entirety. Josie waited for the "but."

"Turn around and let me see you from the side." Katherine looked striking—and intimidating—in her ruby mother-of-the-bride gown, its ruched waist showing off her incredible figure and a front slit opening to reveal a long, tanned leg. "The dress is deliciously posh. However..." she said, hands on Josie's shoulders as she angled her in the light. She rubbed her forehead. "I'm having second thoughts about you wearing white. Anyhow, too late now, isn't it?"

Josie inhaled sharply, refusing to let her mother ruin this day.

"Can't you wear a support garment? Around your middle?"

"I'm four months pregnant, Mother. It's not exactly a secret."

"Secret or not. We're not the bloody sort to display our premarital lust at the altar."

Josie flushed but said nothing. Her mother's barbs and put-on British jargon would not get to her today. She had nothing to hide. It was 1994, for heaven's sake, and not puritanical times when young women like her had been shuttled away to stay with "beloved relatives," code for the Unwed Mother's Home, while adoption was quickly arranged.

She'd gotten pregnant eight months after graduating from Florida State University. The pregnancy, which Frank had blurted out to her mother, sent Katherine into an uproar. She'd insisted on throwing an elaborate wedding, which Josie tried unsuccessfully to dodge, wanting instead to elope in St. John.

She'd been twice to the island, staying in the Maho Bay Campground with its sturdy little tent-cottages, sugared crescent beaches, and the sea turtles she spotted while snorkeling Little Maho Bay. She'd even considered moving there. But now...the baby...Frank...marriage just moments away...

Katherine had paced the floor of Josie's bedroom. "We need to put on your veil and get to the church," she said. "Best be on the early side. You know how Frank is."

No, Josie didn't. Frank was typically between fifteen and thirty minutes late. Josie reached for the sterling tiara woven in silk flowers and crystals and fastened to yards and yards of two-tiered lace, a stunning work of art.

Why was it that she was marrying the man of her dreams, handsome and intelligent, lanky but superbly toned Frank, extraordinary lover (she needed no comparisons), and yet her gut screamed, *It's not too late. Run!* Hadn't they played her wedding song four times before her mother plied her with wine and shoved her through the church doors?

"I'm not wasting $80,000 for you to have second thoughts," she'd said. "Get in the bloody church."

Her father, also a lawyer but with a pianist's soul, had played Pachelbel's "Canon in D" over and over until her mother pushed her into the church. Frank had been standing at the altar with tears in his eyes, his face red with what? Fear? Jubilation? He'd smiled at her and two thoughts ran through her mind.

1. He's the most handsome thing I've ever seen.

2. If it doesn't work, Georgia laws grant a divorce as quickly as thirty days after filing.

Why would a woman in love think such a thing? As she'd walked toward her future, smiling at the Methodist preacher with his open face and Bible, she'd placed a hand on her belly. This child, this baby she loved with frightening intensity, deserved every chance he or she could have in this world. This child deserved a family. A mother. A father. Stability. Josie's needs from there on would always come second.

7

At work, Josie had a hard time focusing. When she'd turned to her online MAC group that morning, the messages left her hollow and whittled.

It's only a matter of time that some of us will lose a child to overdose or crime, or see their kid cuffed and locked up in prison, a woman wrote. *Mine decided he'd had enough with our rehab system that's so broken and ineffective. Last summer, he took his own life to end his pain. The lucky ones,* she continued, *are carted to involuntary commitment and detox centers, many experiencing the revolving doors of rehabs, staying a day here, a week there, only to return to the seduction of their DOC—Drug of Choice. Prayers be with you, Moms! This country needs to change the way it does rehab. It's not working as is!*

Josie thought of the newspaper article and the out-of-the-box rehab that the renowned Atlanta therapist was running. Maybe she ought to look into it. For now, she felt shell-shocked and riddled with guilt. She was fully aware that her impressionable, high-strung son had witnessed his mother relying on a nip of wine in the evenings after work and heard her soft cries behind the bedroom door.

What must have gone through his mind when he'd come home from school and found his father gone and his mother on the south side of sloshed? Had he quickly discovered the answer to feeling whole within the circle of kids experimenting with drugs, those angry or soul-searching adolescents who hated their parents or maybe hated themselves? Some of them way too privileged and entitled with their Xboxes, iPhones, iPads, and i-flipping-everythings. Kids who moved into high school with helicopter parents trying, through their progeny, to get their own childhoods right, parents who did everything for them, kept them from feeling any consequences of their actions. Parents like Frank, who considered a simple time-out the equivalent of child abuse. Frank, who was Finley's best buddy and not parent material at all.

She often thought this: If they'd had a perfect marriage and done everything one hundred percent textbook perfect, wouldn't genetics *still* have slammed a fist into contented living and punched the buttons that lit up the brain's wiring for addiction?

Josie had devoured books on parenting the "difficult child," but none of her disciplinary measures made it to fruition or past Frank's reversing them. It wasn't his fault. He simply loved their son too much to cause any suffering that might elicit change. She remembered a time shortly after Finley turned nineteen and spent four days in jail for pawning stolen goods for an underage friend so they could buy weed, then drove blacked out with an empty bottle of Evan Williams rattling around the floorboard.

Josie had offered rehab. Frank had offered bail. And on and on spun their mismatched parenting styles, chopping their marriage into kindling, then splinters. Until finally, Josie knew what she had to do. She made a decision almost as excruciating as Meryl Streep's in *Sophie's Choice* when forced to choose which child to save. She chose Dottie. She'd raise her baby in a loving and calm environment instead of putting her sweet child to breast with the ambiance of skunk weed and the sounds of sketchy teens pounding on the door at all hours.

With Pauline not scheduled until noon, Josie mindlessly put away stock the dock workers had brought in. When she finished, she might even clean a little. She didn't need Pauline throwing out the insubordination card, not when this job was already hanging by a thread. No employee in recent history, according to Monica, had ever *not* passed and *not* failed certification. "It's one or the other," she'd said. "They're messing with you."

Maybe she should just call Fabiana and get whatever it was over with. But she'd said she'd be in this week "at some point." Pauline said she often pops in and surprises her BAs, trying to catch them violating dress code or other infractions.

Josie found a stool in the shoe department and began sorting eye shadows by number, blushes by alphabet, and mascaras by formulas. She heard the click of heels.

"Hey, did you hear the news?" Monica knelt near the stool.

"What? I didn't see you come in," Josie said, rubbing her neck, sore from bending over the drawers.

"Management has officially named Pauline the new counter manager. Not that she hadn't assumed the role before it became official. I sure miss Kyle."

Josie stood and stretched her back. She'd never gotten to know Kyle, the former counter manager who'd quit to live with his husband in Puerto Rico. The phone rang. "Let me grab this. It might be Fabiana."

"Hola. Buenos dias." Best to answer the official way.

"You need two credits before the end of the day," said Galena, the store's cosmetics manager. "I've set up a table with goodies, and today we're giving associates five dollars for each one they open."

Josie hated cajoling people to sign up for Brigman's cards. She felt like a streetwalker standing at the front of the store, smiling while offering full-size fragrance testers if one would simply fork over a license and social and allow the store to gouge a hole in their credit scores. "I'm on credit duty," she said to Monica.

"Let Carly do it. She loves it up there where she can meet men. We call her the Credit Whore. She'll do it if you slip her a few products."

"That might not be a bad idea. Hey, I better finish putting up stock." Josie thought of the stack of bills rising on her kitchen counter. "I need to stay on Pauline's good side."

Monica grunted. "I didn't know she had one. Hey, after work, some of us are going to that new brewery to celebrate Megan's divorce. You've met her. Works part-time here at Clinique?"

Josie remembered a young woman with an Irish accent mixed with blue-collar Southern-speak. Her first impression hadn't been a good one.

"Divorced? She seems too young to even be married."

"Ah, it wasn't even a year. She found out he was gay."

Josie raised her brows. "Well, that's a good enough reason to reduce a man to public records," she said, shaking her head.

"Least they didn't have kids. Listen, you think you could go tonight? Just for a bit?"

Josie thought it nice how her new friend wanted to include her. "I'd love to but not sure yet. I need to be home for Dottie, my late-in-life little wonder."

"Ahh, I want to meet her. Bet my twins would love her. If it's nice we're going to one of the breweries by the river. And Philly's coming. You've met her, right?"

Josie smiled, thinking of Philly's announcements. "Not formally but I've seen her bouncing around and heard a few of her little ads. They make my day. And she's so exquisite."

"You two need to hang out," Monica said. "I might have problems with online dating but, oh my God, the frogs and trolls she pulls in! And the strangest places she'll go to meet a man." A customer walked up and studied the assortment of Clinique toners. "Be right with you, ma'am," Monica said and returned her attention to Josie. "I'm talking Chuck E. Cheese and laundromats when she has a perfectly fine washer and dryer at home. Last I heard, she joined one of those AA groups and doesn't even have an addiction herself whatsoever. 'Course her daughter was heavy into all kinds of drugs."

Josie had been absently listening to Monica prattle, nodding her head at all the right places, but her mind was elsewhere. When she heard *drugs* and *daughter* she shot to full attention. She'd already thought she and this Philly woman would get along, but now she had to meet her. No other parents understood the torture of this disease, what with their little Ivy League kids studying abroad and skiing winters in Aspen or the Alps.

The morning dragged. After Monica finished with several customers, she continued following Josie around. "I mean we have a *Vogue* and *Cosmo* supermodel working full-time at the Lancôme counter. First Black woman on the cover of one of those high-brow news magazines like *Time* or one of them.

Said her exes ran off with all her money. Something about bad investments and what she refers to as the 'literal skeleton in her closet.'"

Josie had finished the stock and sat at the credit table, surrounded by an assortment of fragrance testers and makeup from the various lines' GWPs, gifts with purchases. She would stay awhile and look the part for Galena but wouldn't approach people. If they showed interest, only then would she offer them a credit card and a partially used bottle of whatever they chose. Now and then she checked her counter, not wanting to miss a sale."Skeleton?" Josie said to Monica, more rhetorically than a question.

"We're not allowed to speak of it," Monica said, picking up a half-empty bottle of Aqua Di Gio and sniffing the cap. "She'd kill us. But I'll give you a hint: her last husband couldn't get over his first wife and robbed her tomb. Put the body in one of their closets."

Josie shook her head, not fully believing this crazy bite of gossip. No way. Yet weirder things had happened over the years she anchored the news.

"Lord, you oughta hear her talk about her more colorful customers," Monica said. "She's got one old lady who buys four jars of that pricey lifting and firming face cream every week and slathers it on those boobs that look like dead trout on a trotline. Thinks it's actually lifting and firming those deflated basset-hound ears."

Josie laughed, loving Monica's colorful descriptions. Only in the South, she thought.

"Come on out with us if you can."

"I promise if I can't tonight, I'll for sure arrange it soon," Josie said. When she glanced again at her bay, she saw Pauline. Her skin seemed to shrink under the goosebumps, her mouth like cotton. "I'd better go. Lady Tremaine is back."

Monica laughed. "Listen, Cinderella, that woman's got her head so far up Mr. Hoven's ass she may as well have given him a colonoscopy."

"I need to start writing down your expressions. You've certainly mastered Southern-speak."

"Yeah, my Asian roots are wearing off, unfortunately. We're a crazy bunch here at Brigman's. Somebody told me old Mr. Hoven has done it again."

"What do you mean?" Josie asked.

"He's hired another one of you celeb types over in Laura Mercier. She made all kinds of news having those twins with two different daddies. One is dark-skinned. The other girl white as me."

Josie thought this would make a wonderful feature for the six o'clock news. She could almost write the story in her head: A store manager some call 'perverse' and others claim is a genius is tackling the rising competition from online shopping with a controversial new approach. Mr. Joel Hoven is making waves—and lots of money—recruiting 'has-been' celebs with fifteen minutes of fame to increase foot traffic—and sales— at Brigman's Department Store in Asheville, North Carolina. The company's other twenty-plus stores may follow suit in the future. In addition to hiring an ex-supermodel, a news anchor who went cuckoo, and a gynecological wonder, Hoven says he has recruited his biggest coup to date, coming soon at the Kiehl's counter. We are all waiting to see who he has…in store, so to speak.

"Time to march to my guillotine," Josie said, pushing back from the table and tripping over one of the legs. Her tights caught on a screw and split. "Jeez. There's no point in my ever buying anything new."

"I laughed so hard when the entire sole of your shoe fell off the other day," Monica said. "I was on the floor doubled over when I saw you use a staple gun to fix it."

"Shoes have never been my thing."

At the counter, the first thing out of Pauline's mouth was, "Quit hanging out with the competition. You know we have to beat Clinique and the others this year."

"Right. I was trying to get credits." A tiny white lie.

"As you know, I am officially the new counter manager." She flashed her Art the Clown smile, red lipstick like blood all over those absurd Hollywood-sized veneers.

"Have you heard from Fabiana?" Josie wanted this certification issue settled. Either way was better than limbo.

"It doesn't matter. I'm in charge and you'll refrain with a capital R from touching a single client's face. You'll clean, organize, greet, and do massages or give them a fragrance experience. We need to get rid of all these Mother's Day sets that didn't sell."

"I've put away all the stock, so I'm going to take my lunch break now that you're here."

Pauline reached for the perfumes to spray the Misty menthols from her clothes. "Make sure you don't skimp on calories," she said sneering. "Wouldn't want a girl of your girth to go hungry."

This didn't bother Josie. People who told fat jokes were pathetic self-haters. "You may be the counter manager, but you need to watch your mouth. Anybody else would be offended by—"

"Remember, you may have a job now, but I'm quite certain your once-charmed life is behind you, Miss Falling Apart on National TV. Or is it Miss Mother of the Year of a son on drugs and a daughter who can't even—"

Josie's blood heated. She stared Pauline down as one would an errant child. "I'll be speaking to Mr. Hoven about your verbal abuse." The nerve of the woman. No one trashed her kids.

"Go right ahead. I opened eight credits in a week, so my job is quite secure."

"I've ignored your digs until now because women of your sort don't usually register with me. They're just insecure little people with overloads of self-loathing. The way you treat the others working here is—"

Josie's cell lit up followed by a rift from Ambrosia's "You're the Biggest Part of Me." She walked off, leaving Pauline pissed. She knew it was Finley, the only person she'd assigned a custom ringtone. The day had been disastrous, so how much more could a serrated knife cutting bone hurt? She quickly answered, but he hung up. And then texted. Shuddering, Josie took cover behind a towering étagère of sneakers. "Mail me money, you bitch. Everyone hates you. Maybe you can find a family that loves you. None of us do. You won't even support your son! YOU TURNED ME INTO THIS FOR LEAVING US."

As she clicked out of the message, the screen brightened again. Her therapist and all those support-group women had told her to block his calls. But she couldn't. No matter how badly he treated her, she knew Ambrosia was her only link, and the song that once soothed her now knocked her heart out of rhythm. "I hate you, Dad hates you, Grampy hates you because of how you treated the Sacred One which is me. Now give me money! You ruined Dad's life and you don't even care. You have no heart."

There was not enough wine or Whoppers in the world to deal with these missives. Josie knew that beneath the enslavement to dope, there had to be a mental illness raging. Or was it the drugs triggering the psychosis? Instead of allowing herself to resent her own child, she remembered him sober: one of the finest young men she'd ever met.

He was in there. Somewhere.

At lunch in the food court, Josie picked at orange chicken from Panda Express, but she'd lost her appetite. She longed to be at home with Dottie, giving her the love her son didn't want. She thought of her little girl, sweet and stubborn with a dash of sass, and pushed the plate of food across the table. She reached for her phone and dialed the store.

"Galena speaking."

"Hi. This is Josie. I'm not feeling well and won't be back today."

"Okay," Galena said and hung up. Nothing else.

Her mind circled back to Frank and their marriage. No matter how often she sifted through the rubble of their last days together, she could not have done it any differently. Not with Dottie in the picture.

8

Pauline hadn't shown up for her shift, and Josie had already sold a couple of things, ringing them in under her name and not caring if Pauline had a fit.

Josie hadn't figured out what to do regarding the woman. Surely she had a good side. Don't all the world's malevolent beings spring forth with at least one positive trait? Perhaps a love of animals? A kick-ass knack for whittling?

"Hey, over there. You." A woman in black and draped in the Clinique lab coat motioned to her. Megan, the newly divorced woman. Josie had run into her a few times since starting her job and tried to avoid her. Megan surveyed her bay, making sure no customers lurked, and ambled over.

"Honey, this is between you and me only," she said in her strange Irish-Southern accent. "Pinky swear you won't tell a soul." She held out her finger which Josie reluctantly took. "I want you to know that Pauline isn't just mean to you. She does this to all of us. It's been this way for a year. Believe it or not, she used to be pretty fantastic. I'm not sure what's happened to make her act this awful."

Josie released her finger. "I'm trying hard to find the good in her. Trying to walk in her shoes as my dad always advised."

"Listen, she waits till we're at lunch or on a smoke break and sneaks over to other counters and steals all our sales. And oh yeah, have you noticed how she leaves right at three fifteen every Thursday?" Megan seemed pleased with herself and puffed like a frigate bird.

"I hadn't thought about it."

"Did you also notice old Hoven sometimes leaves then too?"

Josie tapped her foot nervously. She didn't want to gossip with Megan about the store manager, but the girl wasn't taking a hint and looked both ways as if making sure the coast was clear. "And get this," she continued. "I hear old Hoven's wife is wanting to fire Pauline's skinny arse. But I still don't think that homewrecker's going anywhere. The only way she'll be forced out of here is if the store burns to the ground."

A few others at Brigman's had said pretty much the same thing, that Pauline used to be all right, fun even, but had turned into a vituperative witch a year or so ago. From the corner of her eye, Josie spotted a walk-up and was relieved to get out of this conversation. "Well, good talking to you. I have a customer."

"Be careful over there," Megan said, squinching her eyes.

The woman at La Belleza wore clothes so bright you could have seen her from across town. She lingered at the display of the new three-hundred-dollar facial oils, and Josie watched her caress the products, removing a bottle and reading the label. She had on a trapeze blouse the color of mustard and paired with blinding-yellow jeggings so tight Josie wondered how she could walk. At least, she thought, this one was eyeing the oils and serums and wouldn't be wearing her out trying on every eye shadow in the cases, sixty or more shades, the least expensive product La Belleza offered.

"I don't know why their cheap asses buy those singles and won't fork it up for our palettes," Josie had heard Pauline say. *Because,* Josie wanted to say, *sometimes the palettes have ONE color they'd actually wear and four they wouldn't.*

Before Josie could get to the woman, Megan returned, phone in hand. "I know this sounds weird, but you seem like you've been around the block and know a thing or two about men." Josie didn't know how in the world to respond. "I've got these guys on my phone from this dating service Monica turned me on to. Could you help me screen them when you're done with that lady? You wouldn't believe this one guy whose very first question was to ask if I was on hormone replacement therapy. Here I am only twenty-four." She threw up her hands and shrugged. "Creep must think those things make you horny. Oh, and this other guy's first question was whether I had health insurance and if it included vision and dental. Goodness, these men."

"A woman sure has to be careful," Josie said, trying to break free to wait on her customer. She finally managed to reach the woman stroking the La Belleza products as if she were examining the finest porcelain from the Qing dynasty. The jars and hour-glass-shaped bottles, in that rich lapis blue, were where the money grew.

"Hola. May I help you, ma'am?" Josie always gave her customers space, not making them feel the intense pressure they might endure at another counter or from a sales associate who hadn't hit her goal in a month.

"I was wondering if I might have a sample of this new oil?" she asked. Her lips hardly moved. She had one of those man-made faces, tight and swollen baboon-fanny traits, courtesy of plastic surgery that left her of an undeterminable age and species. Every feature hardened like papier-mâché as if mummified. Oh, and her hair! Josie couldn't peel her eyes from the woman's updo, rising hive-like and so stiff with lacquer a gum wrapper was embedded near the top. Two white petals from the Bradford pear trees had blown in and settled near a neck so tight you could all but see her thyroid.

"Why, we certainly can arrange for a sample," Josie said. "At La Belleza, if you have a seat for a few minutes and give me the honor of demonstrating our award-winning skin care, we are happy to treat you to a gift with your visit."

Into the chair and out with the Brigman's charge card. Twenty minutes later the woman left with Josie's personalized skincare guide, three small samples in a lapis-and-white polka-dotted La Belleza cosmetics bag, and nearly five hundred dollars on her card. Josie rang the sale in her number, vowing not to let Pauline intimidate her.

After the woman left, Josie bristled as she remembered she wasn't supposed to touch a face until certified, but what could she do with Pauline AWOL? She was simply providing excellent customer service.

By lunchtime, Pauline clomped to the counter in five-inch black stilettos suited more for garter belts than standing on one's feet all day. Josie drew the deep yoga breaths Ruby had demonstrated as Pauline threw her clear bag into the cabinet, not so much as saying hello before click-clacking straight for the daily sales sheet next to the cash register.

She sipped her lemon water (lemons burn calories, after all) as she read the numbers. "Wow, it's nice to make money while you're having a massage. I take it this huge sale is under my number?"

Josie needed to think as fast as she did when live at the scene of a fire or murder. "She was in a hurry and knew what she wanted." The omission wasn't exactly a lie.

"So, you didn't touch her, do a makeover or skincare consult?"

"Well, she did want to try the serums and asked for a foundation match. I looked for another associate and couldn't find one free." Tiny white lie.

Pauline punched numbers into the cash register's computer, trying to bring up her daily tally. Instead of screaming and making a scene, she leveled her eyes at Josie and shook her head slowly. "I'm sorry. I'm going to have to report this to Fabiana and Mr. Hoven. You've been told more than once not to do this. And the nerve of you ringing it all for yourself."

Josie knew she'd broken the no-touching-faces rule and owed Pauline an apology, as much as it pained her. "Look. It won't happen again." She thought again of the bills and how most of the TV station's contract buyout went to her three-month stay at Calming Oaks Rehabilitation of Kansas, better known as CORK, a catchy acronym for putting the stopper in the bottle. Insurance went only so far, and her latest bank statement had shrunk to nearly $2,000, including savings.

She heard her mother's voice. *You should have sucked it up like any decent woman with an ounce of pride and stayed with the station, not gone all crackers. It's pure rubbish and not as if you'd shot someone on the air. Give people time and they'll move on to another bit of juicy tragedy and forget the mistakes you've made. I'm purely gobsmacked by all of this.*

Josie couldn't have stayed. She hadn't wanted to, and the station hadn't offered. Her Atlanta had been nothing but a mass of confusing highways, suburbs of pretentiousness, and poor choices, a monumental reminder that no matter the lengths she'd taken to keep up a career, despite all the chaos chasing her son and personal life, no matter how much she longed for Finley's recovery, the city wasn't helping.

"A new set of playmates and a new playground," is the one thing she enjoyed hearing in therapy. And then a couple of months ago, out of the clear blue, Mr. Hoven from Brigman's in Asheville had called. She'd had nothing to lose.

"You came highly recommended by one of our top-selling women in the business," he'd said. "We can't pay your moving expenses but we're sending you to New York for training."

"That sounds wonderful." Josie, fresh off a highway of horrors, had been in a hurry to secure something solid in her life. She could have done as most burned-out or laid-off journalists did—searched for a job in marketing or public relations at a nonprofit, but it was too soon.

Not many were keen on hiring a woman who'd cracked up in her former job to speak about the merits of keeping families together for the United Way of Greater Atlanta. The cosmetics job offered an opportunity to live in the coolest city in the South.

She'd visited Asheville a few times covering news events: the Eric Rudolph "Olympic Bomber" case, and a one-on-one with Jennifer Lawrence when she was filming *The Hunger Games* in a neighboring county.

"I'll start whenever you need me," she'd told Mr. Hoven.

"Can you be here in two weeks? We're super short at the counter and need coverage immediately."

"Yes. I could manage that." A flashing thought of Finley had crossed her mind and she tensed, wondering if moving to Asheville was the same as abandoning him all over again.

Now as she stood before Pauline, her pride lying on the floor, she feared she might lose this job, which had been a way to pay bills and have a semblance of social life. "I'd like another chance?" She hated the groveling in her voice.

Pauline pulled herself tall as those with new power will do. "Ordinarily I would. But since I'm now counter manager, I have a responsibility to make sure everything goes—"

"ATTENTION, BRIGMAN'S BEAUTIES! JOIN US IM-MEDIATELY, AS IN RIGHT NOW, AT THE LANCÔME COUNTER! We have a new salve over here—yes, salve. Let me show you how the products you're using for your talons and hooves, those creams to banish horse feet, can wipe out all the wrinkles under your eyes. You heard it right, ladies. Come see me, Philly, over in Lancôme and I'll show you revolutionary ways to STAMP OUT EYE BAGS! And if you're thinking you haven't got time because your husband's waiting in the car, I have four words for you. Let's say it all together now, ladies: BETTER LATE THAN UGLY!"

"That's it!" Pauline dashed off, leaving Josie hanging. She picked up the phone, her face splotching. "You *have* to do something about her announcements. Well…yes…I'm well aware of her fame, but she needs…Oh, well even so… it's not—anyway, I need to meet up with you later to discuss an issue at the counter…yes, two is fine." She placed the phone into its cradle as if laying down a baby for sleep. "I'm meeting with Joel, um, Mr. Hoven, at two." She smiled in slow motion.

The only thing Josie could do now was plead her case to the store manager, and surely he'd understand and want what was best for Brigman's customers. "Happy customers," she'd heard him say during morning meetings, "means increased business. And increased business means…" He would wait for the associates to dully mutter, "Increased raises." Yes, a whole half-dollar instead of twenty-five cents.

Not wanting to bask in Pauline's gloating, Josie excused herself from the counter and headed for her *office*—the wheel-chair-accessible stall in the ladies' room. She sat fully clothed on the toilet, her black makeup bag, the one that held her brushes, on her lap. Behind the fluffy bronzer and blush tools, under-neath a confusing stack of various eye-shadow brushes, she found her emergency medicine, two mini-bottles of Jim Beam, which she was proud had remained untouched for at least a week. She opened one and poured it down, the heat burning her throat. She reached for the second and paused. *That's it. I've had enough.* She wrapped the bottle in a paper towel and buried it in the wastebasket.

Before leaving the restroom, Josie flipped through her emails, mostly spam for funeral plans and long-term-care insurance due to her current address at the pre-death pit stop. She signed on to Facebook, on the off chance her son had unblocked her. He hadn't. As she clicked the Edward Jones site to check the remains of her funds, a call came in. She recoiled.

Frank.

She almost let it go to voice mail but was anxious to learn anything she could about Finley and if he'd relapsed. "Hello." Her voice trembled.

"I hope you finally realize how YOU fucked up everyone's lives. Mine. Finley's. Running off with Dottie and leaving us here to go broke."

Josie returned to the stall and collapsed on the seat. *Here we go.* He hadn't even wanted to be in Dottie's life and thought it more than admirable that he was a B-and-C dad—cards and small gifts on birthdays and Christmases. Josie wasn't about to go down the "we need money road," not when she'd left Frank with a huge chunk of assets in the divorce, including the Southern Gothic home with all the equity she'd invested. "Is Finley all right? I got these disturbing texts from him that sounded like he'd relapsed."

"Would you be all right if your mother abandoned you?"

Josie thought this ironic. "She *did* abandon me. All the time. I got over it." She wasn't sure there was a lot of truth in the "getting over it" part, but at least she didn't whip out the A-card at every turn. "I want to talk to Finley. Did he get my package?"

"He got your fucking pizzas."

"No need to cuss and act vile. I sent him some new khakis and a gas gift card along with a few—"

"Are you stupid, Josie?" Frank's voice pitched falsetto with anger. "You may as well give him cash because all he does is turn around and sell most of the crap you send."

Her support-group mothers had said the same, but Josie had been naive enough to think, *not my son*. She would remain peaceful on the phone and knew that the best way to calm Frank was placation. "I know it's a lot on you looking after him and dealing with all the drugs and repercussions from the divorce. I was thinking you might need a break." Wasn't that what Frank always wanted? Living just to bolt again?

He grew quiet and Josie's method seemed to work. "Why not let me take Finn for a while here in Asheville. He'd love it here and you could work on your art and even—"

"I don't think he wants to go there. He is still dealing with… all of this."

"Has he relapsed, Frank?" Josie asked in her placate-the-pitbull voice.

"Yes. He didn't come home last night."

"Frank, I think we should try and put our differences aside, stop the blame game, and help our son. Could we do that?"

"We could if you'd send money every month," he said, anger returning to his voice.

"I'll do my best," she said, another white lie, and wondered if she'd even have a job by day's end. "Let's try to meet halfway with this. Tell him to unblock me from his phone. That would be a start."

"I'll talk to him and let him know about the offer to come up to Asheville." Such a different ex-husband when the possibility of cash was in the offing. "He'll probably stagger home in a day or two."

After Josie hung up, she decided to take the allotted fifteen-minute break she was granted per shift. She rode the service elevator to the break room, which was decorated in dismal: two ancient refrigerators—one in that seventies avocado shade—a few wobbly tables, vinyl chairs scratched in frustration and obscenities, and a boxy television set that played only one channel, either old soaps or *Dr. Phil.*

The main purpose of TVs at Brigman's was training videos. All sorts of annoying DVDs ranging from sexual harassment on the job to how to sweet-talk, charm, and cajole people into opening store credit cards. Mercy, how the store drained everything out of its employees but their damned bone marrow.

Several men and women in black or cut-priced business attire sat in the unyielding chairs etched with "Fuck this," and "Die Brigman's." Their eyes were vacant as they chewed food while the TV couples went at it. Most wolfed down items from the food court, the room reeking of spring rolls and pizza and french fries. A few of the healthier employees, realizing their gig at Brigman's leaned toward long-term, tucked into salads and leftovers.

Josie spotted Monica in the corner eating greens and beans from a Rubbermaid storage container. "Hey. Mind if I join you?" She needed to depressurize, and Monica was always good for that.

Monica patted the chair next to hers. "You look like you've swallowed a can of habanera peppers," she said. "Or ran a 10k."

Josie's hand went to her cheeks, as hot as if she had a high fever, courtesy of her conversation with Frank. And the alcohol. "I'm fine. I might be having a hot flash." Monica took a paper plate and fanned her. "How are the Match fellows treating you?" Josie asked, wanting a lighthearted conversation.

"Girrrrrllll. Wait, hold a sec." She pecked a long onyx-painted fingernail at her dating app to refresh the page. "Dang, this cute pilot just winked at me on Match. Oh my gosh, here's a pic of him with his black poodle." She held the phone for Josie to see. "And look, there's one of him without a shirt, and another of him on a sailboat, wearing one of those scrote-totes. I mean, what normal man wears a tiger-print Speedo?"

"Goodness, he's certainly got a healthy sense of self," Josie said, figuring the man was a narcissist.

Monica continued scrolling through her phone, shopping for dates as one might for the ripest tomatoes at a tailgate market. "Oh, check this out. This cutie has winked at me. Uh-oh. He only has one photo, which makes me suspicious." She pushed the phone across the table so Josie could see the man in a collared shirt and narrow tie looking like an accountant or a church deacon.

Monica grabbed the phone back and read the man's bio. "For the love of God!" she shouted, waking up the elderly lady who works in the home department. "Listen to this. 'I want women that cook food like the Cracker Barrel and scorch a mattress like Stormy Daniels. I love Trump, guns, and prefer my deer AND my women with impressive racks."

They both cracked up. "I'm gonna mess with him," Monica said. "I'm going to send him a little message and then block his ass."

While Monica worked on a comeback for this misogynist, Josie's mind veered in all directions but landed in dead-ends. *If they fired her, she could always…what? If Finley relapsed again, she could maybe…what?*

"I give up," Monica said, tossing her phone in her bag. "I'm not giving him the satisfaction." She frowned. "Hey, you okay?"

Josie snapped to attention. "Sorry. I just have a lot on my mind."

"You need a girls' night out with us," Monica said, her eyes empathetic. "Look, I know about your sweet daughter and needing to be home with her when you're here all hours of the day and night. But a woman needs her girl-time."

Josie thought of her dear friend Willa back in Atlanta and her women friends at the TV station. At least every two weeks, they'd get together over wine and tapas, and the shared laughter had always diffused life's worries. "I'll make a point to go with y'all next time for sure," Josie said as Monica popped the lid back on her lunch and rushed to clock in. The only one remaining in the room was the elderly lady who'd fallen back to sleep in the chair, probably dreaming she didn't have to sell K-cups and bedspreads until she died.

She thought of Pauline and wondered what it was about this woman that left her so uneasy. She seemed to know things Josie had never been made public. Maybe Josie should mention her verbal abuse to management. But she'd always hated tattletales and it did seem that Pauline was as golden as Josie's Emmys and could do no wrong at Brigman's.

Before leaving the break room to rejoin her nemesis, Josie slid a dollar into the vending machine for a pack of Doritos. In the hallway she all but collided with Mr. Hoven. "Josette," he said without a smile. He smelled like a gigolo in too much Paco Rabanne cologne. "You got a minute?"

"Sure." It struck Josie how working at a department store was similar to being a kid again, either getting into trouble and going to time-out or being rewarded for good behavior.

Mr. Hoven wore a Ralph Lauren suit, his white button-down slightly wrinkled and tongued in a black-and-white piano-key tie, reminding her of the one she'd bought her father long ago. She studied his face: the trendy goatee groomed to perfection, his sandy hair, slicked back with man grease and combed over to hide his bald spots. She guessed him to be fiftyish, with frat-boy features he'd likely showcased in college still traceable. He reminded her of a suave quarterback gone halfway to seed from too many Bud Lights and a disdain for his life.

"I thought we could go to my office and have a little chat," he said. "Okay with you?"

Josie's heart pounded so hard she felt a pulse beating against her temples. "Yes, sir."

He led her to his office, opening doors as if manners pained him. He shut his door with a bigger bang than necessary and gestured for her to take a seat. Where the main store had soft lighting, row upon row of harsh fluorescent bulbs lined the ceilings in the back offices, which were a catacomb of cubicles. His desk looked as if a copy machine had exploded; so many papers scattered in disarray. A photo of him and his wife, blond and lithe, along with three towheaded boys atop horses, lay sideways in the mess. Dust coated the frame.

Josie braced for what she thought was coming. Pauline's handiwork wrote the script across his pudgy, my-quarterback-days-are-over face. The mug of a man who'd spent way too much time in retail and not enough hours in the sun or with his family.

"Josette," he said. "I need to discuss this…this incident you had at your former job."

"Oh." Her voice squeaked. She'd assumed he wanted to discuss her doing makeovers without being certified and then remembered Pauline wasn't meeting with him until two, so he couldn't know about that yet.

"I was well aware of the viral video and what happened in Atlanta," he said, rubbing his thumbs. "When Pauline suggested we hire you, I was all for it, since bringing in quote-unquote personalities has certainly helped our business." Josie waited for the "but" she knew was coming.

"Corporate is coming down on me," he said, face showing a hint of vulnerability. "I guess they weren't aware at the time of your hiring the full extent of what happened that night on television." Josie flinched. She'd never watched the entire video, unable to face this act so out of character from her true self. "Look. I'm sorry it's come to this, but I'm going to have to put you on suspension until further notice. Without pay, I'm afraid to say."

So, she wasn't fired. Yet. But…no pay! Josie decided to go ahead and beat Pauline to the punch and tell Mr. Hoven about the client she'd consulted. "I, um…I need to discuss something that happened earlier today."

He took out a cigarette and waited. "I did a makeover on a client… She did end up buying a good bit…anyway, Pauline is meeting with you later to let you know I broke the rule and provided services to a woman without my certification."

He blew out a breath and looked Josie in the eye. "That's not my rule. My rule is to keep customers happy. This is a non-issue as far as I'm concerned."

"Thank you," she said, relieved.

"I'll speak with Fabiana about this delay in certification. In the meantime, I'm sorry but you'll have to get your things and leave. We'll be in touch with the next steps." He said this as kindly as one can when delivering unpleasant news.

"Yes. I understand."

There was nothing at the counter she needed to collect, so as soon as Josie left Mr. Hoven's office, she also left the building. She'd drive around and scout for an available phone, where she'd call Finley and ask him to come to Asheville. Beg him to come. It could be her last chance to reach him.

9

Maybe this suspension from work would give Josie a chance to see Finley. She just needed to figure out how to persuade him to come to Asheville. If he refused, she'd hunt him down.

She cranked her car, the check-engine light deciding to cooperate today, and remembered that the members of MAC had told her about a support group that met nearby weekly. "Where is the Mothers of Addicted Children support group in Asheville?" she asked Siri before backing up. An address popped up and she realized the meeting was, fortuitously, today. She had plenty of time to catch the two o'clock meeting at Grace Heart Presbyterian Church a few miles away.

Josie's stomach dispatched a hungry signal and she eased her BMW, now growling with a new noise, into Taco Bell for a Cheesy Gordita Crunch and a large Diet Coke to go with her Doritos from the break room. While eating in her car, she called Ruby to fill her in and let her know she'd be home early.

"Hello there. You've reached Ruby. Leave a message if you find it necessary. Om Shanti, Shanti, Shanti."

"Hey, Ruby. I'm taking a little time off work...frankly, I might not be asked to come back. Well...see you late this afternoon."

Josie miraculously found a parking spot downtown and decided to kill time walking along Lexington Avenue. She checked out all the shops selling vintage clothing and rare used books, the one-of-a-kind boutiques, and restaurants where the food is so local you could hear the carrots rooting in the soil.

Josie loved downtown Asheville and its neoclassical and art deco architecture, with Spanish Renaissance thrown into the eclectic mix. When the crash of '29 hit Asheville, the city had the highest per capita debt in the country. Since the town was too poor for urban renewal, its ancient buildings remained untouched and became a national treasure.

As she navigated the city's hilly streets, the sun against her black clothes became intense. Josie ducked into one of the newer bars in what had been a pawnshop sixty years prior. The only patrons besides staff were what the makeup girls call trustafarians, young hippies with trust funds and who smelled of musty closets and sweat-soaked patchouli.

She was here just to cool off and have a nice sparkling soda or seltzer. She was surprised when the bartender said, "What will you be having?" and without a blink, she said, "I'll try the white sangria."

As she reached for her wallet, she saw six messages piled up on her phone's screen. She quickly finished her wine and ducked into her car to read Frank's latest depressing avalanche.

Message One: "My car is gone. I didn't realize when we talked earlier, but Finley's taken off again and my wallet is missing."

Message Two: "I have no idea where he is. This shit's all your fault. My genes don't have all this crap in them."

Message Three: "You love to ruin our lives. Spending all your money on rehab for yourself and running off to the Caribbean when we needed money to eat and pay the mortgage."

Message Four: "You need to call me and fix this now and not by getting the cops to involuntarily commit him."

Message Five: "I've unblocked you. Call me now!"

Message Six: "It's not fair how you ran off and left me to deal with all this! And don't call me spewing all that 'He needs rehab' shit.' What he needs is a MOTHER!"

No, she wouldn't respond to this. She would not waste what was left of her sanity just to say what was on her mind: *Get a job. Quit relying on art alone and provide for Finley. I paid for most of his college education, not you. I never understood why you can't go back to dentistry. It wouldn't kill you to use your DDS. And as far as Finley is concerned, he does need rehab and has for the past six or seven years.*

Getting to a meeting was critical for her sanity. Josie wondered if she'd have the nerve to talk face to face to women like her, moms who'd lost their babies and who survived on the mist of their yearnings. When she arrived, she parked in the upper lot and walked down the bank and into a church basement half filled with women. She sat in the back, shivering from scalp to toenails despite the temperature in the room, which had to be near eighty degrees. She always got cold when fearful.

The room smelled of anxiety and brewed coffee. Many of the faces at the tables sagged around the mouth, eyes puffed and baggy. Tired. Tired of it all. The fight, the trials, the broken promises, and defeat.

The leader of the group stood and read the preamble. It was similar to the Twelve-Step meetings Josie's counselors forced her to attend in treatment, meetings she discarded once released. Next, she read the prayer. "We didn't cause it. Can't cure it. Or control it. Allow God's grace and infinite mercy to heal our addicts. May we all survive this with courage and strength to help the addict, not enable him or her."

God, how many times did she have to hear this…this word "enable?" It'd had become the noose around her neck. Please just choke me with even more guilt for sometimes giving in.

After the formalities were read, Josie walked self-consciously to the snack table and poured a coffee with two creamers, adding a packet of Splenda. She felt curious, empathetic eyes boring into her as she palmed a pecan sandie and searched the room. Surely this group had the answer, and if she didn't get it fast, she knew Frank's constant persecution would wear her down. He always had a way of harping and badgering until she felt as if she'd been siphoned. Emptied.

The guest speaker reached the podium. "My name is Jordan Brookshire and I'm here today to discuss my child, who died last month from the disease of addiction." She doesn't look like someone who'd lost a child, Josie thought. But what is such a woman supposed to look like?

The afternoon sun caught Jordan's necklace, illuminating the blue stones. Josie knew if Finley had died only a month ago, she'd have been in no shape to choose jewelry and accessories, much less put on neatly pressed slacks and a blouse that matched.

"First," Jordan said, "I'd like to read a short diary entry I wrote. It's to all of us mothers in the trenches, all of us thinking we can't breathe another breath, sleep another night, or eat another meal until we know our loved ones are safe and clean from drugs. So please, allow me. This is called, 'Our Typical Day as Moms of Addicts.'"

She gripped the white notepaper, and Josie saw her tremor. She cleared her throat and closed her eyes briefly. "The alarm clock shrieks," she began, sadness heavy in her voice. "After a sleepless, anxiety-ridden night, she runs down the hall. She flings open her adult child's door and finds what she thought all along; her addict never made it home. Exhausted, she struggles into her cleanest suit and pumps, readying for another day at work, trying not to fall over from lack of sleep.

"The phone rings again as she drives to work, and it's her addicted one, calling from somewhere out on the streets, wanting money yet again. She says no and he's pissed. He screams he hates her and that everything is her fault. At work in the afternoon, the ER calls and says her child has OD'd and needs long-term rehab once stabilized. Yes, she's scared and wants to cry, but she's always jumping into rescue mode, calling institutions and insurance companies, discovering her policy won't cover more than a week to ten days—not long enough to heal or help. Just enough time to get them dry enough to crave the next high.

"They go there for a few days and drop out because, hey, they are over eighteen, and who's to keep them? She can't tell anyone about her child, for the shame is too overwhelming. What kind of mother could she possibly have been to raise such a human being?

"In the evenings, she jumps in the car and roams the streets and haunts, hunting her son or daughter in crack houses, dilapidated buildings, the usual places. She gets home and realizes she's missed her 'good' daughter or son's dances, teacher conferences, or sports matches. Maybe next time. The addicted one consumes what's left of this mother, her emptiness filled only with guilt and regrets.

"At book club, the first time she's been in four months, she sees her friends who brag about their children going off to fancy colleges and studying abroad, the great jobs and grad schools. No one asks her about her son or daughter. They know. They've read about them in the papers. What can they say? Right. So, they say nothing, which hurts the most.

"How could she tell these friends how it felt not to see their children grow up and hit adolescent milestones like middle school dances, the prom, homecoming, state playoff games? She feels envy as if it were twisting vines entangling her. They talk about their fantastic family vacations when she can't even take her kid to Walmart without him or her being too doped up to roll a cart down the aisle, much less rent a cheap condo at Myrtle Beach.

"Later, if she's lucky and her son or daughter doesn't die on the streets, she gets another call. Kid's back in jail. Whew. Safe—like in baseball—at least for now until the next strike comes, the next out. She worries about how her child is treated in jail, yet she's thankful for a few days of relative quiet. Now she can focus on her family, the ones forgotten due to the one chosen."

Josie let out a reflexive cry and immediately covered her mouth. "I'm sorry," she said. "My first meeting."

"No worries," the woman said, her eyes kind and shining with tears. "That's why we're here. This is the place where the pain stops and the healing begins. Remember. It all starts with you. Not your addict."

She considered those words: *It all starts with you.* And at that moment, she knew without hesitation what she had to do. And Frank would not stand in her way. The only way to save Finley was to persuade him (by force if necessary) to come to Asheville.

When Josie returned to 34 Could be Worse Court at four

thirty in the afternoon, she filled Ruby in on everything. "That's why, Josie Divine, I never worked retail. Nonprofits are so damned glad to have you; they don't treat their people like trash liners. Just throwing them out with the garbage."

Josie smiled and looked around the unusually quiet condo. "Where's Dottie?"

Ruby's eyes glittered and she raised her silver brows as if she'd been caught doing something she shouldn't. "Now, I hope this is okay with you, but my neighbor, that crotchety Marybeth Tyner, let me sort of borrow her yappy bichon. Follow me."

Ruby led Josie into the living room where Dottie and the dog were curled up asleep on the couch. Josie's heart warmed and she wished she had the time and money to give her daughter a dog. "That was so thoughtful, Ruby. Look at them."

"Now, I better take the little priss-pot back over to Marybeth before she forgets we have her dog and calls the law. I'll bring her again another time."

"Best take her while Dottie's still sleeping," Josie said. "Otherwise, she'll have a fit."

Sure enough, when Dottie woke up and saw the dog missing, she threw a roaring tantrum. "Honey, Ruby said the dog could come visit again soon." Her daughter wailed and kicked her chunky little legs. Nothing Josie said or did soothed her and the outburst escalated.

Desperate, Josie pulled out her ace card. She'd been thinking for several weeks about taking Dottie to a popular family entertainment center where she could play and run off energy. As expensive as such places were, she'd managed somehow. "We're going to Fun Depot. Right now."

Dottie, forgetting the dog drama, tears abruptly halting, ran to find her Ariel sneakers and dashed to the car. Once they arrived at this vast emporium overlooking the highway, Josie ordered a Diet Coke for herself and lemonade for Dottie.

The place was huge and had a climbing wall, miniature golf course, several rooms for laser tag, Skee-Ball ramps, and dozens of electronic games for kids. Out back was a go-kart track tempting Josie, who'd had a go-kart as a kid. Dottie abandoned her lemonade and went straight for the indoor playground and ball pit.

As she watched her little girl scuttle up a slide, Josie reveled in how well Dottie had adjusted to the move, even leaving her brother and father in Atlanta. She'd never lied about Frank being her daddy, and Dottie never questioned his absence, rarely mentioning him.

She remembered the night she left Frank and walked away from their ridiculously expensive home in the suburbs.

It was on a Sunday. March 16, 2014. At half-past five in the evening under a full Worm Moon, the same moon that upended her career, Josie'd left her Gothic mansion for good, carrying her infant daughter in a butterfly-covered Graco SnugRide. She did not stop to tell her son goodbye. She heard the commotion downstairs where he was smoking dope and God-knows-what else with friends, rap music blaring, the hard bass thumping in rhythm with her heart.

Frank had for too long been her drug of choice, and she'd OD'd too many times on his hopscotching love. His back and forth, "I'm here to stay, I promise." And then a month later, "Just one more retreat to work on myself."

She'd had enough. Their last argument was the fatal blow, a flatliner, and she'd known there was no turning back.

While the marriage had been on unsure footing as Finley's drug use escalated year by year, nothing slashed her heart as much as Frank struggling with Dottie's diagnosis. "You know what we have to do," he'd said during her pregnancy. "It's not fair. Not to us. Not to Finley. Not to her."

"I'm not getting an abortion, if that's what you mean."

"It's exactly what I mean."

The week after that fateful ultrasound, Josie rented an apartment and left the marriage for five months. She begged Finley to join her, going as far as creating a fabulous room for him. And he did come. Twice.

Shortly after Dottie's birth, Frank changed his mind and

showed up with Katherine at the hospital. It was Wednesday, December 18, 2013, one day after the full moon. Dottie had hours earlier made her worldly debut wearing angry purple skin and a scowl and shaking her tiny fist in the air. She was feisty from the get-go, weighing six pounds and three ounces and with a full head of dark wavy hair courtesy of Frank. She had none of the serious heart defects common among babies with Down's but had slight hearing loss and other minor issues.

At forty-two years old, Josie and the baby were both considered high risk, and doctors had performed a C-section. Frank's eyes grew all red and apologetic as he held his infant daughter, tears falling on her receiving blanket. He begged Josie to come home and promised he'd love this child and give her everything he could. He couldn't believe he'd ever considered abortion. He must have been out of his mind with grief, he said.

"I love you, Josie. I've loved you since I saw you at the circus that day. I want my family back."

She'd conceded, as new mothers will when putting their babies first, and moved back in. For the next three months, he and Finley doted on Dottie, and Frank even grew a backbone and banned the druggies from the house. Finley, for his part, returned to his kind and unselfish ways. He gave Dottie a bottle when she wouldn't latch onto Josie's breast. He changed her diapers and carried her all over the house, picking her up if she so much as whimpered. Everywhere Josie turned, Finley was taking pictures of his little sister.

But after twelve weeks, Frank's other side showed up. The side that couldn't face having a child with special needs. He retreated to his studio, surfacing only for food and showers.

On a cool Friday morning in March, a cup of coffee in his hand, eyes smudged with dark circles and hair a mess, he told Josie they needed to talk.

Her heart seemed to power down and she could feel the beats slowing. "I can't do this," he said. "I thought I could, but…I don't know. All these doctors and programs and all the therapies she's going to need. It's…it's…"

Josie climbed outside her body and detached, her heart's way of protection. She methodically walked upstairs, like a robot reading an internal signal, and reached for her sleeping daughter.

That night, as if Frank's second thoughts had some invisible cord yoked to his son, Finley also had second thoughts. He relapsed. Rough-looking boys came and went until well after two in the morning. Music pounded and Dottie screamed half the night. The smell of pot snaked its way into the nursery. Josie ran the air purifier, but the odor lingered.

That was it. She couldn't do it anymore.

For the first week after she left, she and Dottie stayed with Willa. Josie then returned to her apartment near the TV station, called the bank, and removed Frank from her American Express card. She opened new checking and savings accounts.

One week after that, she packed her post-pregnancy body into her Albert Nipon gray-and-white striped suit, wriggled into sheer hose and the black pumps she despised, and entered the law offices of Stern, Wagner & Harrison, a firm her father had recommended. There she filled out the papers she thought would set her free. She had no idea as she gave Bettina Stern a list of her assets that she'd lose her son in the process. Her most precious asset along with Dottie.

When her mother learned of this, hell *and* high water erupted. "We don't divorce in this family," she said in a voice mail so Josie couldn't interrupt. "Do you not think that every day I woke up with your father, I couldn't wait until the day my tickets to London would no longer be round trip? I wanted that one-way flight to freedom, and a good percentage of women in less than ideal marriages have that same fancy. But do we do it? Only a few are selfish enough to ruin their entire families so they can break out of domestic suffocation. You leave him and that child of yours will be the one suffering the most. You think it's bad with him now…"

When Dottie tugged on Josie's arm and asked for a snack and juice box, Josie brushed off thoughts of the past. She opened her Kate Spade, the one missing a foot, produced a

Juicy Juice and Welch's gummies, then navigated her phone to Indeed.com where she scanned job listings, surprising herself by typing "Media, Communication, Television Jobs" into the search bar. Maybe she'd find work off-air as a producer. Maybe it was still too soon to take another shot in front of a camera. She shut off the phone when Dottie ran back to the play area, and after a while Josie floated into a trance, listening to the video machines dinging and the trilling rifts of carnival music, the squeal of kids happily snatching prize tickets as fast as the games spit them out.

"Well, look who's here." Josie felt a pat on her back and smelled the musk of Tresor perfume, the scent she'd worn in college. Philly sat next to Josie and offered a wide goddess smile. "We've not officially met, but I'm Philly, real name is Ophelia. I'm over in Lancôme. I've been wanting to meet you, but my schedule's been mostly nights."

"I'm Josie. Lowest in credit apps, sales per hour, and locating items for customers. You name it. I'm at the bottom." She extended a hand and was uplifted by Philly's surprise appearance.

"Heard what happened," the former model said. "Them giving you grief and sending you off without pay. That place sucks a person dry. I keep saying I'm going to leave but I've been there longer than anybody."

"You heard already? I've only been gone a few hours," Josie said and laughed. "Gossip spreads fast around that place."

"Honey, gossip is the bread and scandals are the butter."

"So true." Josie's eyes followed Dottie, who'd left the play area and was standing in front of the climbing wall. "How long have you been there? At Brigman's?"

"Sixteen glorious, life-wasting years," Philly said, stretching her endless legs.

"But you could do—" Josie didn't finish, but the words were a given. *You could do so much better. And so could I.*

I could figure out a way to be a better mother. To my son. I'll get him here. And it needs to be soon.

10

"I know I could," Philly said, reading Josie's thoughts, "but for women my age, this is one of the only jobs with any security. I need the insurance and benefits. Everything on me is falling but this hair." She reached up and patted her towering hive of coils. "Got hair so high it looks like it took a bong hit."

It took Josie a second to get the joke. "Oh, gosh. That's too funny. Nice to meet you. Officially." Philly sat so close Josie could feel her breath, cool and minty against her face. "I have to confess that I went online and may have done some stalking. I saw all those gorgeous cover shots of you back in the day."

Philly laughed. "Yep. Starved and bulimic. Nose packed with coke and diving into toilets where I threw up New York's finest cuisine, lines chopped on the mirror in wait. Now look at me. Fifty-five and working at Brigman's."

"I had a fairly public past too," Josie said. "Not as famous as yours, but for Atlanta, well...I did all right."

"I know all about it," Philly said, her voice warm. "I did my research on you too."

Josie couldn't decide whether to feel flattered or embarrassed. "Funny how it blows up and all that money and fame, all the good you think you did, just vanishes," Josie said. "One tiny—well maybe not so tiny—mistake, and poof! C'est la vie." For a moment the women were quiet, a companionable silence until Josie raced off when Dottie roamed out of sight.

"I'm probably overprotective," she said when she returned. "Do you have kids playing here?"

Philly's face, ageless and not a single wrinkle roping her neck, fell with sadness. "No. I'm over-the-hill, eggs withered on the vine. My baby's in college now, if you consider the classes at Craggy Prison as the Princeton branch of the North Carolina Department of Corrections."

"I'm so sorry," Josie said, remembering Monica mentioning Philly had a daughter with addiction issues. "I've been there. Not straight-up prison but quite a few jails back in Georgia with my son. He won't even see me, and I've tried everything."

Philly put a hand on Josie's shoulder. "He'll come around. Eventually, they have to grow up, right?"

"If he lives long enough. He can't stop relapsing, and my ex has convinced him rehabs are bullshit."

"Carmen, my girl, she went to five of them. The only rehab that's worked for her is prison."

Josie remembered hearing this same sentiment at the MAC meeting, and she'd recently read a mom's post concerning the relief she felt when her daughter landed in prison. "I know she's safe and not using," the mother had said. "I'm not bailing her out. This is the first time I've slept in years."

"I wanted Frank, my ex, to leave my son in jail this last time," Josie said. "I told him, 'Either he goes to rehab or he stays in jail.' The next morning Frank posted bail."

"I get it," Philly said. "These other women don't understand us moms of addicts."

Josie nodded. "It's so hard to know the difference between enabling and loving your child. I mean, really? How do you just 'let things go,' as they say?"

"They all told me to give up and let it go too, but I didn't listen." Philly fiddled with an earring that looked like a wind chime and made a faint tinkling noise. "I'm never giving up on my Carmen. I go visit every chance I get. She's doing four and change for trafficking meth. Only kid I got. Had her in my mid-thirties." Philly's eyes welled, her irises swirls of copper and gold. She fanned her face to stop the tears.

"Why do you come here, then, if you don't mind my nosiness?" Josie asked. "Sorry. It's a habit from my former life. You don't have to answer. Maybe you love the putt-putt with scriptures printed at every hole."

Philly's laughter was musical, and Josie could have listened to it all day. "Honey, I come here partly to reminisce the past joys with Carmen, when I used to take her to places like this. But to tell you the truth, I come mostly to meet men. Single daddies with no mamas at home. You won't find cheaters here or at Chuck E. Cheese. Look over there." She waved an arm toward the kids and their caretakers. "Somewhere in all that madness might be my third husband."

These past four years were Josie's first without a man and she was finally free to breathe and do as she wished without having to tiptoe around Frank's land mines. "You want to take on another man's brood and troubles? I'd all but rather go to jail myself. I'm done with all that for a while."

"Two reasons, Josie. One, I'm not getting any prettier. I used up most of my pretty on two husbands who bled me broke with each divorce. Two, I need a man to, well honestly, fill me up with his love, devotion, and Amex card. I've stripped the chains from my heart and blown the lock off my panties. I'm good to go."

Josie laughed. "But kids again? I'm worn out with my Dottie. Would do anything for her, but it's not easy." As if on cue, Dottie came running, her dark curls damp against her ears, arms swinging penguin-like with excitement.

"I want climb wall," she said. "Wall, wall, wall."

Josie bent to her level. "Sweet girl. That's for when you get bigger. Here are a few quarters. You can play the games but then we need to get on home and figure out dinner."

"No! I want wall now. I big enough for wall. Now, Mama!"

Josie turned to Philly. "So you want to take some of this on with another man?" Both women smiled, having been down these roads.

"I hope to God if I find another man, he'll have joint custody, so half his time can be spent wining and dining with me." Philly opened her hobo bag and filled Dottie's hands with peanut M&Ms. "Can she have these?"

Well, too late now since Dottie had already popped half of them into her mouth. "You're probably her new best friend."

"She's a beautiful little girl. I'd give anything for a do-over with mine," Philly said. "I did so much wrong with Carmen. She's almost twenty-one. I wrote all this stuff down one time, the mess I'd made. A big-shot publisher wanted me to write a memoir on being a Black supermodel, but I'd rather keep my personal life as private as possible. I do write a running diary of my thoughts on Carmen."

Josie wanted more than anything to hear it. Listening to other mothers who didn't have normal, cookie-cutter, white-bread kids gave her comfort. The sisterhood among moms like her and Philly ran deeper than bone. "I kept a diary for Finley from the time I got pregnant until he was five or six. It's heartbreaking when I read it now, all those plans and dreams I had for him. One day I hope he'll be willing to read it. He'll at least know then how much I loved...still love him."

Philly patted Josie's knee. "I've been posting lists on my bathroom mirror since the six or so years this shit with Carmen has been ruining our lives. Let me think...see if I can remember the latest. Yeah, it went, 'Different friends? A different approach. A few more dollars? A few less dollars. Too many rules? Not enough rules. Setting the bar too high? Setting it too low. Working too much? Working too little. Too many moves? Not enough moves. More ballet lessons? Fewer ballet lessons.' Dang, I can't remember it all."

Tears filled Josie's eyes. "I can relate. All those what-ifs. I'm all for no more self-blame but can't seem to shake it. I learned a long time ago they make their own choices. I've got Dottie to raise now, not that I don't want Finley back in our lives. But healthier. Not living from one high to the next."

"It's hard to know exactly what—" Philly stopped talking. Her eyes flashed and fixed on a man, this one lean and distinguished with a full head of Richard Gere silver hair and a clean, smooth face. "Mighty fine, mighty fine. I wanna take that gray fox and field-dress that man." They both chuckled at the Sarah Palin reference, the humor a respite. "Didn't mean to interrupt you, but I'm here to fish. I'm listening, keep talking. Just got to keep my eye on that one."

It was refreshing to talk about something normal for once, with a woman who understood the tough stuff. "Most of the women I know want them younger," Josie said. "Claim they're done with the whiskey—" She stopped short. *Whiskey dicks.*

"I know, honey. These older ones, soon as they put the pilot in the cockpit, they go limp as an empty Trojan. I'd rather have a firm credit card than a rigid— Look, he's coming over here."

The man walked slowly and deliberately toward them, his suit screaming old money. He paused and pressed his hand to a chin sculpted from the finest bone. Josie slowly, horrifyingly, recognized him, and her head lost all its blood. She felt as if she were about to faint.

Here he was, standing over her paling face. Frank was her one. And this man was her half. That half of her one-and-a-half lovers she admitted to God in her prayers. Thinking of that night together, the blood suddenly returned to her face, and while she was normally not a blusher, she was sure her cheeks said everything.

"Hello, Josette," the man said. "I'd say this is a wonderful coincidence." He held out his hand and Josie relived the calluses and the feel of those hands all over her…her what? How far had those hands traveled along her body? Had he seen the scar running down her torso like a rope? She'd always been so careful to conceal it.

"Hi, um…" How could she have forgotten his name? It was something weird instead of a proper name.

"Paul Oscar Gavins. I go by Pog, my initials." His ungodly blue eyes twinkled with mischief. "I'm glad to see you looking healthy and well."

Josie gazed at Philly whose mouth had unhinged like a ventriloquist's dummy. "Look at you getting all recognized," she finally said.

"Pog, this is my friend, Philly."

Philly turned on the charm as if she were on a Milan runway. "Ophelia but call me Philly. I don't use a last name. Trendy, huh?"

"Such a bonus to see you both." He spoke directly to Josie, only briefly darting his eyes in Philly's direction. "You ladies are the highlight of my day. Other than watching my son scale the climbing wall. Used to enjoy your photos in *Sports Illustrated*," he said with a smile for Philly, who sat up straighter and preened as if she had feathers.

A bell shrilled and his eyes darted to the top of the wall, where a boy of nine or ten called out as he yanked the cord ringing his victory. Pog applauded, his rough hands making a muted sound. Dottie heard the bell and began screaming, "I want to go. I want wall, Mama!"

"Excuse me. I need to go tend to her. You can have my seat, Pog. Philly is known to keep everyone entertained." Philly's eyes beamed the unmistakable sign of gratitude when one woman concedes and hands her catch of the day to the other.

"I'll help her," he said, reaching for Dottie's hand. "I'm pretty good at this sort of thing. Had three kids. Paul, Jr. was my oldest." He searched Josie's eyes again. "Does that sound familiar? You did that series on the opiate epidemic and, well, Paul died at twenty-one from a fatal overdose a few years ago. You came out to the graveside and interviewed me and my wife. So, uh, that's where we met. Then there was that other time when…well…we…anyhow."

She could not have slept with a married man. Noooooo. She squinted to summon the memory. She craved a drink to steady her mental discordance. An image of Pog surfaced, him on his knees staring into the six-foot gouge in the earth, weeping, his shoulders violent with sobs. His wife in the background, her eyes dry and her mouth opening and closing as if she wanted to speak but couldn't find words, her hands scratching at her neck, leaving red marks. And then another memory. The Westin bar, hours after her career casualty, the overfilled comforter on a king-size bed, Pog's head on the pillow next to hers.

"I'm so sorry." She swallowed hard. "Yes, I do remember your handsome son." She left out the Westin part of her recollections. "I hope your wife and family are doing as well as possible under such sad circumstances." Dottie escaped Pog's grip and beelined for the climbing wall, where Josie monitored her every move.

"Doing the best I can," he said. "Got one in college and the other here with me. I won't say it hasn't been a struggle to keep things going. My wife left us six months after we buried Paul. Said she couldn't look at me without seeing him."

Josie knew from MAC and her own research that a good many marriages fall apart when a child dies. "I can't imagine. So, what brings you to Asheville?" she asked, and out of the corner of her eye she saw Philly, who'd clearly deemed Pog a lost cause, and began her predatory circling of the joint to find Mr. Right, or at least, Mr. Amex Centurion.

"I moved here almost three years ago to start over," he said. "I live right outside Burnsville, up the mountain from here. A town so big we got a Western Sizzlin'."

Paul. Pog. Burnsville. Why was this so familiar? This Burnsville reference.

"I've heard of Burnsville but haven't made it over there. Supposed to be rather charming." She combed her brain for details other than frayed images of his greatest grief. And that king-size bed. She couldn't stop wondering if this man had seen her naked or how far they'd gone that night in Atlanta. It hit her suddenly. If he lived in Burnsville, how was he at the Westin the night she'd checked in?

"So," Josie said, fishing around. "You still get to Atlanta much?"

Pog smiled, flashing refreshingly imperfect teeth, a slightly crooked display with one eyetooth heading out of the gate early. "William, my oldest, is at Georgia Tech, so I'm in Atlanta now and then." That gleam was back in his eyes. He'd known why she'd asked about Atlanta. He looked toward his son. It seemed he kept an ever-vigilant watch over the boy as only a man too familiar with loss might.

Josie caught a whiff of Pog's cologne, Chanel Blue, and had a sudden urge to grab his arm and cart him off to 34 Could Be

Worse Court. But that was her body talking. Her mind knew better, and he certainly wasn't part of the No More Men Until I Get My Shit Together plan. Then she thought of Mrs. Young-blood and what *she'd* have to say about this Pog fellow. She'd probably tell Josie to go ahead and service him. At least check under his hood.

"I'm going to pluck my girl from the wall over there before she tries to climb it," Josie said, surreptitiously surveying Pog head to toe and then admonishing that basic animalistic need. When she returned with a protesting Dottie in tow, Pog hadn't moved an inch.

"Josie," he said, head lowered but eyes on hers. "I want to tell you the real reason I'm here, but this isn't the time or place. May I call you?"

Josie's body flexed as if the question had produced a current. Pog laughed and backed away, but he was still so close she could hear the scritch of his leather shoes. "Hey, I don't bite or have rabies. I think you'll find what I'm doing here of great interest. I'd love to talk more at some point, if you'll allow me a bit of your time."

"I'm pretty tied up with work and Dottie," she said, and at least part of the statement was true.

"Where do you work?" he asked, and Josie ignored it. Finally, he said, "I plan to change lives. Help save them too. I'm already well into the process. I believe you, or someone you love deeply, needs my services. Here, take my card, please."

Josie accepted the card and slipped it into her jeans pocket. "I don't know about that, but I wish you all the best. Dottie, it's time to leave, honey."

"I'd appreciate it very much if you'd call me to learn more. I can guarantee this is like nothing you've ever seen before."

"It was nice to see you again, Pog," she said. "I'm glad you're doing well." She shook his hand and searched for Philly to say her goodbyes. She discovered her delightful coworker chatting up a grandpa near the snack bar.

When the conversation paused, Josie tapped her shoulder.

"We're leaving. Just wanted to say how much I enjoyed this today."

Philly waved to the gentleman and followed Josie toward the door. "I'm telling you there's not a single man in here worth even a quick tumble," she said, shaking her head. "Nothing. You took the best, so I'm headed to Chuck E. Cheese, and if pickings are measly there, I'm hitting Wicked Hops for a few beers or an AA meeting as a last resort."

She hefted a Louis Vuitton that must have been as heavy as a kettlebell onto her shoulder, keys rattling in her hand. She kissed Josie on the cheek, her lips sticky with gloss and smelling fruity. "We need to go out and settle our lives. Solve all our problems over a bottle of good Prosecco."

"Sounds like a plan," Josie said, gathering Dottie and spilling from the building into the golden light of a sun winding down for the day. As she unlocked her car, Josie smiled with intrigue. Certainly, it wasn't lusting, her mind whispered as her body shouted an entirely different message.

She reached a hand into her back pocket and pulled out his card: Paul Oscar Gavins, VINTAGE CRAZY: Resort and Rehab. A turquoise retro camper shaped like a canned ham filled the frame. In small print he'd listed a phone number along with a quote: "Real Recovery is Improving Your Cage." Now it all made sense. He was the man in the newspaper article. The paper that someone had purposely wanted her to have. She tossed his card into her glove compartment and pulled out of the parking lot.

By the time they arrived home, after a *healthful* meal at Mc-Donald's, dusk cloaked the mountains. The sun had tucked in for the night, leaving behind eggplant clouds and a ribbon of coral fire painting the mountains.

She opened the door to the condo, and there in her living room, soused with the scent of Beautiful, stood her mother wearing her traditional Jackie Kennedy-style clothing. She held up a garbage bag filled with empty wine bottles, shaking it, and breaking at least a few.

"Hello, Josette. Dottie, sweetheart, come give Mimsy a hug." She swooped her eyes across the condo, taking in the fake tile, the outdated appliances, and the desperate decor. Josie wished, of all days, this hadn't been the one to choose sobriety.

"How did you even get in without a key?" Blood marched through Josie's veins with such force she thought her head might dispatch. "Where is your car?"

"Darling daughter, I'm completely knackered and not in the mood for a row. One question at a time, please."

11

It's strange what you remember from when you were young. Some people don't recall the early years, nothing before they're four or five. Josie's first memory was grabbing the railings of her baby bed and bouncing, laughing when her head hit the plastic butterfly mobile. She couldn't have been older than a year, maybe eighteen months.

Her second memory, when she was two, was terrifying. Someone had left her, and when she realized it, she screamed and flailed in the crib for hours until falling into an exhausted sleep. She awakened wet and starving in her father's arms.

"Where's Mama!" she cried, but Katherine was nowhere in the house.

And this was when she'd felt it: Fear. Its rawness could blister her heart, the scabs never fully healing.

When she was six years old the fear revisited with greater intensity. A door slammed, waking her. A heavy door. Not the more subtle of those in bedrooms. She padded into the kitchen and saw no one, but she smelled the strong coffee recently brewed and the cloying scent of her mother's Yves Saint Laurent Opium perfume. She heard a car pull into the driveway and raced to the window to find her mother ducking into a taxi, her face pressed against the cab window but devoid of emotion. Josie screamed and ran out into the road, crying as the taxi kept going before turning into a slash of yellow and then nothing.

For the next two hours, she alternated between sobbing and watching television. She flung open the pantry and angrily stuffed Frosted Mini-Wheats into her mouth. Around lunchtime, tired of staring out the window and waiting for her mother to return, she crawled into bed and fell into a fitful, dreamless sleep. Later, she was awakened for the second time that day by the sound of a door.

Her daddy was home from work and looked tired. He tried to smile but his eyes were like small, flat stones. "Hey, doodlebug," he said, bending to hug her.

"Mommy. Where's Mommy?" Josie whimpered.

"She's not here? Her car's still—" She saw everything on his face: the shock and hot anger, though he tried to hide it to calm her. "I'm sure she'll be back soon. Come with me," her father said softly. "I'm going to play you a new song on the piano while we wait."

While Katherine had poured her pain and disappointment onto the soil of England, Josie's daddy had found his solace at the keyboard of his restored 1913 Steinway K, his pain transported by the music of immortals. For as long as Josie could remember, her father had played, sometimes for upscale events and at other times various piano bars, even a gig here and there as an orchestral pianist.

"'Sometimes I can only groan, and suffer, and pour out my despair at the piano,'" he said as Josie sat on the bench with him and tried to block the sight of that taxicab from her mind. "That's a famous quote by Frederic Chopin," he said. "It's been saving my life since I was a boy with skinned knees and mud between my toes, two nickels rattling in my pocket."

Her father had begun playing at age five, and by the time he'd turned twelve could perform such haunting and complex pieces as Debussy's *Clair de lune* and Gershwin's *Rhapsody in Blue.* Josie watched as he closed his sad eyes and lifted his face to the ceiling, his fingers trilling Chopin's Étude in G-sharp Minor, op. 25, no. 6. That was his favorite, and hers, too, with its manic arrangement that made her think of cartoon music when something exciting unfolded.

That night in a house heavy with emptiness, they ate Swanson turkey TV dinners and watched the news, where a reporter was discussing the cost of houses and the price of gas.

Then the news switched to a story profiling Elvis Presley who'd died a while back but fans were still converging at his estate at Graceland. Josie took great interest in the beautiful and elegant lady interviewing people who told stories of how Elvis had touched their lives, a microphone in her hand that had seemed so glamorous. "I'm going to be her when I grow up," she announced to her father.

"You'd be perfect." His eyes were still wounded but kind. When the news ended, they played "Pretend I'm on the News," a game Josie invented after watching the lady on TV. She whirled around the house with her hairbrush as a mic, interviewing her dolls and stuffed animals while her daddy pretended to hold a camera.

At eight o'clock, they watched her father's favorite show, and Josie was relieved to see him laughing. "Mama hates this show," she said.

"She thinks it's crass," he said and winked.

For the next eleven months, Josie and her daddy eased into a comforting routine. He'd bought her new clothes for the start of school and drove her there every morning before he went to work. She wasn't the least bit scared as she smiled and posed while her daddy snapped photos with his new Canon camera that first day of first grade, a milestone her mother hadn't bothered to acknowledge. In photos, Josie had worn that haunted pallor of orphans, the ones passed up when the adults chose someone else.

Most days, her father came home early to meet her school bus because he didn't want his daughter home alone or marooned to after-school day care. On the days he had court, a teenager named Becca with bad skin and a matching personality stayed with her for a couple of hours. She was the daughter of one of his paralegals and all she did was drink Coke and watch *Scooby-Doo*.

At night, she and her daddy ate dinner and went over her school lessons before turning on the news and then watching a couple of shows before going to bed. He always read books with her, but she much preferred reading the newspaper and talking about current events. He allowed her a night-light, which her mother never had.

It wasn't so bad after a while, and the blisters on her heart fought to heal. She'd had her daddy's full attention, and he let her interview him for her "news" program whenever she wanted.

"Mr. Nickels," she said one night after a dinner of Kentucky Fried Chicken, canned asparagus, and ice cream sandwiches. "How does it feel having your wife gone for this long?"

He widened his eyes. "Well, Miss Nickels, it feels…well…rather wrong."

"Sir," Josie said, moving in close with her hairbrush microphone, "have you any idea why she left?"

He looked down at his feet. "Miss Nickels, I do have an idea but if you don't mind, this will have to be off the record."

"I most certainly understand," Josie said. "One more question, sir. All of us viewers want to know if you think she'll be coming home any time soon?"

"I have a good feeling she will," he said. "It should be any day now, as a matter of fact."

Nine days later, Katherine Nickels returned as if she'd been gone only two weeks. "Come here, my sweet Josette," she said, hugging her daughter for the first time Josie could ever remember. And the last time, truth be known.

12

Josie was emotionally wrung, having lost her income and then running into her past at Fun Depot, of all places. Seeing Pog had unleashed so many feelings: confusion (did they or didn't they have sex?), mortifications (had he or had he not seen her naked?), and bewilderment (was she or was she not attracted to him?).

And now the worst moment of her day stood in her condo.

"Have you turned into a total alcoholic again?" Katherine asked, rattling the trash in her hand. "Little good that money-draining jaunt to rehab did you." She slammed the bottles into the bin as she called it, several slicing through the bags.

"This child is living with an unfit mother. It's no wonder Finley is in the shape he's in, wherever he is at the moment." Katherine reminded Josie of the evil queen in *Snow White* with her stern, angry beauty. "Last time I visited," she said, "he was smoking pot in the cellar and doing nothing but playing those violently twisted video games. I'm most certain he's bloody depressed living in that dank, infested hole."

She moved to the sink to wash her hands of Josie's trash and sins. "You've no job, no prospects or motivation. And Finley? I love the little sot with all my heart and soul, but I can't bear chatting him up when he's lit sunup to sundown. I can't help but think all this could have been prevented with a hefty dose of decent parenting."

"I am a good mother," Josie said. But you certainly aren't, she almost added.

"And why are you not trying to get back into television? I mean, really. Working retail?"

Her mother, she noticed, had packed two leather suitcases, signs she was staying put for a spell. She ran a hand through her perfect, wavy bob and left it there as if in thought. Josie admired her posture, hair expertly highlighted as if she were still a fury in pumps, one of the most feared prosecutors in Atlanta, tormenting whatever criminal she aimed to see locked up for life.

Even though Katherine hadn't been much of a mother, Josie still loved her in that primal way of biology.

"I can't help but wonder what your sister would be doing with her life had she lived. Most twins feel that permanent sense of loss when one dies, but you never mention Juliette."

Josie's attachment to Juliette wasn't as if she'd lost a part of herself, that phantom twin syndrome. Instead, it was as if she'd *absorbed* her twin, the very soul of her identical sister in her blood and not the cemetery. How can you miss someone you never really knew? Someone you feel became a part of you? When her intuition spoke, she'd assigned the thoughts to Juliette. Juliette watching over her.

"What else are you trying to lose here?" her mother asked. "Have you even thought about calling the station to get your job back? I'm *still* getting fan mail raving over what a humble and caring person you are and how they all miss you on the telly."

"Talent and humility aren't enough to sway news execs these days," Josie said and excused herself to the small bathroom down the hallway where she averted her eyes from the sailboat wallpaper she'd always found jarring in a mountain residence. She released the safety latches on the cabinet and reached under a pile of towels for the pint of bourbon she'd hidden, mostly from herself. She opened the cap and the smell—burnt caramel and roasted vanilla beans—lit up her dopamine receptors. No. She wouldn't. She'd face her mother sober. At least for tonight. One day at a time, as they say.

She returned to find Katherine and Dottie scouring the cabinets for mac 'n' cheese, and she mentally braced herself to confront her mother. "I don't want to go back to anchoring. I'm done being the face of the news."

"Oh, so now you're the face of some rubbish cosmetics line?"

"For now. Unless I lose my job because of what happened in Atlanta."

"I've tried to tell you to get over that. There are other anchors out there mucking up but they somehow pull it together and land even bigger jobs on the major networks." She filled a pot with water and switched the burner on high. "I read about this one absolutely fetching woman here in the States who caught her bloke cheating. She marched to his house, lifted her skirt, and wee'd on his bed. Even left a poo right on his pillow. She went as far as… Let's see now. Where is your olive oil?"

Josie opened an upper cabinet jumbled with spices from the Dollar General. "Here. I didn't know you put olive oil in mac 'n' cheese."

Katherine ignored her and set the oil on the counter. "I'm trying to remember all the details. Oh, right. She then got charcoal and lighter fluid and dumped all his best suits on the bed and set it all ablaze. Word has it she'd intended to burn the bed only, but then the whole house went to ashes. She wasn't even remorseful but right chuffed with herself, so they say."

"And the point or moral of this sordid tale, Mother?" Josie sighed, her emotions whipped into a froth. She'd heard this story multiple times over the years.

"Well, I'm getting there, dear. This little tart is a huge star on cable now. Had offers coming out of the bum and she was a complete twit. You are so much lovelier. You used to be a dazzler with those big brown eyes but now…I'm sure if you just lost a few and put yourself back out there—"

"I didn't have such offers," Josie said, biting her cheek from irritation. "And that woman didn't commit her crimes on air like I did. She at least did it during her time off."

After a half hour of banging pots and pans and rattling plates, ferrying her anger onto the innocent kitchenware, Josie scrounged up the mac 'n' cheese for Dottie and BLTs for her and her mother. Katherine sniffed the sandwich and peeled off the top slice of bread as if it were vile fish skin. She dropped the job-loss conversation, but the air tightened with the unresolved issues between them. Finally, Josie asked again, "I want to know how you found my address, how you got into the house?"

"Frank told me."

"Frank? You're still in touch with him?"

"He's the father of my grandchildren," Katherine said and gathered the dirty dishes and carried them to the sink. She didn't bother to load them into the dishwasher and took off for the living room to join Dottie.

Josie followed, wanting answers. "So you just drove up from Atlanta to surprise us? You missed us so much?"

Her mother reddened. "Okay fine," she said, taking a seat at the end of the couch. "I have moved here. Well, not here as in Asheville proper, but down the road in Hendersonville. They're doing some work getting my condo ready and I didn't want to stay in a hotel. When I heard you were laid off without pay, I decided—"

"How would you even know that?" Josie asked, skipping over the shocker about moving to the neighboring county. Her head reeled, and she dropped onto the opposite end of the sofa. Katherine turned away and glowered out the sliding glass doors. "Mother. How?"

"Okay, fine," she said, swiveling to face her daughter. "Pauline told me."

Josie jumped and her cheeks flamed. "How do you know Pauline? How?" It couldn't be possible.

Her mother's eyes shifted to the floor. She swallowed a guilty lump and brushed sandwich crumbs from her shirt. It seemed a long time before she spoke. "I bought my Estée Lauder from her. She was filling in when no one else was over there."

This made no sense. "Why would you come to Asheville for that when you live in—"

"Hendersonville."

Right. She'd almost forgotten that, with this shock about Pauline. "But you love Atlanta. Next to England. I mean why would you—"

"I'm exhausted, Josie. I hope you're fine with me setting up in the guest room. We can talk tomorrow. Come on, Dottie. Want to sleep with Mimsy?"

"Noooooo!" Dottie bellowed. "Mama, no!"

"She's not used to you. It scares her to be away from me ever since the"—Josie mouthed the word—"*incident.*"

"Blimey," Katherine said. "She and I are tickety-boo."

"Goodnight, Mother. There're extra toiletries in the bathroom cabinets and blankets and pillows in the closet." Katherine nodded once. She took a step toward them, arms almost outstretched, and abruptly stopped. Josie tried to remember the last time her mother put her arms around her. Or Dottie. The last time she ever said "I love you" to either.

Or the first time for that matter.

And in characteristic Katherine fashion, she bore her eyes into Josie's and delivered her closing arguments before shutting her bedroom door.

"What happened to you? A broken marriage to a fine man. One son who no longer speaks to you and our precious Dottie who'll never live on her own. Did we raise you to do all this?"

Josie shook with anger. "No, you didn't. Because *you* didn't raise me."

"That's enough," Katherine said, frowning and pursing her lips. "You should have stayed with Frank, since neither of your kids is, well…you know. You bore two kids with defective genes."

Josie felt as if she'd been bludgeoned. She tightened her fists, and though she wasn't the violent sort, she had to stop herself from busting the condo's cheap drywall. "I want you out of here by morning." An avalanche of icy abhorrence buried any remaining atoms of love she had for her mother. It was true that daughters, no matter their ages, needed a mother's unconditional love. It was also true these daughters didn't need verbal and mental abuse. The only answer in this case was detachment.

Josie would live in the valley of daughters who put their mothers in locked cabinets just like hidden bottles of bourbon.

Hating carved, sliced, and ate souls. But leaving a mother airing in a cupboard was like putting a dangerous weapon in a safe place. Untouched and unattended, it could do no harm.

"Oh, Josie, darling," Katherine said. "My visit has only begun." She smiled and very slowly, for effect, closed the bedroom door, having had the last word so that she could shut her eyes and imagine herself still a winner.

Josie thought of the photo in her underwear drawer, the nameless infant who seemed to have fallen from nowhere. *For Robert*, the envelope read. Josie's mind had careened straight to paranoia, straight to her daddy having stepped out on her mother. Maybe the photo was of Josie as a newborn. The handwriting—what was left of it—on that envelope did seem similar to her mother's. And the baby did seem to have Josie's huge dark eyes.

And her mother could have stopped in Brigman's in Asheville to buy her Night Repair. Thus encountering Pauline. Her mind was merely overreacting, and it had been a long day.

She thought of Pog's business card. "Vintage Crazy." It seemed with those two little words, the card summed up all the generations of kooks and neurotics in the Nickels bloodline. Theirs was a type of crazy that wasn't suddenly applied to the newest generation. Theirs was vintage. Exactly as Pog's card said.

Yes, genetics played a huge role, but it's not just the genes that had upended everything. Josie's mother fertilized those genes with her tongue, what she said and failed to say, and with her actions, what she did and failed to do. Her mother could have nurtured the family. She could have spared them the full brunt of hereditary calamities through loving and motherly ways. Instead, she used her husband's defective DNA as a weapon.

Where she could have saved them, she crushed them with either hurtful words or silence. She withdrew affection as often as she did her husband's money from the ATM. She was a mother who never gave Josie a chance. And it was long overdue for Josie to quit giving Katherine another chance.

Josie glimpsed the faint light through the guest-room door,

a sign her mother was still awake. She was likely on her iPad planning or plotting. Anything to excuse herself during intense moments. Josie found the chardonnay hidden in the produce bin behind a softening cantaloupe and clamshell of liquefying greens. She poured it into a blue tumbler, so full it splashed as she walked into the living room and joined her daughter pretend-reading the new books her mother had brought, the two of them inserting Finley into most of the pages as a character.

Typical Katherine with her withered heart. Gifts instead of affection, as if love is shown via Visa. Josie scooched next to her baby girl and held her as she read.

"Mimsy got me books," Dottie said, resting her sweet head against Josie's breast. "She nice sometimes."

Dottie was all heart, and she and Finley occupied every chamber of Josie's. When she thought of what might have happened had she done what Frank had asked…it made her ill.

After a second tumbler of wine and three more books, Josie heard Dottie snoring like a pug in her beanbag chair. She gently carried her to bed, her lower back catching and left knee shooting pain. Things she never experienced when she weighed one thirty. Maybe she could call Frank and get an update on Finley. Maybe after one more drink, it wouldn't be so dreadful to hear his voice and demands. She snatched what was left of the wine and locked her bedroom door. She tapped in his number. Two rings. Three. Four.

"What do you want?" He had unblocked her.

"I wanted to check on Finley. And you," she added for mollification.

It didn't work this time and Frank laughed with sarcasm. "You left our family. You left your son."

"You didn't want Dottie," she said as gently as possible. "That's what buried our marriage."

"I love her," he said.

"I'm sure you do," Josie said when she wanted to scream: *Is that why you left when she was a baby? Is that why you've never spent a single night with your daughter since?*

"I love both of my children, Josie. And I don't know where Finley is. Car's still missing, and I don't want to report it. They'll arrest him and he'll never get into grad school."

Ah, grad school again. Let's skip right over his rampant addiction and its resulting mental instability. Let's just coddle him so he can sit stoned in class earning a master's he'll never use if he keeps using. "I understand," Josie fibbed. "When he comes home, please help me figure out a way to get him here." She had no idea how to save him if or when he came to Asheville. She *did* know it would not work if he used drugs around Dottie.

"All right, I'll try," Frank said. "It would help to have a financial cushion. I'm paying all his expenses."

"Of course," she lied. "Let me know when you hear from him." After she hung up, Josie corked the wine and kicked it under the bed, the bottle hitting the frame and breaking, spilling what was left into the beige carpet. She cleaned up the glass, sprayed the nylon fibers with carpet cleaner, and then washed, toned, and greased her face the time-eating La Belleza way. She peeled back the comforter and crawled into bed, seeking her daughter's warmth.

Within moments the wine led her to a recurring dream. She was at the beach, *her* beach—Salt Pond Bay in St. John. She snorkeled, only the water churned murky and dark and she couldn't see a single fish. A therapist had once told her this meant that something in her life had blocked her from clarity and would continue to do so unless she fully healed.

Morning materialized with the sounds of Katherine opening drawers and banging tins. Hammers pounded Josie's head, and Dottie threw off the covers and rushed to see a grandmother who didn't seem to give two shakes about her.

No more drinking, Josie told herself. And this time, she meant it. She'd sort things out with her mother and maybe return to the MAC group. That would be a positive step toward regaining some semblance of success and maybe even figuring out a way to navigate a healthier relationship with Frank.

When Josie emerged from her room, Dottie stood an inch

from the television screen and was smearing it with her sticky Pop-Tart fingerprints. "Mama, you work today? I not like you go work."

"No. I'm having a little vacation, darling." Josie drew her close and smelled the artificially flavored strawberries. "Did Mimsy give you that Pop-Tart?" Her headache seemed to have its own heartbeat. *Pound, pound, pound.* She looked at Dottie and was struck by her beauty, her round cheeks with a spray of freckles. How could Frank have once said, "If you must have her, then let's discuss finding her a good home with others in her condition"?

"Mama needs to fix you a proper breakfast, sweet girl. You can't live on those Pop-Tarts, honey. I'm going to make you creamy oatmeal, okay?"

"Oh, for goodness' sake. Nutrition's not going to make a difference in her case," Katherine said, appearing with a mug of steaming coffee in one hand and a glass of green slime in the other.

"No, Mama. No goo."

Josie ignored Katherine's dig. "Well, Mama will throw in maple syrup and yummy raisins." She left Dottie on the Berber carpet, stained here and there from previous owners. No sooner had she trudged down the hall toward her cramped kitchen, made even tighter by her mother's NutriBullet and bags of groceries that only she'd eat, did she hear little raps on the door. Ruby. Thank you, God.

Josie had told her not to come to work but was relieved she was there. Ruby stood with a kind smile, the wind ruffling wisps of her thin hair. In the lemony morning light, Josie saw the tiny broken veins mapped along her cheeks, the age spots near her temples. Even so, Ruby retained a delicate allure.

"Get in here out of that wind. I don't know why these mountains make a fuss like this."

"Good morning, my Josie Divine," she said and stepped into the kitchen. "I thought I'd take you to yoga today, since you aren't working."

Josie threw Ruby a look and hoped she'd get the drift. "My mother is here," she whispered. "Don't know how long she's staying, but I barely survived night one."

When Ruby sailed into the living room for introductions, Katherine stood with both her Louis Vuittons at her side. "I've changed my mind," she said, not acknowledging Ruby's presence. "This child doesn't seem to like me, and honestly, there's not much I can do for you considering you don't seem to even want to help yourself."

Josie's breath caught. She felt a strange mix of relief and that age-old shame. Once again, she'd failed her mother. The first time had been when she survived the surgery that Juliette hadn't. This time, she vowed not to care.

"I'll be at this address." She pushed a piece of her expensive stationery into Josie's hand. "The house in Atlanta is on the market because your father, the impuissant man he was, has left this world with the last word."

"What does that mean, 'the last word'?"

"Until you get yourself sorted, Josie, this isn't something I can discuss with you. We both know if you don't get help, you'll lose the rest of… Well, not that there's a whole lot left to lose. And by the way, lock that bay window in the back bedroom. I can't believe it wasn't latched. I hope the neighbors didn't see me crawling hither and thither like a guttersnipe. From what I've gathered about this place, I'm certain their cataracts have spared them such a sight. Regardless, anyone could just barge into this hovel."

Hadn't the worst already entered?

13

Wicked Hops Brewery on Biltmore Avenue buzzed with singles and young marrieds on this Friday night. Ruby insisted—threatened, rather—that Josie carve out a night with her friends.

"You never go anywhere but work and home," she'd said. "If you don't join these women, I'm going to force you to sing at open-mic night." Ruby and Dottie had planned what Ruby named, "Dottie's Paint and Pizza Night."

"A woman needs her girlfriends like a Birkenstock needs a foot," she said and shooed her out the door.

The sun was setting as Josie arrived at the brewery, leaving behind its own personal paint night, the magenta and tangerine sky its canvas. Monica and Megan were already there and well into their first beers.

"Get over here now," Megan cried out, motioning for Josie. When she'd greeted them and ordered her beer, the conversation turned to what they had in common: Brigman's.

"Let's make a promise not to talk about Brigman's anymore," Monica said after a few minutes, and she blew a sigh, her cheeks puffing. "This is your night, Megan. We're here to celebrate your divorce, yet again, and check out this town's eligibles. Josie, that goes for you too."

"I'm not looking at another man," Josie said. "My heart's wrapped in crime tape, I assure you." She thought of Pog, and for a fleeting second, she imagined him with a giant pair of scissors, the kind from a ceremonial ribbon cutting, as he snipped the tape from her heart and stepped right in.

"I'm still looking but I don't think I'm over Lowell completely," Monica said. She turned to Josie. "I don't think I told you about him, did I?"

Josie shook her head. "What happened?"

"Cheated."

"I'm sorry."

"Oh, it gets better," Megan shrieked. "Tell her what you did, Monica."

Monica's smile started slowly and then spread across her face, showing every tooth in her head. "Well, Lowell must have decided he was sick of feasting upon Kobe beef every night and was hungry for canned Spam. He took up with my former best friend, who I'd worked with at Dillard's. When I heard about it, I got me a bunch of poster boards and taped my message all over town."

"Oh my God, you won't believe this message," Megan shouted.

"I got out my staple gun, and any street pole and bulletin board with an inch of space was real estate for my anger," Monica said, taking a small drink of her beer and scrunching her face from the strength of it. "It said in giant letters, LOST DOG: LAST SEEN HUMPING HIS WIFE'S BEST FRIEND. ANSWERS TO LOWELL. Big mugshot of his Spam-loving face taking up half the page."

Josie sputtered with laughter and nearly choked on her IPA, a beer so bitter it tasted like a juiced pine cone.

"I miss you at work," Megan said and tilted her head like a little dog. "I hope you get to come back."

Josie nodded and wondered how many divorce parties Megan planned on having. "I hope so too," she said.

"I'm telling you now," Monica said. "La Belleza is going down the can. There's nobody over there with you gone and Pauline leaving any time she feels the urge to bounce." Monica's eyes landed on the table where a dozen men in cycling Lycra grew boisterous, flights of no-doubt high-octane beers fueling their testosterone. "Here we are yammering about that damned store again," she said.

"When did *you* get a divorce?" Megan asked, and Josie hoped she wasn't going to meddle all night as she had at work last week.

"Let's put it this way," Josie said, checking her phone and wondering if Dottie was having a good time with Ruby. "Not soon enough. Frank and I never agreed on anything except naming our son."

"I know the secret to this now," Monica said, returning her attention to the women. "Here's the deal. See those men over there looking all fit and squeaky clean? Well, instead of meeting someone and tallying up all their fab qualities, you've got to pop that lid and dig in. You know how you go to a restaurant and order the World's Best Hamburger? It looks scrumptious, so you open your mouth big as it will go and bite down?" She paused for dramatics. "Problem is, we women should always lift that bun and check out the goods first. An entrée never looks as perfect when served as it does on the menu."

"I hear ya," Megan shouted. "I just need to meet a fellow before all my eggs turn rotten. I'm pushing thirty."

"For the love of God," Monica said. "You're barely in your twenties. Children will break your heart. Let me tell you, when your kids do you wrong, it hurts much worse than some man doing it. My twins are getting old enough to sass me and refuse to mind."

Josie jumped in. "And then when you think you can't take another minute of it, those same kids will turn around and fill your heart right back up. There were times I thought I'd run out of love for my son. Next thing I knew he'd picked every flower in the yard and put them in a vase on the dining room table for me."

"Mine are refusing to bathe at night," Monica said. "Throwing fits so massive they look like screaming eggplants."

Josie smiled as she thought of the time when Finley was nine or ten and decided to stop bathing. *We have a swimming pool, Mom*, he'd protested. *Chlorine cleans better than Dove.* After a week of this, she suggested they go for a little day trip in one of the golf carts prevalent in her ridiculous neighborhood.

After enjoying an alfresco lunch and shopping for a new tennis racket, Josie steered the golf cart into the Splash and Dash car wash. She slid her debit card into the slot and selected Ultimate Wash offering buffing, waxing, and a protective coating.

Ready to bathe now? she'd asked. And instead of balking, Finley's eyes lit up.

"What's got you all happy?" Monica asked, motioning for a waiter. "I'm going to send my cherubs over to you one evening at bath time."

"I was thinking about the time I threatened to run Finley through the ultimate cycle at the car wash if he didn't start showering. When he saw all those bristles and flapping things hitting the cars… I can still see his face. He was excited and wanted to do it. Always was one for danger."

Josie longed for the laughs and fun she and Finn once shared. It's odd how she could pinpoint exactly when things went wrong for him. It was a week after he had his wisdom teeth out. He was fourteen and begged Josie to call the doctor for a Vicodin refill, claiming his mouth wouldn't stop hurting. If she had put her foot down, said no…*if this and if that.* Most kids started with beer, then moved on to pot. If wired for addiction, they climbed that drug ladder to reach the opiates at the top. Finley's pattern was the reverse, beginning with hydrocodone for vacant teeth and graduating to everything else for a vacant soul.

All that would change once she got him to Asheville and talked him into a recovery program, one that included lots of outdoor activities and sunlight. She'd found several during her Google searches, but for now, she remained a mail-in mother who sent her son letters and care packages filled with books on addiction, along with clothes and toiletries, even a Groupon for a fitness center membership. She knew from Frank that he sold it all for drug money. But it didn't matter. The act of caring for Finn, even from afar, sanded the sharp corners from her guilt. On those here-and-there sober days, Finley might send a text of thanks and gratitude or one of remorse and apologies, promising to turn his life around, go to grad school, get a job, find Jesus. She'd saved every text he'd sent, her heart puddling with hope when he'd said: "I love you so much, Mama. I'm clean and going to meetings. I get all my drive and passion from you."

That was before her TV drama, before he'd cut her off for good.

Monica flagged the waiter to bring mayonnaise for her fries. "I'm going to tell my twins I have a friend who'll run them through a car wash if they don't start sinking their little asses in the bathtub," she said, offering the delicious-smelling fries to Megan and Josie.

When the band fired up its first set, loud in that way of too much ego, the women gave up trying to scream a conversation. "I'm going to dance," Megan said. "Y'all wanna come?"

"I'm not drunk enough," Monica said, eyes back on those athletes in Lycra. "Go on. You always draw a crowd when you dance. Next drink's on me."

A blasting techno-beat pounded the Wicked Hop's cavernous space. The place used to be a warehouse, but a few years ago a group of beer-loving yuppies hired crews to transform it into a showplace with its expensive bar inlaid with ancient kauri wood, the oldest workable wood in the world, and beers so strong one could get a DWI just smelling them.

"Look at her," Monica yelled over the music. "You ever seen such a display?" A crowd formed a semicircle around Megan, gawking as she dirty-danced solo, sporting moves that could get her either banned or dollar bills stuffed in her hip-huggers. "I'll let her ride this song out, then I'm going to get her," Monica said. "I believe she missed her true calling."

The women laughed and nursed their beers. An hour later they hit up the Waffle House because Megan, still sweating from dancing, had said, "I can't get full on bar food."

"Nothing's as good as bacon and biscuits, red-eye gravy," Monica said, reading a large laminated menu.

Josie ordered waffles and to-go pancakes for Dottie, remembering she was out of breakfast food. She needed to get home. When she arrived just after ten, Dottie was still up.

"I tried everything to get her settled," Ruby said. "She's been checking the front door and windows like a little puppy missing its mother."

"It's fine, Ruby. I just appreciate all you do for us."

"I hope you had a delightful evening," the elderly woman said, threading her arms through a boho backpack seen mostly on hikers or Asheville's trustafarians. "I must say this little one sure loves a pizza smothered in black olives. Oh, and our paint night was spectacular. Check out the Van Goghs on the fridge."

Josie walked to the refrigerator and admired her daughter's suns and moons. "What's this?" she asked Ruby, holding up the other painting as Dottie rushed into the kitchen and squeezed Josie's legs. "Maybe I should ask, 'Who's this?'"

"That Paul Carty, Mama," Dottie squealed. She clutched Mary-Mary, pizza sauce on the doll's face.

"It was supposed to be Sir Paul McCartney, my dream man before my liberal lawmaker phase," Ruby said, bending to kiss Dottie goodnight and suddenly hurrying out the door as if she had someone waiting for her at home, which could be possible knowing Ruby. "Toodles," she sang into the darkness.

When Dottie finally fell asleep, Josie crept into a Rubbermaid tub of memorabilia, searching for confirmation of past joys with her son. She discovered Finley's clay handprint, the thumb crooked from a T-ball mishap. The one he'd made for Mother's Day scripted with blocky handwriting: *I love you, Mama.*

She pulled out a finger painting splashed with the pastel swirls of an innocent child, the world his for the taking. Searching deeper in the bin, she found the Christmas decorations he'd crafted from preschool through third grade, including a reindeer made from a clothespin, an angel resembling a ghost, a paper-plate Santa with his cotton-ball beard in shreds. She shut the lid and knelt at her bed. The ceiling fan whirred, and its chain clacked against the wood like an antique clock ticking.

"Dear God, help us all," she prayed. "Please help me to find a way and a path to save my son. Help me to become a better mother to Dottie and not a boozer, wallowing in what was, what is, and what might have been. Bless our family and others needing you most. Allow me to see the blessings and not the battered parts of life. I give you my will, dear God. I'm not sure I'm praying the right way. Maybe it's all in your time, not mine. Maybe I need patience. I know I need sobriety. Help me get there, sir. Or ma'am."

Instead of climbing into bed, she flicked on a lamp and reached for the DVD—her final moments on camera—that split-second brain crash that got her fired and sent to rehab, never to be allowed back on the air anywhere reputable.

Since everyone else had seen it, maybe she should finally force herself to watch it. Her team of therapists and doctors suggested viewing it multiple times. They'd said it would weaken the impact, and that things are much worse if we don't face them head-on. We build them much bigger in our minds and way out of proportion to the actual event.

Now her heart skittered, and her mouth dried as if it were stuffed with breadcrumbs. She could do this. She *needed* to do this. She hit the play button.

"Good evening. I'm Josette Nickels and tonight we bring you a story of loss and laws never before enacted until now. For the first time in decades, a district attorney's office has charged a suspected drug dealer with murder following a heroin overdose." Her voice cracked on the video. She vividly remembered her stomach churning and her entire body radiating heat as if melting from the inside.

"According to arrest warrants, Adam Lamond Richardson, nineteen, of Courtside Drive in Dekalb County, reportedly killed twenty-year-old Grace Turbyfill with 'malice' caused by the unlawful distribution of heroin. Detectives believe Richardson administered the narcotic himself, causing the fatal overdose of the young woman, a sophomore at the University of Georgia studying psychology."

At that point in the tape, she'd stopped reading, talking, breathing. She panted and sucked at the air, trying to get oxygen into her lungs before she passed out. She wiped her wet hands on her pink Calvin Klein skirt, then across her mouth, smearing her matching lipstick. This was when she lost it. "The average woman will eat four to seven pounds of lipstick in her lifetime," she said, staring zombie-eyed into the cameras.

The young woman, dead from a single bad hit, had once been her son's girlfriend in high school. She was class valedictorian, a straitlaced girl known in the choir for her perfect soprano and riveting solos. Josie had heard the news earlier that day. She vowed she could still report the story with the required disconnect. She could contain her blistering emotions stemming from the frantic calls from Finley, missing in action and crying on the phone, cursing God and everyone else for Grace's death. Finley, who'd gone on the run again four days earlier and sounded garbled and over-drugged when he'd called. How could he have done this to her again? She couldn't take it. No, she had to take it. She had to keep pretending to be the calm and composed Josette Nickels everyone expected when she spoke into the camera.

She remembered seeing the shock in her producer's eyes. As Josie gasped and froze on camera, producers had scrambled and motioned frantic cues. In retrospect, sure, she should have listened. She'd held up a hand and said aloud, for all the viewers and God to hear, "Stop. I've got this." She closed her eyes, counted three breaths, then faced Atlanta households with the eyes of a woman gone mad. To hell with the script.

"This was my son's friend. He's on drugs. Lots of his friends are on drugs. Maybe your kids are on drugs. Maybe they aren't. Not yet, anyway." The producers waved hands behind the cameras, signaling her to get back on track. She ignored them.

"You may recall the series I did on the opiate epidemic. It's not over, is it? It's a nightmare growing worse because slimeball dealers are bringing in fake heroin—nothing but pure fentanyl. This drug is the thief of souls, snatching the breath out of those who use. Their hearts just stop. And so do ours—those of us who love the addicts."

A brief wave of equanimity had returned, and her voice evened. Always able to separate her personal life from the job—until that day—she allowed that control a single crack.

And through the opening, she saw the face of her daddy holding his pretend camera as she interviewed him. God, she missed him. He'd died unexpectedly two weeks prior, and the numbing shock of his death had worn off and left debilitating grief.

She'd felt her head bobble as she stared into the cameras. She thought of her daddy, cold in the Georgia dirt, and Finley, who would likely be on this very news channel for his latest drug-related crime—smashing car windows and stealing valuables from a mall parking lot.

But she continued. Viewers had admired Josie's strength in crisis, her measured grace, and genuine concern during other people's tragedies. They loved her down-to-earth style and how at the end of every broadcast she'd share a story highlighting her fashion finds or disasters. Like the time she'd visited a cosmetics counter and the makeup artist had taught her how to "draw" eyebrows with just the right arch. She'd swept her bangs to the side and the camera zoomed in on not two, but four eyebrows adorning her forehead. Viewers had loved it when she said, "This is what happens when you forget to take one set off and you find yourself at the Dollar General buying Metamucil and cat food and the checkout girl says, 'Did you know you have four eyebrows?'"

Josie had ventured off script and ad-libbed successfully for more than twenty years. Until that day, the day she broke. Right there, right then. On air, as she tried to report the death of yet another victim of drugs. Drugs which turned good into hideous and sons into savages.

"I knew this girl," she said, still ignoring her producers' cues. "Never in my life would I have thought her capable of using anything stronger than a Bayer aspirin. But as with the others, it probably started with a little drinking, then on to pot, maybe a sports injury, oral surgery, and a careless doctor prescribing Percocet. Next thing you know these newly addicted kids are begging for refills, and when that well dries up, they score street Percs laced with God-knows-what for exorbitant amounts of money. Pills poisoned with deadly fentanyl. When they run out of money, where do they go? I'll tell you where. The Heroin Highway beams its headlights."

Cameras still rolling, she'd paused before flinging herself down more avenues of uncensored commentary. The producers had given up by then, figuring this was another of Josie's brilliant moves, foraying into the unknown designed to sky-rocket the station's ratings.

"It all started in the 1980s." She leaned closer to the camera as if she wanted to lunge from her desk. "Doctors were told by the drug makers that opiates weren't addictive. Then comes the cartel, producing black-tar heroin...and their aim was the mighty dollar and to fill in the gap when an addict couldn't get his highs from a pill."

She'd cleared her throat and tasted the chili powder from the fajita salad at lunch and the rot of tequila. She rolled her head twice as if warming up for Pilates. She held up a hand and gave the camera a *one moment, please*. And that's when she'd felt the seams pop, allowing images of the son she couldn't reach, her precious father stiff and lifeless in his coffin, her beloved Dottie, a child her own daddy had never wanted.

Josie couldn't watch another second of the video. She knew that in a matter of seconds the awful climax would roll: those eighty-four seconds that ruined her forever. She ejected the DVD and crawled into bed, seeking the kind of deep sleep where everything is forgotten or forgiven.

When sleep eluded her, thoughts of Finley pushed up like flowers before the final frost. She traced those old memories to a time when she was the Good Mother, the one who'd taken him to zoos, held his hand on roller coasters, taught him how to swim at the local country club and how to ride a bike. That mother had climbed into his bunk bed each night and smelled the soft curls at the nape of his bath-dampened neck as they read books together, sometimes the same one until the pages softened.

Josie flicked on the lamp and reached for a small heart-shaped picture frame. Inside was a photo of Finley, around age nineteen, during a brief stint of sobriety. His hair was long, his face and eyes clear. He smiled with tenderness and held his newborn sister. He'd nuzzled Dottie's cheek and cut his eyes to the camera as if to ask, *Am I doing this right?*

Every night Josie kissed that photo seven times for good luck, believing her rituals kept her son's heart beating.

14

Josie swore off alcohol and planned to ante up her good-mother status. She'd already spent the past twelve days of not working as if she were the newest recruit in the Mother Scouts of America, trying to earn a dozen badges in as many days.

Badge One—The Tenacity Badge: She'd called Finley four times this week from various phones.

Badge Two—The Handles Disappointment Badge: Every call had gone to voice mail.

Badge Three—The Face of Hope Badge: She'd left messages for Finley to come to Asheville.

Badge Four—The Acceptance Badge: Frank said Finley was home and doing well. *Liar.*

Badge Five—The Generous Badge: She'd promised to Pay-Pal Frank a grand.

Badge Six—The Follows Through Badge: She'd said she'd pay upon delivery of her son.

Josie was still working on what the other six badges entailed.

She opened the sliding glass doors and stared into the sky, a full Flower Moon hanging fat and low.

Full moons over Josie's head were like thieves in the night, warning her of their shifts and pulls. She'd lost her luminous career on the edge of a full phase. Her marriage to Frank had dissolved four years ago when a March Worm Moon ripened and sagged in the sky as if too heavy to rise. Both of her babies debuted into the world squirming and mewling when stout moons lured them like the tug of tides.

Tonight, she wouldn't let that moon rob her of joy with Dottie.

Josie had bought new crafts projects and Sculpey Clay with her Michaels forty-percent-discount coupon. She and Dottie spent the evening kneading the firm rectangles into animals and creatures and cooking them in the toaster oven until they were hard but a tad burned around the ears and tails.

"Now you'll have a whole farm to go with your Barbies, sweet pea," Josie said, taking three hot bunnies from the toaster oven. Dottie ran splay-legged to her bedroom and returned with a bucket spilling with tangled and disheveled dolls, including Mary-Mary, half of her sequined scales missing and her scalp nearly bald from Dottie's hair-salon games.

"Where Aunt Ruby?" she asked. "She gonna take me to the zoo to see otters and bears."

"Well, Dottie. She met someone on a dating site for the elderly and said she deserves one last crack at love before she departs this earth." Oddly, Josie had never seen Ruby in a car. It was as if she just walked into the night and vanished. Or appeared at her door like an ancient fairy. "She'll be back, so don't you worry."

And she would. Paid or not. *She's a wonderful little child, a real delight*, Ruby had said daily. *You needn't worry about her missing out on all the educational therapies. I'm teaching her enough until you find the right program.*

By the time she and Dottie finished their roasted menagerie, Josie managed to push aside her worries over money and jobs and owing Ruby a week's salary. She listed her BMW for sale on Facebook Marketplace and Craigslist. She'd barely thought about her mother's bizarre move to Hendersonville, and realized that she could, as Ruby was quite fond of saying, *Be in the moment. In the present.*

She didn't need the wine to feel the blissful effects of mindfulness. An evening with her baby girl, doing normal mother-daughter activities, felt right. She watched Dottie bend her Barbies to interact with the clay animals and her heart expanded. Sweet and innocent Dottie, having no idea of her mother's failings.

She had a sudden thought about Finley, remembering the old diaries she'd kept from his conception to that first day in kindergarten, when she laid her forehead against the steering wheel and sobbed after delivering him to a stranger. She could still see him standing at the door of his new classroom, looking back only once, the *Star Wars* backpack towering over his sun-honeyed head.

Every word she'd written was filled with love and admiration for her child. She should have shown him these years ago, but would he have read them? Didn't teenage boys have more pressing concerns than a mother's butterflied heart, split wide open and releasing every emotion ever stored?

But maybe, now that Finley was older, he'd read them and seen firsthand the infinite capacity of her love for him. She reached into her purse for her cell and a packet of mustard squirted in her hand. (Gosh, she needed to quit carrying around condiments.) She wiped her hands on her tights and dialed Willa, whose own son had nearly died of a heroin overdose.

After catching up and promising each other a visit and Girls' Night Out soon, she shared her idea. "If I mail these diaries to your house, could you put them in another envelope, so they have an Atlanta postmark? Maybe Frank won't know they're from me. He opens everything and selects what he deems fit for my son to see."

"I can do one better," Willa said, and Josie knew friends this tight were mortal angels. "I'll use the Coca-Cola business envelopes where my cousin works. Surely that won't interest him enough to tear into Finley's mail."

"You're so good to me, Will. How are the boys?"

"Great. Both clean...at least for now. It's like night and day. I finally have my sons back. Oh, I'm sorry, Josie. I didn't mean to bring that up, not when you—"

"It's okay. I still have hope as long as he's breathing." On the MAC site, it seemed a mother lost a child to drugs every day, and the others in the group posted heartfelt comments about how sorry they were and how they were praying. Deep down these mothers were relieved it wasn't their horrible news to report, that it wasn't them who'd gotten *the call.*

Josie quickly changed the subject. "You won't believe who's moved to the mountains," she said.

"Let me guess. Your boyfriend, Bradley Cooper?" Willa knew Josie had fallen in love with Bradley and the movie *Silver Linings Playbook* because it so closely mirrored her own effed-up family.

"Nope."

"Hmmm. Let's see…"

"You won't guess."

"I give. Let's hear it."

"My mother," Josie said with a nervous laugh.

"Dang. She still a piece of work?"

"Worse than ever. She must have a dictionary for every slang term used in Great Britain and Australia. I can't figure out why she'd move this close to us. She's been acting so odd since Dad died. Remember that witch, Pauline, I told you about? The one out to take what little of me is left and bury it?"

"Yeah, but you can handle her, hon. What's that got to do with Katherine?"

"Not sure, but I'm planning to find out. Something's not right. They know each other."

"They do? How bizarre," Willa said.

"My mother's hiding things for sure and could win a gold medal in secret-keeping. I never know what she's thinking or doing."

"You just focus on Finley and send me those diaries. Let's make a point to get together. I can't believe it's been this long."

"I will," Josie said, picking at a speck of mustard drying on her tights. "If Finley isn't here in Asheville in a few weeks, I'm coming to Atlanta and hog-tying him to the back seat."

Willa laughed. "I can see that now. You sure love that boy, Josie. I've never seen another woman do all you do for scraps of love here and there."

"A scrap is *something*."

After they hung up, Josie's phone vibrated. She didn't recognize the number.

"Hey. I hope I didn't wake you. It's Philly."

"What a nice surprise," Josie said, remembering exchanging numbers at Fun Depot. But people did that all the time and never had intentions of calling.

"I need to tell you something. Remember that man, the yummy one with the weird name from the arcade place?"

"Pog?"

"Well," she said with an air of conspiracy, "that dude waltzes into the store today looking for you. Jesus, that's one fine-looking fellow with that head full of hair and smelling all edible. I got a sense he was making more than a booty call. He asked for your number. Of course I didn't give it to him, but he said if I talked to you to please, please have you call him. I got his number."

Josie thought for a moment. "So, he came to the store? I wonder how he knew I worked there?"

Philly grew quiet and then said, "I might have mentioned it when you went to get Dottie from the Skee-Ball area. You should call him, Josie. There's a kindness in his eyes."

"Yeah," Josie said. "Kind eyes are often deceiving." She'd felt an attraction to Pog and wanted to shut it down while she dealt with matters more important than squelching her parched libido.

"What could it hurt to call?" Philly said. "He wears those fabulous clothes and smells like money, but Lord knows, have you seen his hands? He has oil stains underneath his nails."

"I saw them." *And I very well may have felt them all over me too.*

"And all those blisters? I'd call him anyway because he at least seems straight. Didn't get a gay vibe from this one, and I'll tell you, this town has only four types of men: gay, married, old-as-dirt, and total freaks. You have to take what you can and lower your standards. This isn't the big city." She finished her little monologue with a riff of laughter.

"All right. I am curious about him. Can you text me the number when we hang up? I left his card in my car and I'm sitting in bed without a pen handy."

"Sure thing. Hey, I heard through the ol' cosmetic grapevine they were going to call you back to work."

Yay, I'm not fired! "I could use the income. I'd considered stripping in our community center. 'And here she is, folks. Please give a warm round of applause for Josie and her special guest, Mr. Poler, who's oh-so-much more than her former shower rod.'"

"You're crazy," Philly said. "We need to hang out more. Swap our celebrity war stories. I can tell you things that happened in the modeling world that will make your little televised trip-up seem like a time-out in kindergarten."

"You saw it? The video?" Of course she had. Who hadn't?

"It's all over the internet."

"You know, Philly, I've never even seen the entire disaster." And just then Josie had an idea. "My therapist said I need to watch it repeatedly, so it gets all watered down and doesn't have a hold on me. One of those exposure tactics that shrinks use. I have a DVD of it here at the house."

"If it's any consolation, you looked breathtaking in that pink suit with your hair all dark and sleek and you were skinny as a—shit. Sorry to have implied that you're not beautiful now. You've got those full lips with a perfect cupid's bow, and you're perfectly proportioned even at your size. God, I'm digging myself in deeper here."

"I'm going to do it," Josie said, Philly's weight and beauty comments not registering. "I'm going to watch the flippin' nightmare. And I'm going to google Pog." She wasn't ready to admit she might have had sex with him. "I may not call him, but I'll least look him up on the internet."

"Good girl! I can't believe you haven't already. I meant to look him up, but we're swamped with GWP right now. Oh, when you come back, you wait and see what I've invented for that TV show, *Shark Tank*. I plan to test-drive it in Brigman's."

"Can't wait to hear the details. Hey, I have a question a bit off-topic. You said your daughter's been clean since you took that different approach. What was it?"

"Right. I'd always heard from people that love is a verb," she said, her voice softening. "I thought they were dumb do-gooders who didn't understand the magical feelings of love from the heart. Once I started treating it like a workout program and forcing myself to do everything love requires, Carmen started getting better. Prison and my love-bombing worked for her."

"That's inspiring," Josie said, wanting more than anything for Finley to be here in Asheville.

"Here's the thing. We go crazy when our kids first start using and messing up. We lose our minds and hearts for years trying everything we know of to get them to stop. And then…well, I don't know about you, but I got numb as a rock."

Josie remembered that same feeling during the months she'd checked out of the marriage to raise Dottie. "I get it," she said. "So did I."

"After several years of Carmen's shit, I just threw in the towel and ignored her. Stopped taking her calls, stopped falling for her lies and cons to get money. I pretty much gave up on her. I loved, best I can describe it, from a distance. Maybe all of us get to that point. Maybe it's God's way of protecting us from the pain we no longer have the strength to bear. Once we get to that threshold, a fuck-it attitude comes in. For me, I stayed on pause for a year or so." Philly exhaled deeply. "Then I started my new approach where love became an action akin to a kickboxing class.

"I had to physically and emotionally *love* my baby back so she could love herself enough to stop. You white mamas… no offense, but tossing a kid out into the streets isn't the answer. You all act like *enable* is a dirty word. Do you know what that word can mean? It can mean *empower*. Once I taught my Carmen how to get her power back through God, through my love-verbing and through anything but drugs and thugs, it… well, *she* changed."

"Wow. Incredible," Josie said, pressing a hand to her forehead as she remembered the years of ultimatums with Finley. "My methods certainly haven't worked: 'Do this or else,' 'Sit up in jail and learn your lesson,' 'Use again and you can sleep on the streets.'" What had that ever gotten her? How had it ever helped her son?

"Josie?"

"Hmm?"

"If you want, I mean I don't mean to pry or impose, but I don't mind watching the tape with you if you need moral support."

Josie felt a surge of love for this woman and her eyes filled. "Sounds like a 'Girls Night In' to me. I'd be up for that."

"More like 'Girls Gone Wild.'"

When they hung up Josie booted her laptop and typed "Vintage Crazy" into the search bar. She couldn't remember what the rest of his card had said. The search brought up clothes and quilts, not what Pog had been peddling for sure. What else did that card say? Rehab. Resort. Wait. Wasn't that in the newspaper article? She typed it in along with his full name. And there it was: "Vintage Crazy: Resort and Rehab" with a link to Pog's TED Talk.

TED Talk? What in the world?

15

When she awoke the next morning, sublimely rested from not drinking, she saw three missed calls and a voice mail, all from the human resources manager at Brigman's saying she could return to work today and would be re-employed until further notice. Wow, *further notice.*

Josie thought of the bills and their second-notice stamps and knew she didn't have the luxury of time to sort out another job path. The women at the other counters—Monica, Philly, and even Megan—made the work more tolerable, an almost social-type venue. The support of girlfriends proved as healing as any therapy or SSRI streaming through her veins.

She phoned Ruby and announced that she could start paying her again. "Money is the worst discovery of human life," the woman said, quoting Buddha. "If it takes money to be happy, your search for happiness will never end."

Josie had savored this great day so far and didn't want a power struggle with Dottie. Instead of forcing oatmeal, she zapped a Pop-Tart and sliced half a banana for good measure. She settled her down with watercolor paints, a sketch pad, and a stack of basic math flash cards.

She dressed in her best black jersey knit with a matching duster. No one would even notice that the hem had unraveled at the bottom. She also took extra care with her makeup, which surprisingly, glided on much better without the welts of a hangover. If she didn't know better, she had every symptom of a woman on the verge of falling in love. How many times had she watched Pog's TED Talk? Mercy, he'd looked delicious in that white shirt and those snug faded jeans.

But more than that, Pog's talk had given her an idea that might save her son, if Finley would open his mind to the possibilities.

She drove to work smiling in the rattling BMW she hoped would sell quickly. With time to spare, she made a cup of hot green tea (turning over a new leaf, so to speak) before heading down the escalator.

"And a happy good morning to you," Monica said, looking like Morticia in her tight dress and winged sleeves. "We're all thrilled you're back. Everyone but *her*," she said, tilting her head to indicate Pauline, who was ringing up an Estée Lauder customer and taking the credit. "Want a Starbucks?"

During more solvent days, Josie didn't blink when spending six bucks on a cup of joe. With the coffee shop and pretzel place closer to her bay than the ladies' room, the mall had become a financial and dietary land mine. No wonder more than a few get the Retail Body—skinny legs from running around the department store hauling stock and fetching this and that, and tubby arms and tummies from shoving down carbs and salt at the food court.

"My arms look like a pelican swallowed a flounder," Josie said, tapping a fallen tricep. "Why not have a sugary jolt? Here's my debit card. Let me find something to write this down." She tore out a piece of register tape. "Hazelnut mocha macchiato, iced, almond milk, and no whip cream." So much for the green tea regimen.

Monica waved off Josie's Visa. "Just ring Clinique in my number when I'm out getting the coffees. Good luck with old Succop today." After Monica left for Starbucks, a woman dumped a heavy Brigman's bag onto the counter.

"Hola, and welcome—" Josie stopped talking. What was wrong with this woman's face?

"I have a return," the lady said, rubbing her swollen eyes. "Pauline told me this crema de whatever would transform me so I'd never need a face-lift. I used it for three days and look at me! My face itches so bad I thought I'd scratch it to the bone."

Josie scanned the receipt: a complete set of Hermosa Piel Radiante and a jar of Bella Mujer. "You spent eight hundred dollars on this?"

"She said it would work miracles. She told me if I didn't buy these, that I'd regret it and would for sure be needing surgery. A face-lift! Look at my eyes! I look like I stuck my head in a hornet's nest."

As Josie told the lady how sorry she was, Pauline instantly materialized, as if she sensed money. She circled the bay like a shark and spotted Josie with the woman. Her eyes glimmered at the bounty of creams, most still in shiny packaging. Thinking these were soon-to-be-purchased items and not returns, she pushed Josie aside and smiled at the woman.

"I've got this," she said. "She's one of my best clients. Aren't you Mrs....Mrs.... Seems I've forgotten your last name, sugar."

Josie couldn't resist. "She's just here to see you, aren't you, Mrs. Roland?" She'd read the name on the Brigman's charge card.

"I need to return all of this," the woman said, clearly losing her patience. "I'm going back to Origins because this clearly doesn't work with my skin." Josie could see Pauline's brain ticking. She'd try to find a loophole so this return wouldn't take a chunk out of her sales-per-hour numbers. Her hands trembled as she scurried and lined up the products.

"Are you sure I can't put this all on a nice Brigman's gift card for you?" she asked, her voice taking on a desperate tone.

"Do you *think* I want a useless gift card? I want it all back on my Brigman's card. Then I can afford that face-lift you told me I needed."

"Now, Mrs. Rowan—"

"Roland," the woman snapped. And with that, neither woman said another word. They stared at each other through narrowed eyes. As Pauline processed the return, she banged her register as if she were trying to kill it. She slid the return receipt onto the counter and didn't give the woman another look.

When Mrs. Roland left and Pauline dropped her slightly used products in the damages drawer, Josie knew she'd have hell to pay. "I need the rest of the customers this week to make up for this disaster."

If you'd quit overselling you wouldn't have such astronomical returns, Josie thought. *And I'll be damned from here on out if I give you a single customer I work with.* Another woman appeared and Pauline jumped on her like a tick on a shelter dog. "Hola, and welcome to La Belleza. How can I help you look and feel more beautiful today than you already are? Not that that's possible, honey."

The woman must have been pushing eighty and had gorgeous cream skin set off with a shimmering turquoise scarf. She wore the bright colors of happy women, aging ladies who reach a certain birthday and realize accessories and bold hues redirect the eyes from time's handiwork.

"I don't know," she said. "I'm just browsing and killing time until I meet my daughter for lunch at that Asian place."

Pauline wasn't about to let this one go. She eyeballed the woman's floral Coach tote and the sparkling half-dozen carats stacked three-rings high on her third finger. "Here, take a seat and let me pamper you, baby doll," she said, all but pushing the woman into a chair. "What kind of skin care are you currently using, angel?"

Good Lord. Josie forced herself not to roll her eyes at Pauline's baby talk: honey, angel, sweetie, darling. It was nauseating.

"Nothing but Ponds Cold Cream," the lady said, smug with satisfaction.

Pauline's face dropped and she stretched her lips over those massive teeth, trying to purse them into concern. She looked exactly like an egret: tall, every feature pointed and sharp except that weak chin. She'd caked on the makeup today, even more so than usual, trying to do the cat-eyed look and failing miserably. She also sported two circles of pink blush, not even smoothed out, and looked as if she'd just crawled from two sleepless nights at a Motel 6.

"Do you mind if I take off your makeup and treat you to a little demo?" she asked the woman who clutched her Coach as if Pauline might snatch it from her hands. "I can also give you a hand massage with our new Dulce Rosa perfume. It means 'sweet rose' in Spanish and is heavenly."

The woman settled her purse and folded her arms. "I don't need all that nonsense. I only came in for an eyebrow pencil. I'm more than happy with the five-dollar Ponds I get at Walgreens."

Pauline wasn't going to settle for a measly twenty-five-dollar sale. "Well, honey, your skin is looking drier than a Pentecostal wedding." She laughed at her rather inappropriate joke, but the woman didn't crack a smile. "I'll just treat you to our luxurious serums and creams and let you feel how wonderful they are. It'll be the same as getting a free facial, lovie."

Pauline set her trap. While layering everything but cadaver skin on this poor woman, she barked orders at Josie when customers walked up. "Ring that up under my number, and I mean every word of it in large caps." Every time she saw someone ease toward the counter, her eyes flashed. Josie had had enough of Pauline and rang the sales for herself.

The cold-cream woman grew restless and tried to stand. "Wait a minute, sugar doll, we're just getting started." Pauline all but strapped Mrs. "Ponds" in a straitjacket to keep her seated. The woman stole pleading glances at Josie, but half an hour later, she stood before the cash register as if facing execution. With every barcode zapped, a rush of pleasure flooded Pauline's clown face.

"You putting this on your Brigman's card, sweetness?"

"I don't have it with me. I don't even know if I have one."

"Sugar, that's not a problem. I can save you twenty percent on all this fabulous skin care if we just take two minutes to get you one of our rewards cards." She leaned into the poor woman as if talking to a child. "Honey, they are wonderful. You'll get so many more coupons than the other Brigman's shoppers and you'll get free bonus dollars to spend on anything. No exceptions or exclusions."

Josie was tempted to add, *Don't dare bring bonus dollars to the makeup counter when Pauline's presiding. No way is she allowing them to eat away her commission.*

The elderly woman's head bobbed in confusion as Pauline scanned items and crowed about the virtues of a Brigman's card. She'd come in for her brow pencil, and Pauline rang up nearly seven hundred dollars' worth of products she told the woman were must-haves because that Ponds would eat her alive.

"I have enough cards," Mrs. "Ponds" said suddenly as if Pauline's words had just sunk in.

"Lovie, you need a Brigman's card. Now let's get you signed up so you can save that twenty percent."

When it was all over, the woman, whose mind earlier had been sharp as a five-blade razor, slipped into a stress-induced daze. Her head twitched and she tottered toward the doors opening into the mall. She peered into her Brigman's bag as if she'd just bought a python.

"This…this is how you do it," Pauline said with a snarky grin. "This is why I'm top dog around here. I'm going to smoke now. One celebratory cig. When I get back, I want you to have a living, breathing body in the freaking chair. That's the only way to make it in this business, and we're trying to take over the Big Three."

Josie thought she heard incorrectly. "I'm not certified," she said.

"You are now," Pauline muttered. "Mr. Hoven pulled rank on Fabiana."

Josie wondered if this was another of Pauline's tricks. "And ring it in under your number?"

"Not now," she said with a smirk. "I'm being generous while on my little break."

After Pauline left, Josie found her mind rolling from Pog to Finley and wondered if what Pog proposed in that TED Talk was ludicrous or genius. She'd work up the nerve to call him later and delve more into his out-of-the-box ideas on treating addiction. Her thoughts broke when Philly's booming voice rang out over the intercom.

"ATTENTION, BRIGMAN'S BEAUTIES! Are you listening? Let's all pause and get quiet. Okay, good. Now that I have your attention, I want you to come *directly* to the Lancôme counter. Today only, as in right now, we're having a Go Fishing booth.

You remember that one from the carnivals of yesteryear? Well, march over to Lancôme and with every *free* foundation match and *free* ten-day supply of our makeup, we'll let you go fishing. Everybody who fishes gets a fabulous prize. ALL FOR FREE! Come on over and get this free mud." Philly giggled. "Mud, you say? Yes, that's what my daddy always called foundation. He'd say, 'Girl, whatcha doing with all that *mud* caked on your face?' So come on down, ladies. You are the next contestant for FREE MUD and Go Fishing at Lancôme! And as always... we'll be happy to service you with our free facials. Yes, ma'am, we'll WIPE YOU DOWN and GREASE YOU UP. You'll be slippery as a salamander and glowed up in no time. Remember our motto: BETTER LATE THAN UGLY!"

Josie couldn't help but laugh and was still giggling when Pauline returned, smelling like breath mints and cigarettes. She plopped down her clear bag, pack of Misty's in full view. "So how did it go while I was on my break? Did you sell anything?"

"One woman stopped by, but she just wanted a free sample."

"Did you log her name and information in our sample book?"

"Well, I was going to but—"

"Cheap-asses only wanting samples. I've told you, sampling should always, I mean always, lead to selling with a capital *S*. Don't let them get the free shit and leave." Pauline opened the sample drawer and removed most of the items. "Use these *only* if someone sits down for the full La Belleza experience."

"Pauline, we have plenty of samples, more than we can use," Josie said, standing up for herself.

As Pauline rustled around the counter, a customer stood near the back with a list. Yes, a list! The most beautiful sight for a cosmetics worker. And on that list was a column of products.

"May I help you with La Belleza today?" Josie whispered, praying Pauline wouldn't overhear with those bat ears of hers.

"Yes, I need to replenish." Words of gold.

"Hey, sugar," Pauline said, rising from the cubby where they stashed coats and personal belongings. "I *thought* you were coming to see me today." She turned those soulless eyes on Josie. "I've got this."

Josie groaned and headed to the Lancôme counter where Philly stood poised over pen and paper, probably working up more announcements. "I'm going to call him," Josie said. "I mean he did a groundbreaking TED Talk and his website is fascinating. You should hear his ideas on addiction and rehabs."

Philly set down her pen and pointed across the aisle. "I don't know a thing about TED Talking but no need to call him. Look to your left. He was coming to see you, but that new woman at Estée snagged him."

And there he was. Paul Oscar Gavins. Pog.

16

Josie drew a Ruby Necessary-style breath and rounded the corner to find Pog sitting in one of Estée Lauder's makeup chairs. He was patiently listening to a striking middle-aged beauty adviser Josie'd never seen.

His Chanel Blue seduced her, and she reminded herself, *No men*. And certainly not now—with Finley's condition and their estrangement. Even so, she'd be lying to herself if she didn't imagine her son happy and thriving at Pog's unconventional rehab.

Josie double-checked La Belleza to make sure Pauline was still occupied. As Pog conversed with and smiled at this deeply tanned woman, Josie overheard her saying something about her former job as a Miami Heat dancer and her past relationship with Tiger Woods.

Old Hoven's at it again, hiring those with high-profile pasts, Josie thought and cleared her throat. "Pog?" He turned around and flashed his sweeping smile.

"I tried to give him a facial," the Miami Heat woman said and held her shoulders back so her breasts inched farther out. She cocked her head and sucked in her stomach, posturing as if to assert dominance.

Josie nodded and smiled. She lifted Pog's hand, surprised by her boldness. "Someone needs to give him a thick cream for these ranch paws."

"Never trust a man whose hands haven't seen a good day's labor," he said, azure eyes shining. "Cowboy hands equal a prince's heart." He swiveled in the chair, so he was fully facing Josie. "I trust you've seen the talks and website. You may have questions."

He certainly got right to the point—even assuming she'd already ventured into Stalk Town. "Questions wouldn't begin to cover it," Josie said. "Why do you want *me* to see and hear about all this?"

The Estée Lauder lady had strutted to another client, leaving Josie with Pog. "Have a bit of faith," he said. "Let's talk and I'll explain everything and where you come in. I take it this isn't the place for such a conversation?"

"Where *I* come in?" Josie had so many questions for this man, some she wouldn't have the nerve to ask. Questions about that night at the Westin. "I was wondering why you—" The cell in Josie's pocket vibrated against her thigh. She froze and nerves thumped at her chest; she never knew from day to day what such messages would entail. She always feared each time it rang or buzzed that it was her due date for *the call*.

She picked it up.

A text from Finley read, "I need money!! What kind of mother won't even give her son a dollar? I'm asking one more time nicely. Are you willing to help your son? This is a messed-up world that has mistreated me. Thanks for the last batch of groceries and clothes. BUT I NEED YOU TO TRUST ME WITH FUCKING MONEY!!!"

This wasn't her boy, her Finley. This was the drugs talking. She willed a calm, trying not to let his words take root and choke off love. She remembered what Philly had said: love is a verb. Philly had forced herself to actively love Carmen while she was using.

"You okay?" Pog reached for Josie as she teetered. "Should I get you water? Do you need to go outside for air?"

She braced herself on the chair and her heart twisted. She thought of Finley's escalating drug use and erratic behavior. His messages had disintegrated from horrible to heart-shattering. He was advancing toward death or imprisonment, and she knew, with the powerful instincts of a mother, that her time had run out.

"I get off at six," she told Pog. "Here, I'll write down my address. Don't come before eight. Please. I have to get my daughter to bed."

Another text pinged. "BUT YOU don't care DO YOU!!!"

Josie shut off her phone and remembered her son as a little boy, smelling like sunshine and dog, wet mud and joy. Some nights Josie's dreams were so real she could smell him in her sleep, as if he were on the pillow next to her: the Aveeno baby shampoo and Dreft detergent; the waxy crayons and tempera paints; the Axe deodorant heralding his early teens; and finally, Polo colognes and the odor of skunk from blunts and bongs, and the last time...that chemical ammonia smell she couldn't identify.

After leaving work it took everything Josie had not to stop by the store for wine. Once she got home and fed Dottie supper, played Barbies, and amped up their reading and math lessons with Skittles as rewards, she watched the TED Talk. Again.

She revisited the Vintage Crazy website, shaking her head in disbelief and wonder at much of it but finding so many aha moments in what Pog proposed. She poured a lemon La Croix and jotted notes from the talk.

"Nothing we've been doing in the United States to treat addiction is working," Pog told his audience. "Addiction and recovery are not one-size-fits-all." He strode across the stage under dim lighting, wearing those faded jeans that caught his sculpted legs without being obscene. His white button-down shirt skimmed his broad chest. Whew. Josie needed to focus on the message. Not the messenger.

"You can't cram the Twelve Steps down a person with aversions to the spiritual component of the program or who shuts down at the words, 'You can never drink or use again in your entire life.' We need treatment centers in this country that offer more than one method of recovery.

"Let's end the utterly dismal failure called the 'War on Drugs' and quit punishing those with addictions." The camera panned to a rapt audience. "It's time, my friends, to give addicts a rich life that includes an environment to support meaningful connections and work—real jobs and careers. Got a felony drug charge? Too bad. No career for you in life, but hey...if you'd want to stand in front of a conveyor belt for eight hours putting pieces of Styrofoam on bottles of ibuprofen, we have a job for you.

"Don't get me wrong. There is absolutely nothing wrong with honest work. But for many addicts, opportunity just isn't there. Why not train them? Educate them? Give them opportunities?" He shook his head and paused. "Our country punishes and incarcerates people with addiction, pressing charges that forever ruin their lives. Even companies that say they hire felons, often don't."

It seemed each time Josie watched the segment, she learned something new. Of particular interest was Pog's description of the Rat Park experiment conducted in the late seventies by the Canadian psychologist Bruce Alexander. A researcher had separated rats into two cages: some in a stimulating one with wheels and tunnels, cool things for rats to do; the others in a boring, isolated cage. He then gave the rats morphine to measure the effect of the environment on addiction rates. The 'Rat Park' experiment was intended to discredit the flawed understanding concerning addiction. Because during that time, every specialist thought the drug itself was the most important factor in whether someone became addicted. But it wasn't.

"In this experiment," Pog said, "the rats in both cages became physically dependent on the morphine, but the Rat Park rats with lots to do in their tricked-out cages consumed far less morphine than the group in the boring cage with nothing to do. So, what did Alexander conclude?" Pog raised his eyebrows and pressed his lips. "Alexander famously said, 'Addiction isn't you—it's the cage you live in.'

"At our facility, Vintage Crazy: Resort and Rehab, we're providing those with addictions a human version of 'Rat Park,' complete with education, careers, and a breathtaking place to live for up to a year. Thirty-day rehabs are too short and aren't working."

Josie's hand cramped from scribbling notes. She checked the time. Pog was due in less than ten minutes. She thought about

Finley's cage, the dark basement where he played *Mortal Kombat* and *Call of Duty*, not coming out of the house for days (weeks?) at a time. He had a college degree in video game design, but no one would hire him because of his criminal record. Or so he said. Maybe he wasn't even looking for jobs.

"Enhancing the environment is another tool," Pog continued. "Maybe the most important at knocking out addiction. There isn't *one* right way to treat this epidemic," he emphasized, the audience fully engrossed. "And now, I'd like to talk about my new treatment compound, two years in the works and already with promising results. I'm asking that you open your mind as we take a tour of Vintage Crazy: Resort and Rehab." He clicked on a PowerPoint presentation, beautiful images coloring the large screen. "Tucked away in the quiet mountains of Western North Carolina, Vintage Crazy offers—"

The doorbell rang at two minutes until eight. He was certainly punctual. Josie stood before her mirror and tousled her hair. She quickly topped her lips with a shimmery gloss, swept highlighter across the area where collarbones once protruded, and slowly, calmly, walked to the door, noting that Pog had yet another good quality. He was patient and didn't ring the bell twice.

The condo was so quiet and cheaply constructed she could hear the laugh track on her neighbor's television and the sound of popcorn in the woman's microwave. And even though the house was warm, a shiver zipped through her body.

"Would you care for leftover pesto and pasta?" Josie said, guiding Pog into her living room. She handed him a cold La Croix, though he didn't ask for one.

"Thanks. Full as a tick on a hemophiliac," he said, patting his flat abs, those Carolina-blue eyes on hers. "The kids at the resort put on a big spread with our grass-fed chickens and beef. We teach them organic farming and gardening and offer culinary classes. Did you check out those vintage campers? Boy, they're something else."

"I did," she said, not adding how she thought the entire

operation was fascinating. "How many of those campers do you have?" Josie had once done a news segment on the vintage camper craze. All those Shastas and Scottys from the '60s had been fully restored mini-havens and painted in beautiful teals and pinks and every other color in Dottie's Crayola box.

They sat opposite each other, Josie on the recliner and Pog at the sofa's edge. She suppressed a smile when she saw he wore one white sock, the other a deep gray.

"We have twelve up and operating and six more units the kids are refurbishing. What we have is a full-on business venture. We teach our clients, if you will, life skills they can use, such as construction, plumbing, and electrical for the hands-on types." He gulped his beverage as if he hadn't had water in a week. "Then we have an entire marketing department where they learn skills in public relations and website design and operation, social media for the place. Everyone pitches in.

"The adjacent farm is another area where we're teaching all the agriculture classes. We let them choose where they want to contribute, and nearly everyone who comes here to teach and work with our clients does so voluntarily."

They were silent for a minute and Josie took it all in. "I'm a little confused about the resort part of this," she said. "I mean, how can you keep an eye out when couples and families all converge and are possibly smuggling in booze or drugs? Couldn't this lead to a lawsuit?"

Pog reached for a throw pillow. He spun it in his hands like a pinwheel. "Our guests are in recovery. Must have a year clean and sober. We monitor what they bring with diligence, but we certainly don't strip-search them." He smiled, and that one crooked incisor tempted Josie to strip-search him. "Since we had our first guests, around a year ago, we've had only one incident."

"Isn't that one too many?" Josie felt herself going into journalistic mode as naturally as a luxury car (not her own, of course) shifting gears.

"We discovered it within hours. Pot. Could smell it all over the place. Luckily, it never made it into the hands of our recovering addicts. I hate calling them this. Wish there were a better way to put it."

"Using the word 'recovering' does soften the blow," Josie said. "So you've got the farm, the resort, the detox, and regular rehab and a team of therapists and doctors offering three or four different avenues and programs geared toward wellness."

"Yes. They choose the program they feel best meets their needs once we get them detoxed, if they need that protocol. We offer the standard Twelve Steps and abstinence that the vast majority of centers push. But we also offer Rational Recovery, Smart Recovery, and moderation techniques as well as the harm-reduction approach because, in all honesty, some of them will never have loads of clean time. We try to take a more holistic view of recovery."

"You mean through herbs and oils?" Josie asked, raising her eyebrows. That certainly was the Asheville way.

Pog laughed and hugged the pillow, and Josie was charmed by his fidgeting, reminding her of a nervous little boy with a favor to ask. "If that works for them, hey, go for it. What I mean is that we have yoga and meditation. We promote physical fitness and self-confidence. What it boils down to is finding natural highs."

"Sounds like a spa," Josie said and smiled. "When I did my news special on the opiate epidemic, the recidivism rate was through the roof. I think you're right that it's time our country woke up and implemented a more 'cafeteria' plan of treatment. Every person is different in terms of what they need."

"If one method doesn't work, they can switch to another plan," Pog said. "The key here is to expose them to as many natural highs as possible, trick out their inner and outer cages if you will. We have massage students from the tech school volunteering for their training hours and offering massages. We have future chefs from the same school who teach those who're interested in culinary arts. All these programs and skills are aimed at fueling them with dopamine through means other than drugs or alcohol. The beauty is that it's working. Much better than your general rehabs."

"A utopia for recovering addicts," Josie said. "Or anyone, for that matter." She closed her eyes and imagined Finley in such a place. "I guess my only concern is that you might be playing with fire having that moderation approach. I mean music to every addict's ears is, 'I can still drink or use. In moderation.' I bet they all try that method, right?"

"I'd say half choose it, but after a week or so, most realize it's easier to stay away from a substance than to moderate it. They come back to full-on sobriety and find joy and purpose in running this place and learning a new trade or career. They discover how to laugh again and feel good from something as simple but powerful as the sun on their faces or fish biting in the river. The taste of what their own hands have helped grow and prepare."

"Why not call it a more appealing name? I mean, 'Vintage Crazy' seems to imply all of the clients are off the rails."

Pog chuckled and drained his sparkling water. "It's a play on words. We've got people going nuts over these vintage campers. It's got an edge of humor to it. We've been experimenting, with great success, by adding programs that bring about laughter. Once a week we invite a stand-up comedian and even have an open-mic night with our residents. Did you see all the arts we've added?"

"It looks amazing," Josie said, wondering how this operation was funded.

"We've got the famous Rockland School of Craft in the neighboring county. They teach pottery and drawing, painting, glass, iron, and woodworking...you name it. The clients ride over in one of our two shuttle vans. Next month we're adding dance classes. A lot of those with addictions like to joke and say, 'How am I ever going to get the nerve to dance sober?' We're teaching them to cut loose without substances."

"Well, if that's 'Rat Park,' I almost want to get hooked on meth just to come vacation there," Josie said, regretting sounding so flippant. "How in the world are you even breaking even or not completely going under?"

"Lots of money up in these rural areas of the mountains," he said. "Millions in Mason jars buried on their land. Except for a couple of our medical staff, a huge chunk of our expenses is covered by donors. Some of my counseling staff are grad students working for credits. The biggest expense is the cost of the buildings. The land's paid for."

"How?" Josie asked, trying not to stare at his pecs straining against the crisp shirt.

"I've owned that property for twenty-odd years, and it was sitting empty except for people trespassing to fish. When my son died and I got divorced, I decided to use my CBT training—that's cognitive behavioral therapy—and set up a rehab like no one had ever seen."

He stood from the couch and sat on the floor, leaning back as if all this talking had tired him out. "We make a good bit of money from the resort and farm. We get lots of donations from Atlanta's wealthiest when we take on their kids. We're not getting rich, but we're bringing in enough to grow and offer scholarships to those without insurance."

"You mean insurance covers this…this experimental-type program?"

"Some do. Some don't. We don't focus on that. The bulk is covered by the resort and working the farm. An egg from a free-range chicken is like a nugget of gold."

"Farm to table. Seems that's the Asheville motto," Josie said and laughed. "That and 'Dog is Love.'"

"I can do you one better. One of our residents has a sticker on his old Subaru that says, 'Make it Organic: It'll Give You a Hippie Boner.'"

"Save me one of those for my next car. I'm getting rid of that pretentious monstrosity in the driveway. Only one person has even come to look at it."

More than an hour passed, though it seemed only minutes. Pog continued talking up his vision, but not once did he mention why he wanted Josie on board. When he finally finished speaking, he stood and reached for her hand. His warm touch awakened urges she tried to douse.

She quickly withdrew from the clasp. "Well, this certainly is interesting work you're doing. I still don't understand why you wanted me to know all about it."

He stared into her eyes and didn't break the contact. "You don't remember. Do you?"

"Remember? Remember what?" Oh, God. Not *that* night.

"At the Westin in Buckhead. After your mishap on TV. We had drinks at the bar, you did anyway, and then we spent the night..." He stopped, probably sensing he'd gone too far. "I have always wanted to see you again, Josie."

A force pushed through her body and she gasped. "Pog," she said, her heart drumming. "I have way too much going on with my son to backtrack down...to start a relationship."

He walked to the door and turned back; his sad eyes focused on hers. "I want to help you with your son. If you'll let me," he said and stepped outside without another word. Five minutes later as she splashed warm water on her face and scrubbed exfoliant into her skin, her phone buzzed with a text.

"Don't panic. We didn't have sex. I stayed with you and you cried in my arms all night. My true intent to see you was to offer you a job. And offer your son a spot here. I'm sorry I brought up our night in Buckhead. Think on it. You'd be a great asset. We can talk more when you're ready."

A spot for Finley. Had she drunkenly told him all her sordid secrets while at the Westin? She envisioned her son at the resort/ rehab—working on campers or in the office with computers, kneading his hands in clay to make pottery. A much-improved environment. Or "cage" as Pog's TED Talk had said. It was a chance to learn new skills and possibly discover a meaningful life.

She lay under the cool sheets thinking that maybe, once she got over the shock of this night, she'd consider the offer. Not the job, but the placement for Finley. Well, maybe the job.

17

Brigman's Corporate decided to compete with Amazon Prime Day coming up on the sixteenth because other department stores were jumping the gun, not wanting to lose leverage to online merchants. So when Josie walked into Brigman's she was discombobulated.

A giant "Christmas in July" banner hung from the front of the store, and everywhere Josie looked were decorations: silver trees dripping with red ornaments, hanging white lights, Santas, and festive scenes throughout the store.

Pauline, who'd been calling in sick frequently the last couple of weeks, showed up looking as if she were recovering from the Ebola virus. Her hair hung in greasy sheets and her makeup sank into her face as if her pores had absorbed it. Josie almost felt sorry for her after seeing her dry heave over the La Belleza wastebasket.

"Shouldn't you go home?"

"It's not contagious," Pauline said, sitting on a stool with her head in her hands. "I can't afford to be out anymore with all this going on." She threw her eyes toward the countless gift sets that arrived for La Belleza a few days ago. "I'm at the point of getting on that phone and barking out a round of Philly-style announcements to get this stuff sold."

This was a rare moment of Pauline showing a vulnerable side. "I was wondering," she said, eyes on Josie, "if you were close to your father."

Now that was certainly out of the blue. And weird. "Why would you ask?" She hoped her voice didn't sound as threatened as she felt.

"I don't know. I was thinking about my father and how I never had a chance to meet him." It appeared Pauline's sickness had mellowed her.

"I'm so sorry," Josie said. "I miss my dad. He died of a heart attack over a year ago."

"I know. Your mother told—I mean, I read it somewhere."

Josie reeled. Her mother had visited only twice since her arrival in Hendersonville (if you count her break-in as a visit), sparing no slashing of Josie's remaining self-esteem with jabs about her being "one stone shy of fat," and sinking to a new level selling cosmetics at Brigman's. Now it seemed she was spending more time with Pauline than her own family. Which was fine if it meant fewer of Katherine's taunts hurtled Josie's way.

She'd stopped by the condo last week to grace Dottie with a brief visit and a CD of Disney princess songs. Later that afternoon she'd breezed into the store for a bottle of Beautiful and Josie witnessed her talking to Pauline, taking her off to the side for privacy.

"What is it with you and my mother?" Josie asked. Her mother's uncharacteristic open body language when around Pauline spoke volumes. It seemed as if the two were more than acquaintances. She stepped back and cupped her throat. "I don't understand how you even know each other. And don't lie and say she happens to be a regular customer. I'm not stupid."

Pauline clambered from the stool. She rubbed the back of her hand across her forehead and waited for what seemed like forever to speak. "But it *is* from here, mostly," she said, and Josie could tell by the quiver of her lip she was lying. "She buys a lot of Lauder." This is what her mother had also said, but it felt spongy, full of holes.

"I knew you'd say that. It's bullshit."

"I always make it a point to have a more personal experience with my clients."

Josie's heart banged through her veins. *Let it go, let it go. For now.*

Pauline sat down again. "I need you to go out into the store and recruit people back to the counter. We're hiring a part-timer soon, but our numbers are down."

What nerve she had. At least she'd asked nicely without the demands to also clean, scrub, dust, and empty garbage. "All right. I'll hand out those cards we have for deluxe samples with a visit."

"Thanks," Pauline said, a hand on her flat belly. "I'm going to get a Coke to settle my stomach."

"A real Coke?" Josie asked, stunned she'd consume empty calories.

"Yeah. The doctor said I needed to gain weight. She was worried about my health and the health of—" Her face reddened. But Josie understood without her saying. She was pregnant. How was that even possible at her age without fertility treatments? And could it be Mr. Hoven's? He was the only man she'd seen Pauline have much to do with.

"Anyhow," Pauline said, "I'm going up to the break room for ten or fifteen."

During work Josie felt solid, almost content. She'd put down the bottle and continued with her support group, mostly online because she didn't like leaving Dottie after having worked all day. She'd joined Ruby for several gentle-flow yoga classes and discovered a relaxation that rivaled that of her old buddy chardonnay.

And while she hadn't spoken to Finley *live*, the scorching messages had stopped and he'd promised he was sober. She still longed for him to take her up on the Asheville offer, maybe even agree to check out Pog's rehab. As for Pog, they'd spoken a few times on the phone, but Josie told him her son was doing better. So really, there was no other reason to meet up with him. Well, there was another reason, but Josie suppressed it. She was in no place emotionally to start a relationship

When he'd suggested lunch twice, she gave excuses: "Dottie and I are going to the movies," and "Dottie and I are at the park." She realized she couldn't keep using her daughter as an out, but she wasn't strong enough to be around him. He had the power to turn her one-and-a-half into a straight-up two.

Things had been going well, everything considered, and

starting an affair, or whatever, would do nothing but distract her from this mission to get Finley to Asheville. Plus, Dottie had been accepted into a preschool program this fall, paid for by the good old state of North Carolina.

And the good news kept coming. Her BMW had sold too, and she'd taken the cash and bought herself a used but decent Toyota Tacoma. A truck! Of all things.

"I always hated trucks," she told Philly before leaving work. "I saw the ad and it was like a spiritual force told me, 'Buy this. It's what you need.' Another voice urged me to head down to the U-Haul place and put in a trailer hitch. Why in the world would I get a trailer hitch? But I did. The guy asks me what I was planning to pull because I guess they come in different weight capacities. I told him, 'Put the medium size on because anything medium has always been my go-to.' I guess I'm now a stick-driving redneck and love it."

"I kind of adore what's gotten into you lately," Philly said. "You're either secretly in love with that silver fox or sucking the Zen fumes at those yoga classes. And after tonight when we watch the DVD—"

"Oh, gosh! That *is* tonight." With everything going on, Josie had confused the dates, thinking it was this time next week. Maybe she'd repressed it, hoping her friends would forget.

"Don't try to back out," Philly said, wagging a finger.

"Don't you all have something better to do?" Josie asked, a flitter of nerves prickling her core.

"No. And neither do you." Philly frowned, hands on her hips.

"I'm bracing myself and going home now to get things ready."

"Ahh, don't knock yourself out. We're happy with cheap hors d'oeuvres and world-class wine. So if it doesn't come in a box, forget it. Corks are so overrated."

Tonight was the night. Josie wondered as she stepped into her tiny kitchen to prepare food if she'd have the fortitude to stick it out until that final scene on air. "Here we go," she said aloud as she turned on the oven and set the frozen mini-quiches and crab-stuffed mushroom caps on a baking sheet.

A wheel of brie, an artisan loaf, and Trader Joe's cracker assortment gave the spread a touch of sophistication. She chilled a 1.5 liter of screw-cap wine for the girls and splurged on real Perrier for herself.

Ruby had taken Dottie to see an animated dog movie and made plans to visit that mangy mutt down the road afterward. The quiet condo soothed Josie's jitters. She plugged her phone into her Bose speakers and pulled up her eighties funk playlist while setting out the food. The air thickened with smells of baked bread and cheese, the fragrance of contentment. She kept thinking of Pog and how it really wouldn't hurt to see him. She'd remembered parts of their night together: the intoxicating smell of his skin as he stroked her hair, the warm, strong arms that held her as she wept. She admonished her brain, quelling its primordial side. I mean, sure it had been over four years since she'd had sex. Talk about born-again virginity. She was unquestionably more than attracted to him…but…this had to be about Finley's recovery. Nothing else.

She heard rhythmic knocks on her door and her fleeting Pog fever dispersed. Monica and Philly arrived bearing paper hats, horns, and blowouts as if invited to a kid's birthday party. Philly held a bag of other delights she was saving for the grand finale, as she called it.

"These will bring our evening more of a celebratory tone," Monica said, placing a conical hat on Josie, its rubber band popping against her chin. "Not a birthday party per se, but a re-birth-day affair!"

She slapped Josie on the back like a man greeting a buddy. "The hat does you justice."

"Something needs to," Josie said with a nervous smile. "You all help yourselves to the wine and food and let's head to the living room and get ready for my judgment day. I'd prefer getting it over with as fast as possible so we can enjoy the rest of the evening."

As the women drank their wine and dove into the hors d'oeuvres, Josie studied her new friends. She thought of all those who'd borne and survived worse than she had. And as she savored these new friendships, tranquility enveloped her, and she realized there was little to fear. What was the old saying? Comedy equals tragedy plus time?

They sat on pillows around the coffee table, eyes cleaved to Josie's flat-screen TV and the disc in her hand that felt like a loaded gun. She checked her watch, worried she'd change her mind if she didn't let the momentum of her good health and elevated mood propel her into further healing. Her heart galloped into the starting gates of panic. "I guess I need to explain some things before we watch this. Give you the background. Nothing just happens out of the blue."

"So the stories on the internet aren't true?" Philly asked, unfolding her long body into a reclining position, head propped on her elbow.

Josie caught her breath. "It's not the whole story," she sighed. "I kept as much as I could from the press."

For the next half hour, she shared everything. From the beginning. She told them about moving out when Dottie was a baby. How she'd decorated one of the three bedrooms for Finley, furnishing it with a TV and Xbox, a laptop—all the comforts a man-child could want. Everything had cost her a fortune, and she'd drained a good chunk of savings to maintain the exorbitant downtown Atlanta rent while keeping up the mortgage on the house for Frank and Finley.

"I told him he was loved and welcomed here. That it was also his home and he could stay there all he wanted to," Josie said. "But I also told him I wouldn't allow drugs or criminal activity in my house." After two days, Finley had bolted and never returned. He missed his man-cave and his bongs and booze and increasing dependence on pills. He'd come to dinner or for an hour or so but squirmed and twitched the entire visit, itching to get back home to feed his fiends.

Philly and Monica fixed their eyes on Josie, neither of them saying a word, which was highly unusual for those two. They stopped eating and drinking, waiting for her to continue.

Monica cleared her throat and twisted her hair into a clip. "I'm so sorry about your son. I think you're a wonderful mother."

"You did nothing to cause this," Philly added. And then in typical Philly fashion, she said, "All right, ladies, let's get this show rolling so Josie can see it wasn't as bad as she's built it up to be. We got a surprise for you at the end." She raised her wine glass. Monica also lifted hers. "Salud!"

"Better make sure at the end I haven't had a coronary," Josie said, toasting with her sparkling water before inserting the disc and turning on the TV. And there she was, perched behind the anchor desk for her final broadcast. She focused on her screen persona, the pink suit, and smeared lipstick.

She watched herself as if she were looking at a stranger. She remembered that by the time she positioned herself for the evening broadcast, she'd downed the tequila shots. She'd been drinking nearly every night that year, more so in the weeks after her father had died, finding she couldn't go to sleep without at least two or three glasses of wine, but the booze before work had been a first. A woman is an indomitably unbreakable creature who can endure mountains of burdens until losing her balance at the top. Josie's point of no return had happened, unfortunately, on the job. And on television.

The familiar beginning of her demise flashed, the volume too loud for her liking. "Good evening." She smiled into the cameras. Josette, eyes burning with passion and anger and veering off the teleprompter. Josette, writing her own broadcast on live television. Part brilliance, part madness.

Her heart sped up as she saw herself as others must have: a woman crumbling one word at a time.

Her daddy was newly dead. Her son was missing and running from his latest charges. Her daughter had been rejected by her father, a man who wouldn't stop with demands for more and more money.

Josie had faced viewers that night with her head filled with more blood than it could hold, her heart ripped with more breaks than it could bear. And now, as she observed the screen in front of her, saw her friends glued to the broadcast as if seeing it for the first time, her head filled again.

She paused the DVD, the remote shaking in her hands.

"Josie, you can do this," Philly said. "Please, we're here with you, and you know if you watch it, well…it'll lose its noose around your neck."

"No one is going to judge you, girl," Monica said. "We judge ourselves far worse than others do. Turn it back on and we'll hold your hands."

She gazed at the empty fish tank she'd been meaning to fill with tropical fish—a reminder of the peace she'd soaked up in St. John. She clicked the remote and felt like she was choking. She held her friends' hands, Josie's clammy and sweating. Again, she pretended that the woman in the pink suit had no relation or connection to herself. She made it to the parts she'd watched in late May and then she tensed. Here was that final moment.

"I imagine," she said to the camera, "a lot of you see me in these happy-looking suits and all made up and accessorized and think, *Wow, she's got everything, the little bitch. I'll bet she has a thigh gap. I bet her house costs over five million and she never has to clean poop from a bidet or scum from her sunken marble tub.*

"Let me tell you, gentle viewers. I have mopped up more than my share of shit and scum in my life and, starting tomorrow, you'll hear about my wonderful son shattering car windows for valuables. Valuables to buy dope with! It's time to stop this now, son. Come home now. I love you and want to do all I can to help. I know this isn't your fault, this addiction."

At this point, the beeps were scattered throughout her monologue, but anyone with a brain knew the words behind them. "I have one thing left to say. Frank, you can kiss my tight little Pilates ass and go…go…fuck yourself. And, Finley, you can either get your ass in rehab or—" *Beep, beep, beep.*

She jerked as she saw the conclusion. How could she have

done this to her child? Or Frank for that matter. If only she could take it all back. If, if, if, if.

On screen, Josie took out a fifth of Gray Goose she'd hidden at her desk and eyed the cameras as she would an errant lover. She threw back a long slug of vodka, stood from her chair, pulled a Dior lipstick from her bra and wiped it all over her mouth. "Here goes another pound of lipstick down my throat." She slammed her microphone onto the desk and flashed the camera a wink.

The DVD went black. It was over. She'd watched the entire grisly horror. Shaking, she faced the women. Their heads were bowed. Their shoulders shook. Were they crying? Surely they weren't laughing. Were they?

"I'm...I'm so sorry," Philly said, rolling over and grabbing her stomach, twisting her face into pretend anguish. "It's just when you tell Frank to kiss your tight little Pilates ass and then your teeth are all hot pink...I lose it."

Monica let out a great snort and writhed near the base of the sofa. And then Josie fell to the floor in a fit of mirth and liberation and laughed until tears ran down her face. Hilarity and deep shame intertwined, and the potency of regret diminished.

The two women topped off their wine and Josie filled them in on the rest of the story. Relief engulfed her as if a surgeon had carefully excised a tumor, releasing her of the constant pressure. She had always found strength and healing in the power of girlfriends. What better way to mitigate a catastrophe?

"I ran off to St. John and stayed buzzed on Painkiller cocktails the whole time," Josie said, feeling the need to give her story an epilogue. "That's the official drink of the island. I swam and hiked and snorkeled, but mostly drank from sunup till sundown. Did that for two weeks before Mother flew down and committed me to a rehab ward."

"Well, you're beyond fine now, so congrats, Josie," Philly said, rustling a plastic bag she hid behind her back. "You are officially cured of dishonor and have a colorful story that will make you the coolest chick in the nursing home. Okay, Monica, let's do this already." Monica dashed to the kitchen and returned with a pink and white frosted birthday cake she must have stashed when Josie wasn't looking. Then the two performed a rousing rendition of the birthday song with new lyrics.

"Happy re-birthday to you. You should feel like you're new. You look like a survivor, and you live like one too." They lit a single candle and Josie blew once. A curl of waxy smoke rose and then disappeared.

"All righty then," Philly said. "We, the makeup bitches, are now about to honor you with this state-of-the-art plastic trophy." She pulled something bulky from the bag. In place of the standard cup on a pedestal, a giant tube of hot-pink lipstick ascended. The trophy's inscription read: THE AVERAGE WOMAN WILL EAT FOUR TO SEVEN POUNDS OF LIPSTICK IN HER LIFETIME! And below: *We love you! Philly and Monica.* Josie couldn't stop laughing and thanking them.

After cake and conversation, the women stood to leave. Josie loaded them leftovers and made sure they took the wine. She felt she'd never be able to repay them for all they'd done.

Later that night, with Dottie home and asleep, Josie sat in her empty living room. With the lights out, a glow from a nearby streetlamp illuminated a framed photo of Finley holding his sister in his arms, a rare photograph in which his eyes weren't half shut from sedation.

Josie felt a rush of air pass over her body although the doors and windows were shut and the air-conditioning unit not running. It suddenly hit her. She'd never fully supported Finley. She'd been pushing and punishing. Do-this-or-I'll-do-that. Sorrow settled over her heart. She had, throughout Finley's later life, the years he'd been on drugs, become a version of her mother: a criticizing parent promising love only if he complied with her rules. *Come to Asheville now Finley and we can start over.*

She thought of Rat Park and how she'd give anything, everything, to see him flourish in such an environment. She knew his latest stint of sobriety wouldn't last. That in a matter of days, maybe hours, his monster would once again seduce him.

18

Word had gotten around about Pauline's pregnancy and rumors circulated that the baby was Mr. Hoven's. Josie had recently noticed the two leaving together every Thursday, as Megan had said.

Her mother had dropped by a few days ago, once again bearing gifts and snide comments. She'd brought clothes and educational toys for her granddaughter. And for her? A copy of *Women Who Think Too Much*, and a memoir aptly titled, *Drunk Mom*. She also bequeathed Josie six new packs of black tights and leggings, Spanx, of course, and as many new pairs of panties, which in Josie's eyes appeared beyond colossal.

"I'm tired of being embarrassed by all the holes in your garments and the Spanx should give you a bit of tummy control," Katherine had said with a smug tilt of her chin. *Great. I'll have to cut them off within an hour of wearing them.*

Today at work Pauline was feeling better, thus giving her the energy to return to Lady Tremaine status. She told Josie to clean this and that and grant her every sale because her numbers had plundered. "You're almost ahead of me," she whined, her hand caressing a barely visible baby bump. When asked about the child, she brushed it off, saying, "Can't a woman over forty have a baby without a husband? Mind your own affairs. Nobody knows about this so keep your mouth shut." But people did know.

Lancôme was in free-gift-with-purchase mode, and Philly asked Josie to help out if it was dead at La Belleza. The Lancôme counter crawled with women hustling to get more gifts than allowed. A certain few drove the beauty advisers nuts trying to come within a dime of the minimum thirty-seven-dollar purchase.

"I'm a good customer and my Rénergie cream costs over a

hundred dollars," a woman shouted as soon as Josie went to help. "Put more free creams and an extra lipstick and mascara in my gift. Philly, tell her I buy big." Philly smiled and busied herself with another draining customer who flat-out told her the shades weren't complimentary for women of color and that she *also* wanted a customized gift. Well, it was true and she deserved one, so Josie took her aside and obliged.

After another half hour of this bedlam, Philly grew more flustered. She snatched the phone and announced: "ATTEN-TION, BRIGMAN BEAUTIES: Bonjour! As you know, it's free gifts over here at Laaaaaaaamb Comb!" She pronounced it like a sheep baa-ing. "We have your DREAM CREAMS and colors to make those peepers *pop!* But please, please, please don't try to squeeze *more* gifts out of us. We are bound by Lancôme law to hand them out according to the rules. When you spend *more*, you get *more*. It says so right there on display at the counter. Three extra pieces for a purchase *over* seventy dollars. No more trying to con us! Oh, and don't *even* think of trying to return your qualifying purchase next week and then nabbing the gift. We *are* keeping track! Return your products and the gift comes back too!"

She put the phone down and laughed until her eyes filled. "I'm so fired," she said to Josie. "Let's go to lunch in fifteen. The others can cover." Six customers later, they clocked out and sat in a booth at the Asian Dragon where sushi was half off after two o'clock.

"That was some announcement, Phil. You trying to one-up my final exit from TV?"

"I'm leaving the counter," she blurted out. She wielded chopsticks over her Boston roll. "Going back to New York this summer."

"Wow. Didn't see that coming. Are you leaving Lancôme altogether?" Josie's body drooped with the news.

"Got a shot at modeling again. Senior modeling is heating up and an agent contacted me a week ago. I'm shooting test pics in two weeks. Pays better than this."

"This is wonderful, Philly. You'll be huge!"

"Carmen is getting out of prison in September, so we're uprooting to the big city later that month. We're applying for a probation transfer. Both of us need a new start, and I'm tired of pimping firming creams. If only my *Shark Tank* invention had taken off."

Josie laughed, thinking of Philly's "Affirmation Mirror." She'd sketched out a full-length slenderizing mirror for department store dressing rooms. The idea was that the mirror would talk to the ladies, saying things like: "Wow, that looks sublime on you," and "Goodness, that makes your butt look fabulous." When Mr. Hoven didn't want it, she figured no one would.

She poked at her wasabi and put down the chopsticks. "Lord, I need to lose a few."

"Philly, you're what? Five eleven? You can't weigh over one thirty."

"I'm tall enough but have gained quite a lot since this menopause. I need to lose fifteen pounds."

"I think those Whippet-thin women look older," Josie said, wishing she could lose a few. "Don't starve like Pauline. I bet she hasn't put on five pounds during her pregnancy and what is she now? Three months?"

"I won't miss that stick witch. Carmen and I just want to—" She instantly went silent. "Oh, my God. Look two booths behind us. Try to be cool."

Josie pulled out a compact and tilted the mirror to spy. And there he was. Paul Oscar Gavins sipping soup with a girl who looked college-aged—a barely dressed young woman with tats up her arms and tits spilling over fried rice.

Well, it didn't take him ten minutes to point his obsessions elsewhere. How long had it been since she'd heard from him? A month? Not that she'd been counting, and anyway, she couldn't blame him when she'd spurned all his texts and let his calls go to voice mail.

"Let's go," Josie whispered. "I don't want him to see us."

"Too late. He's been cutting his eyes your way. You should

give him a shot. He's a decent guy and clearly he isn't over you."

"He's not over me because it never started." She thought about the flowers he'd sent Dottie. Nice gesture but on the cheesy side. She couldn't count the number of times she'd reread his texts, especially the one professing all. "I can't fully explain the attraction I have to you, Josie. In part it's admiration. For all the good you do for people. I watched you on the news. You had a genuine love for those suffering and didn't stop until their lives or situations had improved. The evening at the Westin…I saw how vulnerable you were. It's honestly not a physical thing. It's a weakness for that heart and mind of yours. Please call or text."

"Heeeeee's coooooming," Philly sang. "Stay cool."

Pog stood before Josie, scrumptious in his boot-cut Levi's. He greeted Philly warmly, taking both of her hands in his. Josie looked into his eyes and steeled herself against mixed feelings. Here was a man who could save her son but possibly destroy her if she let herself get romantically involved. Heartbreak wasn't what she needed.

"I've been hoping to run into you," he said, grinning, his hands clasped and rubbing two banged-up thumbs. His lunch partner, whoever she was, stayed at the table scrolling through her phone. "I could use your help and expertise."

Josie felt the breath leave her body as if she'd hit a drop on a roller coaster. She wondered if Pog noticed a flush splotching her cheeks. "I'm listening." Gosh, she sounded like a bitch. And to be honest, seeing him with a skinny young thing tinted her soul green. She most certainly wasn't jealous. Yes, she was. Why, she doesn't even like the man. Not in *that* way. Never.

Or maybe she did.

"My help?" Josie asked.

"A crew from the local TV station is doing a series on the rehab, the resort, and farms. I'm not good at this PR stuff and would love it if you'd come out and see things. Maybe give me pointers. I've been trying for weeks to get you over there. See if your son might benefit from what we have going on."

Josie's first instinct was the same. No. No way in hell do I want to hook up with you no matter how gorgeous and kind and outrageously delectable you are.

"I'd love to see it. When did you have in mind?" She had no control over what had sprung from her lips. It was almost as if someone else was speaking for her. Same as when she bought the truck and trailer hitch. Who was that woman?

"How's tomorrow?"

It was Josie's day off. She certainly had other things she needed to get done that day. "Perfect." Mercy, she needed to shut up whoever was doing the talking. "How's early afternoon? Say, one-ish?"

"We're on," Pog said, shaking her hand. The woman with the low-cut peasant blouse and floral tattoo appeared by his side, still on her phone. "Josie, this is Zenith. She's our new graphic designer and graduate of our program. Been clean and sober over a year." *So, she's not a date.*

"Nice to meet you, Zenith." Now that the girl wasn't competition Josie could play nice.

"Likewise," she said, tucking her phone away and smiling.

Philly pointed to her watch. "Well, we need to get back to work," Josie said. "Look forward to seeing you and the compound."

That night after Dottie had fallen asleep, Josie thought about her stint in rehab and how traumatic it had been. Maybe Pog's place *was* different. With the way some of these traditional rehabs were run, not many troubled souls were voluntarily clamoring for beds.

She slipped under the covers and reached for Dottie, hoping the touch of her daughter's skin, the weight of her little foot against her own, might lull her to sleep. But her mind kept returning to the failing rehabs in this world.

She gave in to the thoughts of those days after her televised debacle: the crushing blame she felt for subjecting Finley to her "falling ass over tit" as her mother colorfully put it, and those haunting weeks spent in detox and rehab.

She wondered how many of the others from her group had failed to remain clean and sober. She knew through her news reports that up to eighty-five percent of those in treatment relapse within the first year. And many leave after a day or two.

After finding her drunk in St. John when Josie had called crying, her mother had thrown her into the emergency room for stabilization before getting her into a treatment center. Forty-eight hours later, in a papery green hospital gown stained with vomit, she rode by ambulance to an unassuming red-brick building that easily could have been an elementary school or government offices.

After an attendant buzzed her in, Josie crumpled in a chair next to a middle-aged nurse who wore her hair too long for a face etched in hardship. She bagged and tagged her belongings, all the leftover swimsuits and summer clothes from St. John. She beat the emptied suitcase over the trash can, and Josie could hear the faint rustle of white sand falling and smell the hot sun and tropical air in her clothes.

She'd tried to stand and staggered. The scents of salty air and coconut tanning oil coalesced with the soporific effect of the phenobarbital prescribed every few hours to prevent seizures. Withdrawal was a nasty business. She took a step forward and spiraled against a wall.

"Sit," ordered the woman who wore a badge Josie's vision was too blurred to read. "In a minute you'll be searched just like everyone else who comes through these doors."

Josie nodded and her head felt as if it weighed more than a ship's anchor. She tried to speak but the floor seemed to rush at her, and the walls wavered. She desperately craved sleep.

Time passed but Josie didn't know how much. The nurse led her into a windowless space much like an interrogation room at a police station. "Take everything off," she ordered. Her eyes, like tiny lasers, scrutinized Josie as she removed her clothes, her body deeply tanned and way too thin, the white outlines of her swimsuits contrasting with the rest of her. Josie knew what this woman was thinking. *Rich, entitled little news lady ruining her life over problems anyone with a decent mind would trade for without hesitation.*

"Now squat and cough."

Josie, high from the phenobarbital, had jumped up and down, knowing but not caring how obnoxious this appeared. She frog-hopped into a series of limber squats, at which point her keeper said, "That's enough. Have you ever been diagnosed with a mental illness?"

"Madam," Josie said with theatrics, "my family is riddled with every disorder and defect known to humankind." After she dressed, with the nurse's help, a male technician walked her to her room where she slept for the next twenty-one hours until someone roused her for dinner and groups.

She didn't know pajamas weren't allowed except in bed. They'd pumped her with so many drugs, she tottered into the social room scattered with tables and the other addicts who stared at her hippo jammie bottoms. She'd paired them with a silk button-down tucked in as if she had half-dressed for an important meeting. It was the shirt she'd worn under her pink suit that last night on the air. Lipstick smeared into the collar.

She accepted a dinner tray, a plastic spork like the kind from Taco Bell, and a Styrofoam cup of watered-down tea. Since no one offered her a seat, she ate alone on the vinyl sofa. As she bit into the toughest chicken she'd ever tasted, her brain suddenly fired, as if an old blockage had begun dissolving. She remembered that horrible nurse who'd held up one of her nightgowns in mockery. "Nice choice," she'd said, tossing the oversized T-shirt in a black trash bag with all the other contraband identified as possible conduits for drugs and booze. The shirt said, "It's Five O'clock Somewhere," in hot-pink writing above a giant green margarita.

By the third day, the staff had tapered her phenobarbital, and Josie's senses and awareness exploded with intensity. She heard the whispers.

"What is Josette Nickels doing in this place?" they asked, referring to the state-run facility.

"God, did you see her shit-show on TV?"

"She don't look like no celebrity without her makeup, does she?"

Josie was allowed no toiletries and only four of the following: tops, pants, and pairs of panties. The staff removed all laces from patients' shoes, but Josie didn't have sneakers, having always preferred at minimum a two-inch heel. Even the flip-flops she wore in St. John sat atop a foamy wedge. And those doubled as hiking shoes.

By the end of the first week she noticed people had begun behaving like caged rats. They lined up for everything and seemed to crave order and routine as their newest drugs of choice. Lined up for the med window. Lined up for the snack time when the staff threw chips and Nutri-Grain bars across a table like birdseed. Lined up for groups and sessions with the robotic psychiatrist, pleading their cases for legal meds of choice.

Most of her fellow rehabbers were hooked on heroin, oxy, crack, meth, Xanax, or a combination of substances. She befriended a young woman named Jennifer, who drove a new Mercedes and owned a real estate firm. It had been her fourth time there, and she looked as if she'd fallen from her posts as head of the Garden Club and president of the Junior League.

Her other friend, Krista, was in her late twenties and a former high school math teacher whose DOC was crystal meth. She kept them all laughing with her wild sense of humor and uncensored mouth. "I want a cigarette so bad; I'd just about suck a dick to get one," she joked multiple times daily, getting high on the laughs.

For the first time in her life, Josie felt acutely aware of simple pleasures: the luxury of lotion on her bare legs, damp from a hot shower; the taste of coffee when restricted to one cup a day; hearing a group of hard-core addicts, clean for the first time in years, singing *Do-Re-Me*, their innocence returning.

By the end of the second week, Josie's doctor had diagnosed her with anxiety and depression (wow, huge surprise) and placed her on a regimen of Wellbutrin and Trazodone. He strongly suggested she enter a long-term program to treat her addictions and PTSD.

"PTSD?" Josie had covered plenty of post-traumatic stress disorder cases but never thought of herself as a victim.

"You lost a twin sister and your father. You lost a husband a few short years ago. Your son is on drugs and your daughter has a disability. In addition, from what you've shared, you've destroyed your career and your mother sounds like a narcissist."

"What a life," Josie said, the shrink's little summary like a stab in the stomach. "I can't go to another rehab. Who will take care of Dottie?"

"You won't be much of a mother until you get these demons under control."

After eleven days in the state institution, Josie flew to Kansas and entered CORK for the next ninety days. She'd asked Willa to shut down all her social media accounts and arranged for her mother to keep Dottie, which completely displeased Katherine and ripped out Josie's heart.

19

When Josie pulled into Pog's resort and rehab, what struck her first, other than the enchanting mountain views, was the odd layout of the campus and farm. Five long ranch-style log cabins and an auditorium formed a U-shape around parking areas. Behind the cabins, the campus stretched for acres. There were basketball and tennis courts, a twenty-five-yard swimming pool, a softball field, and covered shelters with grills and picnic tables. Josie could hear laughter and the slaps of rubber soles as patients (clients) walked or jogged the perimeter. A class, possibly group therapy, was meeting at one of the shelters.

The scent of charbroiled meat suffused the air and Josie noticed several grills smoking and hissing with the grass-fed beef Pog had mentioned. She heard cows in the distance, a lazy moo here and there, resembling black dots as they grazed in the field beyond. She listened as chickens clucked, reminding her of a gathering of elderly women at a covered-dish supper. Now and then a rooster let out a bossy plea. Red barns rose like tulips from the flat parts of the land, and she saw the lake shimmering beyond. Somewhere a river babbled.

When she looked right and up a hill, her eyes widened. There, in aqua and pink, in cardinal red and lemon yellow, painted in waves, zigzags, and polka dots, a dozen campers in various sizes colored the vista. Within another expansive red barn, Josie saw more campers in stages of repair. She spotted guests sunning or reading in lawn chairs, enjoying one of July's more charitable days. She hadn't heard anyone behind her but sensed an intoxicating smell.

"Hola," Pog said, using the Spanish greeting La Belleza required. "What do you think?"

"I haven't." Josie turned to Pog and smiled. "This is…well… it's just unreal. It's a modern-day Garden of Eden."

"Allow me to be the first to warmly welcome you to Vintage Crazy." With that he led her on a tour of the cabins, two of which housed the men, and two, the women. Josie was impressed by the cheerful recovering addicts, the joy in their step. But it was their eyes that gave her pause. They sparkled. They seemed luminous and alive, with pupils neither constricted nor dilated. She hadn't seen Finley's eyes like that in years.

At the end of the tour—after she'd viewed everything from organic farming to pottery glazing, glimpsed the clients renovating campers, and visited the offices—Pog escorted her to the compound's coffee shop.

There, the former heroin, oxy, and meth addicts steamed milk and presented delicious lattes and fragrant offerings. "Lots of places don't even allow caffeine," he said. "Who could live under those draconian conditions? Here, try one of these scones Tia and Crook make."

"Crook?"

Pog grinned. "Old nicknames die hard."

"I don't know how you can afford all this," Josie said and blushed. "It's not my business, I just—"

"Like I said, I inherited the land and had a bit of pocket change. The majority of all this has been donated. That brick building over there, it houses the auditorium and gym and many of the educational classes. The kids helped build that last year. There's a special section that's locked and sequestered where we let the moderators try out their techniques. They have one week and are allowed up to three drinks in a day. If they want that third, we know they're unable to successfully moderate."

Pog stopped talking long enough to pop half his scone into his mouth. "Mmm. Delicious," he mumbled, mouth full as Tia appeared with two ice waters in handmade pottery tumblers. "The staff closely monitors and supervises the moderation group. Most do end up over on the sober side. They don't like being shuttled away and limited in activity. So in essence, if you want the full Vintage Crazy experience, you have to choose and commit to sobriety."

"I don't know why other places aren't doing this," Josie said, sipping her mocha latte and biting into the ripest blueberries she'd ever tasted.

"Money. We're lucky in that the surrounding art and technical schools are allowing credits for doing internships and work over here. The two docs are paid, but we have a couple of older retired shrinks who volunteer. We have a few cabins by the river and let them stay rent free. My place is there too. We could head down there after—"

"Oh, thank you, but I should be getting back to Dottie pretty soon." There was no way she was traipsing into this man's personal space. She didn't fully trust him. No, that wasn't true; she didn't trust herself.

Pog crinkled his forehead. He knew what she was thinking but kept the subject on recovery. "Look, I've been working on presenting this type of treatment compound to other cities and states. It can be done if area schools and colleges donate their students' time in exchange for course credits. We've gotten grants and this type of program is possible all over the country." He wiped crumbs from his mouth, which for some reason, pulled at Josie's heart.

"Once a patient is here ninety days, they have the opportunity to stay on and work and pay rent like at a halfway house. They live in our Airstream campers on adjacent land. Others complete the program and go out on their own. And a few, sadly, leave right after detox."

"What about the successful moderators?" Josie asked. "Where do they go?"

"Most can't control it. I'd say less than three or four percent can pull it off. We give them information on moderation meetings and harm reduction. They leave but our doors are always open. Some have already returned."

Josie thought of the addicts who use rehabs as revolving doors. In and out multiple times. "What's the success rate?"

"We're still new, but we're at over eighty percent still clean after a year. We're using medications in many cases to suppress cravings. A lot of traditional rehabs won't touch that one, and I believe that's part of the reason their success rates are so low. People need to open their eyes and minds and support this more medically sound and holistic program."

"I think people would want to help," Josie said. "This epidemic isn't going away. Not with the majority of treatments we have now so rigid and stuck in ancient models. I'd be more than glad to write legislators and—" She stopped herself. That was her old life, campaigning and fighting for causes and the underdog, and she missed it more than she'd realized.

Pog offered a half-smile. "You'd be wonderful persuading the tough current administration. It's proven that in more lenient countries, the drug addiction rate for the harder stuff can't touch our rates here. We're four times higher than in Europe. I'm telling you, Josie, it's all about their environment and not self or societal punishment."

For the first time in over a year, Josie wished she had a mic and cameraman. "You have me convinced." But what she thought about most was Finley, visualizing him here on this beautiful land, learning new skills and ways to manage his inner pain and cravings.

"If the environment reeks," Pog said, "people are going to use more drugs. Every addict in the world should have a reason to get out of bed every morning. Something to do. A purpose. Threatening doesn't work. We should all be saying, 'I love you and if you need me, I'll be there.'"

His words shot through her heart—a love story to everyone broken. She fought tears and picked at her pastry. "You don't need any coaching," she said and met his eyes. "You've got this interview. Just show them what you've shown me. Let's hope it goes viral and the big networks pick it up."

Pog leaned forward. He reached for her hand and her skin blazed beneath his palm. Flashbacks of that night at the Westin strobed. Whatever had happened, Josie almost wanted an encore. "Let me walk you to your truck." Before they made it outside to the parking lot, he asked if she'd come to his office.

For what, she had no idea, but she agreed. Well, maybe she did have *some* idea on a base level. When he shut the door and gently pulled her toward him, she didn't resist. "Josie, sweet Josie," he whispered. "I've always wanted a second chance to—"

"I can't," she said, retreating, though her body was sending an entirely different message.

"Why not?"

She left without giving him an answer. Because she had none to give. She'd been besotted—as her mother would say—with this man since she'd seen him striding across the stage telling his audience why addicts need love.

The next day, Josie's hands were deep in the dough when it hit her. Her entire body rumbled like a quake's aftershock. It was Finley. Something wasn't right and her intuition never lied.

She removed her trembling hands from the cookie batter and was washing them in the sink when a second jolt stole her breath. Light-headed and panting, she sat at the kitchen table where Dottie colored and ate Goldfish crackers. She had that awful brittle feeling, as if her bones would splinter.

It was a full moon, a blood moon eclipse, shining red and visible only in the eastern hemisphere. But even though she couldn't see it, she felt its stirrings in that deepest part of her.

Her soul seemed to brew. A tug, a premonition riding on the hem of her brain, all but told her Finley was close to death. She sat trying to catch her breath, and at the same time, hatched a plan to call him from an unrecognizable phone.

The lady with the dog. Yes, she'd compose herself and borrow the woman's landline. As she considered the plan, her cell rang, and music from Ambrosia filled the air. She jumped and seized the phone, which slipped in her damp palm. "Finley!" she cried, scrambling to answer.

"Hey, Mom," he said as if they'd just spoken the other day, as if he were a normal son calling his normal mother for a normal conversation. "How's it going?"

Tears sprang fast. "I'm so glad you called. Oh my God, I've been so worried." She had to be careful, tone down the fear in her voice and say the right words, or he'd hang up.

"I got your messages about coming to Asheville," he said but didn't elaborate.

"I've always had a place for you wherever I've lived," she said and silently thanked God she was finally hearing from her boy and not just through texts or the random voice mail. Dottie ran into the room, and it wouldn't be long before she caught on and begged to talk to her brother. Josie eased from the table and entered the foyer.

"I know, Mom," he said and waited. He sounded sober, his voice free of the thickness and slurring.

Josie rallied her courage. "Are you going to come up here, sweetheart?"

"Mom?" he said, his voice now childlike.

"Yes?" She could hear her thundering heart.

"I keep messing up. I can't stay sober. I mean I'm clean right now, but it's always on my mind to use again. I thought I'd take you up on it and get away from Dad and all this drama around here. The drug crowd. Two people I know died in the last couple weeks from overdoses. It's that fake oxy. Pretty much pure fentanyl. It's bad, Mom."

She closed her eyes and chose her words as carefully as one would a last meal. "I can't imagine how hard it is," she said. "But I think you'll love it here. There's something so restoring here in these mountains."

"Yeah. I remember going with you guys a few times. I was thinking I'd be there tomorrow night if that's all right," he said.

Tomorrow. Tomorrow! Her son was really coming to Asheville. She broke into a little dance, raising an arm in victory.

"I can't wait to give you a giant hug. Oh, Finn. Everything's going to be okay. I feel it."

Josie heard a loud commotion in the background followed by a blast of rap music. "Tell Dottie her big bro is coming and give her a hug for me," Finley said.

"I will. Be safe driving. Go the speed limit or lower."

The music grew louder and she barely heard Finley say, "Gotta go, Mom. See you tomorrow," as he rushed to hang up.

She didn't like how things ended, but he was coming. That thunderous music could have meant anything. Maybe a You-Tube channel abruptly clicking to life on his computer. And not the blasting score of a pre-drug binge as it had been during the dark years.

She returned to her daughter, her eyes shining. Relief flowed through her. And excitement. Finally, after more than a year, she'd see her son. She began singing "Three Little Birds" by Bob Marley, forgetting she even knew this song until calling to mind Finley as a toddler bouncing up and down to the reggae beat. She wondered when she'd last sung anything.

"Bubby's coming," she said and sang those words as Dottie reached for the batter spoon.

"Bubby!" Dottie cried, waving the spoon and dropping a glob of dough. She ran in circles before grabbing Josie's thighs.

As the cookies baked and the air took on a rich nutty fragrance, the scent Josie assumed happy homes emanated most afternoons, she thought it uncanny how she was here in her kitchen baking, almost as if knowing her son was coming. Peanut butter was his favorite.

"How about we get everything ready in the guest room? Make it look nice for him."

Dottie sprinted to the back bedroom and returned with Mary-Mary. "Bubby wants her," she said and placed the well-worn mermaid on the bed. As they happily prepared for Finley's arrival, the small beige condo seemed to grow larger, and Josie's mind swarmed with ideas of what to do during his visit.

In addition to the usual tourist attractions, she wanted to slip in a visit to Pog's resort, which she couldn't get out of her mind. It was just so idyllic. Maybe Finley would decide to get help if he saw the place firsthand. She knew better than to push it, but it couldn't hurt to plant the seed.

As Josie stripped the bed and tossed sheets in the washer,

taking special care to use fabric softener and the good detergent she'd bought on sale, she said a quick prayer, thanking God for her sixth sense which had alerted her to something major, an almost seismic shift, but not to the doom she'd come to expect.

Maybe this was the beginning of the end.

Of the drug life. Of her son's suffering.

20

Josie woke up feeling like a new woman, a smile on her face before she even lifted her head from the pillow. Finley was coming today.

She chose her best outfit and arranged her hair (still in need of a major reno) into a loose, motherly knot. She'd given Ruby her credit card to shop at Publix with a list of all of Finley's favorite foods: Doritos, Chili Cheese Fritos, dark cherries, red grapes because he thought the green ones were subpar, rib-eye steaks she'd take to the community grill next to the pool, jumbo potatoes, sour cream, and Silver Queen corn on the cob.

At work, she couldn't still herself. She jumped from client to client, chirping like a teenager pumped with Ritalin.

"Why are you so giddy?" Pauline asked, a hand on her belly which was commencing a desperate rise from prenatal starvation. "Did Mommy finally give you a compliment?"

Josie would not allow Pauline to spoil the day. She'd been good to this woman, not gossiping about the baby who was no doubt struggling to survive Pauline's near-empty placental pipeline. Today, she'd at least brought a little more to feed the fetus: two extra carrots in her little baggie and a tin of StarKist tuna. Guess that was her upgrade from a tablespoon of hummus. At least fetuses knew how to survive their hosts' restrictions.

"I'm not sure why you always ask about my mother—or my father, for that matter," Josie said, checking her reflection in the mirror and pleased her no-booze routine had done such wonders for her complexion. "It's none of your concern."

"Is that right?" Pauline asked, ignoring a young woman who was rummaging through the bronzer testers.

"I'm leaving early today," Josie said. "Do you want to help her?" She nodded to the college girl dressed in Lilly Pulitzer's brightest and tightest.

"Not especially," she said, but then the Prada handbag caught her eye. "All right, I'll check on her since you seem jacked on caffeine or *whatever.*"

Josie left her with the preppy girl and found Monica and Philly chatting at Lancôme. Megan had quit. She didn't show up for a shift and never returned, never called or turned in a notice.

Josie danced over and propped her elbows on the counter while waiting for them to notice the big secret on her face.

"Girl," Philly said. "You're up to no good." Monica stuffed her mouth with a bagel, covering her Brigman's rule-breaking with a napkin.

"No, it's good," Josie said. "He's coming."

"Who? Oh, I know. You're in love," Philly said. "With that Pog dude."

Monica swallowed her food. "I can see it," she said. "She's got that horny halo rising above her granny bun."

Josie smiled. "I might be in what you'd call a fondness with Pog, but this is better." The women waited, eyes big. "Finley. He's coming today."

"Oh, my Lord in Heaven," Philly shouted. "I told you he'd come around." She grabbed Josie in a hug that left her breathless. Monica set her bagel down and hugged Philly.

"Damn," Philly said, breaking the embrace. "We look like those beetles I saw on my deck last week that honest to God were having a threesome. When's he coming?"

Josie tucked a wisp of hair behind her ear. "He called last night and said he'd text when he was on the way. I told Pauline I needed to leave early."

"She's been acting strange," Monica said. "I saw her frantically doing sit-ups in the dressing room."

"God help her," Philly said. "So unfair to that poor baby."

"You heard about the baby?" Josie asked Monica.

"Everybody knows. Oh, Lord. She's coming. Y'all shush a minute."

Pauline stood before them like a judge holding a gavel. "Glad you all are having fun on Brigman's time and dime," she said. "Josie, you need to come back to our counter. It's important with a capital *I*."

Philly rolled her eyes. "I'd better head to the stockroom with a fucking capital *S* and get more gifts before the crowds come," she said. "Find me later." She looked at Pauline and said, "Get ready for plenty of fabulous announcements today."

"I'm thrilled you're leaving in a couple of weeks," Pauline said, referring to Philly's return to modeling.

"I'll miss you so much, my little windbag," Philly said, making a pouty face. "My little ray of sunshine no longer in my life."

Pauline flipped her off as she walked away, Josie following. She wore flats today—a first—and clothes that draped instead of glued themselves to her body.

"It's your phone," she said. "It's been buzzing nonstop for the last ten minutes. Whatever it is, don't deal with it out here on the sales floor."

Josie's heart fell. She couldn't bear it if Finley was canceling on her. She quickly picked up her cell and saw four missed calls and two voice mails from an Atlanta area code. A number she didn't recognize. Her stomach fishtailed and she rushed from the store and into the parking area out front. Without listening to the voice mail, she jabbed the redial.

"Sergeant Pearce, APD."

Josie backed against the building to keep from stumbling. Her gut churned and she couldn't control the shaking. "This… this is Josie Nickels. I saw that you've been calling?"

"Is this Josette Hope Nickels residing in Asheville, North Carolina?"

"Yes."

"Ms. Nickels, I have some…there's been an accident. An incident, if you will."

She thought of the call from Finley last night, how he'd sounded good and everything had gone great until the music started. That sudden, deafening bass beat and her son rushing to hang up.

She slid down the storefront and sat in the mulch. She rocked from side to side, hand across her crashing heart. She released an anguished moan.

"Please try to remain calm. It might be a good idea to have someone there with you."

This is it, she thought. This is *the call*, the one all the Mothers of Addicted Children feared most. The call saying her son had overdosed or died. She knew intuitively this wasn't about larceny or DWI or an arrest for possession, all of which seemed simple and even desirable right now. Comparatively.

That feeling last night as she stood with her hands in the dough. That electrifying jolt of intuition when she knew without a doubt Finley was in trouble. And then thinking she was wrong when he sounded sober and said he was coming.

"I'd prefer you have someone there," the sergeant said, voice firmer.

"Please," she cried and everything around her—the people who walked by and stared as she wept in the boxwoods, the sound of cars coming and going, and the oppressive humidity making it harder to breathe—ballooned with intensity. "Is my baby alive?"

"Ms. Nickels, he is, but I need you to slow your breathing and focus, okay?"

"Yes," she said, panting. Ruby breaths. Ruby breaths.

"Your husband—I'm sorry, your ex-husband, Dr. Frank Chapman, is in the ICU at Grady Hospital here in Atlanta. He's in and out of consciousness and listed in critical condition. He's alive but you need to—"

"Stop," she said, and for a moment she closed her eyes, head bowed as if in prayer. She willed herself into reporter mode and that equanimity before delivering a tragic piece of news to her viewers. And then it hit her. This was about Frank and not her son. Finley was safe.

"Ma'am, we need you to get down here right away," Sergeant Pearce said. "He's been, well, he's been shot."

Josie bit into her cheek and tasted blood. "Shot? Frank?"

Why would anyone call her about the very man who couldn't sustain intimacy in the marriage for more than a month without running away? Just like her mother. The man who said to Finley almost daily, "Your mother chose to abandon us and leave us struggling financially."

"Look, he isn't going to want me anywhere near him, and if you knew Frank as well as I do—"

"Ms. Nickels, Mr. Chapman gave us this number and said to call you. I'm afraid he's sustained multiple gunshot wounds. A couple are superficial, I'm told, but one's serious. I'd highly advise you to get here as soon as possible…and…well, there's more…Ms. Nickels? Are you there?"

Josie realized she hadn't spoken for a full ten seconds. "I'm so…so sorry to hear this," she managed to say, struggling to her feet and brushing off the dirt. "I can't believe it. I mean, he was an artist, he *is* an artist…he's a sculptor and a great one at that, but…I don't know. Do people get shot over art deals? Or dime bags gone wrong?" She regretted saying this but seemed to have plunged into shock.

She walked back to the store on trembling legs and found an empty bench near the shoe department. Frank had been shot—shot!—and all she could think of was her son, wrapping her arms around him. "I'm probably not going to be able to come right away because my son is on his way here at the moment and—" What was she thinking? This was her husband of twenty years, and she knew she and Dottie needed to be there. Estrangement didn't count when a family member gets shot.

"Ma'am, there's another matter. I need you to please remain calm. Is there someone you can get to be with you?"

"I don't have anybody," Josie said. "Look, I thank you for your call, and I'll be there to check on him as soon as I can pack a few things and get my daughter ready. Please call me with updates, or do you have a doctor's name at the hospital?"

"Ms. Nickels, I need you to sit down and catch your breath. You tell me when you're ready."

"I am sitting," she said, her voice barely audible.

"Now I need you to focus on what I'm about to say. Do you understand, ma'am?"

"Yes."

"Are you the mother of Thomas Finley Chapman, a twenty-three-year-old white male born October 11, 1994?" *Here it comes.* She could feel its edges, the pounding fear kicking her with steel-toe boots. Her senses sharpened. She heard two sets of high heels marching down the center aisle and the air-conditioning units hum to life. Elton John crooned from the store's speakers about Daniel and red taillights heading for Spain.

Her body detached from her mind, eyes on the ceiling where the tiles appeared to move. He was asking if she was Finley's mother, that precious little boy who grew up and chose drugs over family. Drugs over full music and tennis scholarships. Drugs over the sweetest young woman now on her way to becoming a pediatrician. The boy who'd once loved art time in grade school so he could craft his mother mementos was now...

She remembered a little cardboard box encrusted in fake gemstones with his smiling five-year-old face on the lid. "Open it, Mama," he'd said, as excited as if it were his birthday. Inside, love notes folded a half dozen times fluttered like dove's wings. *I luv you, Mama. You cook the goodest makeroni* and *Yur the butifulest and best mama on the planet.*

She tried to summon words. "Please...he can't...tell me he's not involved in..."

Sergeant Pierce cleared his throat. "Ms. Nickels, as this young man's mother you need to know he's in a coma for what appears to be a drug overdose. He is also at Grady. Both father's and son's conditions are very serious. I'd advise you to get down here soon as you can."

Josie dropped the phone. Sweat pricked her neck and soaked her blouse. The words floated and swam from consciousness, her brain protecting her heart. Every organ in her body seared as if it were over an open flame. If she allowed this cop's statement to fully register, the weight of it threatened to crush her. She'd operate in her former Emmy-winning mode. Don't break down until the situation is under control, hover above emotions, flip the switch.

"Ms. Nickels? Did you hear what I said? Ms. Nickels, are you there?"

She grabbed the phone. "Yes." She felt as if someone was strangling her. "Did they give Finley Narcan? Because it's the only way to reverse an opiate overdose and save his life. Please. Oh, dear God. He has to have Narcan."

"Ms. Nickels, I'm sure they did. And, if I may say, how sorry I am and will be praying for you all. I know as a mother you love your son. I used to be a big fan of yours from the news. All those reports you did on addiction and everything you contributed to the Atlanta area." He cleared his throat. "Anyhow, try to remain strong and be careful driving."

"He needs Narcan!" Josie shouted, paying no attention to the customers staring at her.

"As I said, I'm sure they gave it to him. It's a standard procedure. I'm sorry to have to call you with all of this," he said, and Josie dropped her head between her legs.

"Please God," she cried to this man she'd never met. "Please don't let my baby die."

"Ms. Nickels, I'll keep you all in my thoughts and prayers."

Thoughts and prayers. Thoughts and prayers.

She despised those empty words politicians spouted during every flipping tragedy. Sharp pains shot through her chest as if a knife-thrower had bull's-eyed her heart. She struggled to her feet, clutched her growling bowels, and rushed to the bathroom.

God, please don't let him die. I'll do anything, and I mean anything you ask if you keep him alive. I am so close to getting him help.

In the ladies' room, Josie rinsed her mouth and scrubbed her hands. Staring in the mirror, she took a deep breath and steadied herself. She could do this. She walked back to the sales floor, her knees gelatinous, bypassed Pauline, and explained to Galena that she had a personal emergency and needed to leave right away.

She understood in that moment how families of the victims

she'd interviewed could fill the tea kettle or pour hot coffee with a steady hand as they discussed their newly deceased loved ones. Their minds protected them from the gouge their hearts would never stitch. Shock's numbing grace allowed them to open photo albums and yearbooks and click on videos of their dead kids singing or playing ball, describing their children as though they were simply on a short vacation, living as if their entire futures had been promised. The unimaginable grief would come later.

"When will you be back?" Galena asked, without a trace of empathy.

"I don't know," Josie said, her body trembling from the toes pressed into her Herman Munsterish clodhoppers to the top of her head, almost as if she were seizing. *Reporter mode, flip-the-switch mode.* She needed to rely on the two decades of her former training, separating her emotions from situations much in the way one removes the yolk from an egg.

"I'd advise you to call us. You may or may not have a job when you return."

"For God's sake," Josie said and rushed up the escalator. She left behind her clear tote, makeup brushes, the random pairs of reading glasses, and Pauline's curious stares. All that mattered was Finley's survival and getting to him as fast as possible.

At home, after shoving random clothes—she had no idea what—into suitcases and frantically answering questions from Ruby, she pried Dottie from *Shrek 2*, bribing her with half her toys just to get her into the car.

Within an hour after getting the call she'd feared for years, she and her daughter were on their way to Atlanta. She hadn't told Dottie all the details and wouldn't. Not until she could sort how much her little girl should know at this point.

Once on the Interstate, her hands clamping the steering wheel, Josie's tears spilled. She aimed her Toyota truck past the familiar landmarks leading toward Atlanta. When she left North Carolina and hit I-85, she tapped her cell, knowing Willa would answer on the first ring.

"Josie!" Willa exclaimed. "My God, you're on your way, right? Did you not see my million texts and calls?"

"I…I haven't had…it's just that. Oh, Willa. Do you think he could have really—"

"They're alive." She paused. "I'll meet you at my house. You can't go to the hospital without cover. The media's swarming and those bottom-feeders are already going wide open with this. Your picture is on every major channel and cable network in the country. They're also running the segment where you… you… Just come straight to the house. Mom said she'd keep Dottie."

Josie glanced in her rearview mirror at the little girl who had sutured her world and prevented the last seam of it from ripping. "We're going to see Bubby and Daddy," she said. "They both got boo-boo's so you pray with Mama that God will make them well."

"Bubby hurt? Me and Mary-Mary help him, Mama." Dottie had been playing with her VTech laptop and searched Josie's face with her crescent eyes, a blue so dark the pupils disappeared.

"Everything'll be okay, sweetpea. You know how we pray all the time? Well, let's just do it extra hard."

"Josie? Hello?"

"Sorry, Willa. God, I forgot I was on the phone with you. Look, I'll call you back when I'm a half hour from the house."

"You're strong, Josie. I'm here for you, and the staff at Grady—" She mercifully left out details of which Josie knew her nurse friend was privy.

"Call me if you hear anything," Josie said. "Please."

After they hung up, she checked on Dottie and said, "Keep praying, baby girl. God's all we got most days."

"Nam-nasty," she said, meaning Namaste, which she had learned from Ruby. "Om and om and om. I love you, Mama."

"I love you more than Snicker Bar Blizzards, princess," Josie said, her sobs on hold. She couldn't get to her son soon enough and pressed the gas as she changed into the faster lane, gripping

the wheel as if tight hands would ground her. Her phone dinged. She saw the number. She reached for her cell and hesitated.
He'd have to wait. Other messages flashed, probably reporters.

In the passenger seat sat a thick envelope with a manila
folder inside. Josie angled it toward her. "Hang on, Finley," she
whispered. During her packing frenzy, she'd somehow had the
fortitude to collect the diary she'd printed for Willa to mail,
having never gotten around to sending it. On every page, was
proof of her unconditional love, proof of a mother incapable
of abandonment.

21

As Josie approached Atlanta, where both her son and ex-husband fought for their lives at Grady Memorial Hospital, she forced herself to remain in professional journalist mode, despite this being her personal tragedy. Dottie slept in the back seat, her mouth open and eyes fluttering.

She'd called Willa fifteen minutes earlier and now pulled into her white brick ranch, watching her friend running toward her, arms as open as her smile. Long braids trailed colorful beads down her back.

Josie stepped out of the car and the women embraced. It had been months since they'd seen each other. Willa squeezed her shoulders and wiped a tear from Josie's cheek. Then, like past generations of women who'd anchored their upheavals with shared strength, they pushed grief into a corner and got down to business.

"Let's get Dottie inside," Willa said. "Mom's here to look after her and we can head on over to Grady. She's got the dolls out and the brownies baked. She also ran off two reporters with her DustBuster and pepper spray. Must have been your ex-cohorts."

"Even your closest will turn on you when you become the story," Josie said. "None of them contacts me anymore. Come on, Dottie. Let's go inside."

After a few protests and an ear-splitting wail, Dottie settled down when Josie promised she'd bring her to see Finley as soon as he stabilized. What she didn't say was *if he stabilized*. Willa's mother had adopted two kittens, and within minutes Dottie had forgotten everything else.

In her best friend's Honda, as they made their way to Grady, Josie suffered a series of raging panic attacks. She choked and couldn't force air into her lungs. Her long hair stuck to her sweat-drenched neck and the more she tried to inhale the dizzier she became. That end-of-life feeling overcame her.

"Baby, you gotta calm down and be strong," Willa said. "I checked before we left and Frank was out of surgery and stable. Look in the side pocket and get that grocery bag. You need to breathe in it slowly until you get yourself straightened out."

She grabbed the paper bag and began inhaling. After a moment, the attack abated. "Did they say anything about—" Her voice splintered as if everything inside her had fragmented. And it had. How could any mother's voice sound normal if her heart and mind couldn't pull cohesive strings?

"He's a fighter, Josie. I know he'll get through it." Josie knew she meant Finn. But it was what her friend failed to say that said the most. Josie didn't ask questions because she didn't want to face the answers. Not yet. The women turned onto Jesse Hill Jr. Drive toward Grady's main campus. Her heart kicked against her ribs, and she wiped wet hands on her jeans.

"We're parking in the employee area," Willa said. "You need to crouch in the seat 'cause there's a ton of media trucks all over this place. Having you at the center of all this makes it much more interesting than any regular OD and shooting. Plenty of all that here in A-Town."

Her phone vibrated. Her mother's number. "Mom?" When had she ever called Katherine *Mom*? In weakness, in crisis, even bad mothers are elevated from past wrongdoings.

"I'm coming tomorrow."

"I can't believe what the cop said—" She spoke from the car's floorboard, hiding as Willa suggested.

"I talked to the doctor on call. They said Frank is conscious but didn't offer much about Finley due to their bloody daft rules. I'm just worried Fin—"

"I know. But he's going to make it." She aimed her tone at confidence and found terror instead. "He has to."

"My whole church is praying," Katherine said. And Josie wanted to say, *church*? Since when did Katherine Nickels darken God's doors?

"Please. Come as soon as you can." Josie was surprised by her words and the sudden primal urge to feel her mother's arms around her. She could count on one hand the number of times Katherine had held her. Maybe that hand minus a finger or two.

Willa reached under her seat and gave Josie a bag containing an auburn wig, a tennis visor, and sunglasses. They bypassed the main entrances and checked in through the administrative offices. Frank had been moved to the ICU and Finley awaited transfer from the Trauma Center to a critical-care floor.

They made it inside without incident, and Josie pummeled the woman at the ER desk with questions.

"You'll need to speak with their health care teams to get the details," she said curtly. "I'm not at liberty to say. Go down the hall and to the left. Someone there will check you in."

"I need to see Finley," Josie begged, her chest aching. She clutched Willa's arm for support as they made their way down the hallways crammed with wrung-out family members and the sickly lying across chairs. "I don't think I can do this."

"Yes," Willa said. "You can."

Once inside the trauma center doors, the hallways blinked with blinding fluorescent bulbs and Josie smelled death and disinfectant, blood shed and blood delivered, flesh ripped and flesh sewn.

In a corner, a woman squalled, and nurses led her to a family room. Machines beeped, phones rang, but the voices, in low and hushed tones, reminded Josie of a wake.

Willa took over. "We're here to see Finley Chapman. This is his mother, Josie Nickels. They said we needed to speak with the medical staff about his condition."

The hospital was cold, and Josie shivered. She backed against the wall and doubled over, trying to stop shuddering and calm her body's fight-or-flight response. After righting herself and going through more identification screenings, Josie followed a woman who ushered them into a private room. Five minutes seemed like five hours until a doctor in a tie-dye scrub cap and matching Crocs greeted them without a hint of compassion. His face, like a Vegas blackjack dealer, revealed nothing.

"Mr. Chapman presented ten hours ago with opioid and alcohol toxicity and in respiratory failure," he said. "We've administered multiple doses of naloxone, had an initial response, but are now giving it in low doses through his intravenous tube."

"A tube," Josie cried. "Is he on life support?"

"We've intubated him for airway management and correction of hypoventilation. He's had a few seizures and we've given him anti-epileptic medication. He presented with a blood alcohol level of nearly point three five and a large amount of fentanyl in his system, likely from fentanyl-laced Xanax, from what his father was able to tell us. We've done kidney function testing and haven't ruled out dialysis—"

"Please, I need to see my son now," Josie said, her legs all but giving out as she tried to hold back a sluice of emotions.

"First, I want his nurse to come in and let you know the background and what we've ascertained about this incident— what we're facing." He said this looking down at his shoes, making no attempt at eye contact.

Willa reached for Josie just as her anchorwoman facade buckled and she broke down sobbing. "I can't lose him. I don't even have him, but I can't lose him."

"He's in the best care possible," she said, then whispered: "Dr. Hollings isn't the chattiest, but he's the one everyone wants on their team and taking care of their loved ones."

Soon after the doctor left, a woman in blue scrubs, wrinkled and soiled in places, appeared. She smiled and extended her hand. When Josie took it, the nurse brought it to her heart. Josie felt the cold metal of the woman's wedding ring.

"I've been taking care of that precious boy of yours. Please, sit."

In fifteen minutes, she laid out the entire scenario, her face honest, open, and freckled like Dottie's. Josie had never met a mean person with freckles. It seemed to her that God sprinkled saints and sweethearts with these spots.

"The police have a young man in custody as the possible suspect in your ex-husband's shooting. We heard from Mr. Chapman that the dealer had come to get his money for the pills he'd sold your son. Went downstairs and found him barely breathing. The dealer couldn't wake him up. He ran and found Mr. Chapman and they both went to work trying to get him to come to. They put him in the shower, turned the water on him... I'm sorry. I know this is hard. We could pause here and—"

"No. Please," Josie said and leaned into Willa.

"The juvenile's version is that Mr. Chapman threw him to the ground and tried to choke him, so he pulled the gun and shot him. That's what we know so far. Not sure as to the full truth of the situation. Somehow, Mr. Chapman managed to dial 911 and when paramedics arrived... Are you sure you want to hear this? You look like you're going to faint."

"No. I need to know everything."

"I'm going to get you something cold to drink," Willa said. "You're white as paste."

"I need you to stay with me." Josie faced the nurse. "Go on."

"Your son's respirations had fallen to a few breaths per minute. Paramedics arrived within four or five minutes and gave him Narcan to reverse the opiates. They rushed him to the ER, all the while giving him oxygen."

"So, this means he doesn't have brain damage," Josie said. "Please, tell me my son's condition and his prognosis."

"Kids your son's age are extremely resilient. I've seen hundreds of overdoses and many that looked hopeless. The doctors are doing everything they can to rid his body of all the substances. Narcan only addressed the opioids in his system. He had a cocktail of other drugs in his body. He's on a twenty-four-hour watch. We're doing ECGs, chest and abdominal X-rays, CT scans, and other testing. I assure you these doctors are going beyond thorough, Ms. Nickels."

She couldn't swallow and felt as if any minute she'd collapse. She had to get a grip or she'd be no good for her son. She'd heard that unconscious people are still aware. Josie needed her A-game and a positive attitude to help her son pull through this. "I'd like to see him now. Please," Josie said, drawing herself up taller and assuming the posture of an optimistic mother.

"I understand. Come with me."

As Josie put her arm through Willa's, everything suddenly felt dream-like. She'd detached from her body and observed from above. *Look at this broken woman walking toward "the call."* Everyone else's tragedies had now become her own.

And there they stood—in a place Josie begged God she'd never be standing—at the room where her son fought for his life and where an officer and nurse stood sentry. After scanning their hospital passes, the nurse stepped forward. A frown tugged her brow. "Ms. Nickels, you can't go in just yet. They're working on him now to get him into the ICU for dialysis."

That's when Josie Nickels climbed back into her body and lost it. Her detachment disappeared and the terror of a mother who could lose her child reached its boiling point. She pushed past them and tried to open the door to Finley's room. She heard a woman screaming. She felt nothing when the security guard grabbed her arm with force and pulled her away. And then she heard the screams again.

And realized they were hers.

"Josie, honey," Willa said, sliding an arm around her waist.

"You need to settle her down," the nurse at the door ordered. "That screaming won't help, Ms. Nickels. We're getting someone to assist you in handling this. We have counselors and medications to—"

"Stop! Please! Willa, please get my phone from my purse. There are a bunch of texts and missed calls from Pog. Can you try to reach him?"

᮫

"Here, sit and drink this," Willa said, handing Josie a cup of hot tea and a low dose of Ativan which Josie accepted, then tossed, thinking of her see-sawing struggles with addiction. Isn't that what typically fanned the flames? Telling the soccer player who broke his shin that an Oxycontin or Percocet every four hours would relieve the pain? And two refills later that soccer player taking them every two hours to relive the high. Until the dose is doubled, tripled, and addiction plants its roots. Everybody relying on substances instead of the body's own inner mechanisms and neurotransmitters.

Josie sipped the tea, feeling it warm her in the Arctic-like room. "Did you call him? Pog?"

"I did. He's almost here. Half hour or so from Grady."

"What? How could he have gotten here this soon?"

"Your friend Philly was worried and told him."

Paul Oscar Gavins. There for her when her career ended. And coming for her if her son's life…no. Finley would pull through. The nurse said his brain was functioning and that because CPR had begun so quickly, he'd had oxygen. But the toll of all those chemicals ravaged his kidneys. His heart rate was slow. His blood pressure low. They were pumping him with fluids and antibiotics, getting him stable so she could see him. Her boy. Her sweet, sweet boy. He remained unconscious, and the next forty-eight hours were crucial.

"The press is blowing up your phone," Willa said. "They are asking for an interview or even a statement."

"I'm wondering how they got this new number. I threw my old phone away." She set her tea on an end table and heaved herself to her feet. "Guess the press has always been resourceful. I'm going to see Finley now. This is ridiculous; it's been over an hour."

"Josie, honey. They said they'd come get you. Let them get him stable first."

"Stable? What an oxymoron for a drug overdose patient! I'm sorry. I'm not yelling at you. It's unconscionable to make a mother wait this long."

"I'll go see what's going on, okay? I'll ask them if you can see him. Bless you, poor girl."

Ten minutes later Willa returned with a nurse. "You can go

in, but you'll need to keep calm in there, Ms. Nickels. We don't want your son upset, so we—"

"I need to see him. Right now."

Within minutes the door to his room opened. She tried to focus. She heard the click of an IV and the Darth Vader wheeze of an automatic blood pressure cuff. She saw snaking tubes and white. So much white. She moved closer and bowed, leaning into her son's face taped with tubes. Instead of falling apart, she reached for his hand. It was warm. And dry. His lips were cracked and crusted in the corners. More tubes in his arms.

"Mama's here," she said, her voice torn. She felt the roughness of his unshaven face against hers. "I'm never leaving you again. Ever." Hot tears surged but she held it together. She saw the bag with his personal belongings on a counter and pulled out a red Polo, still damp from the shower. She held it against her chest and breathed in her son's scents. She sat in a chair and began singing one of his favorites from childhood, "Baby Beluga," while clutching his shirt, not wanting to let go.

For the next half hour, she sang all his beloved songs, including "Three Little Birds," the tune she'd sung as she baked him cookies, believing he was coming to see her in Asheville as planned. At no point did his eyes open or his fingers move. Wherever her boy was, it wasn't here.

A nurse quietly came into the room and placed a hand on Josie's shoulder. "We're giving him lots of glucose and are hoping he'll wake up soon," she said. "I'm sorry, but we need you to leave for a bit so the doctors can do more assessments."

Willa hurried to her side as Josie stepped into the hallway. "Pog's here. In the waiting room. You okay?"

"He looked...so..." Josie closed her eyes and drew in a forceful breath. "Like he did as a little boy. Sweet and innocent with a full life ahead of him. Oh God, he's still unconscious."

"That's okay. He'll come around, so don't lose that faith. Let's go see Pog and get you a bite to eat. I called Mama, and Dottie's having a big time with those kittens. A woman named Ruby also called and said to give you her love and prayers."

"How's Frank?" Josie asked.

"He's stabilizing. The wounds weren't all that deep. He's giving them a hard time, trying to jump out of bed and come down to the ER to see about Finley. They had to restrain him." Willa shook her head, rolling her eyes.

"This...all this was inevitable," Josie said, sighing deeply. "I'd been toying with time, hoping for more, hoping I would be the fortunate mother who wouldn't get this kind of news."

In the waiting area, she spotted Pog right away. He hadn't bothered to sit and walked toward her with his arms outstretched; Josie fell into him and held on as if he were the only life vest in a boat going down. His grip, gentle yet firm, glued her to semi-sanity.

"Let's sit you down."

"He's so frail," Josie said, her voice a whimper. "I don't know if he's going to make—"

"He will," Willa said. "I know he will. Why don't we go to the cafeteria and get coffee and a bite to eat."

"No. I'm not leaving." Josie slumped, hands in her hair, legs jiggling with anxiety.

"You can stay right here, and we'll bring you something back," Pog said, stroking her back.

"I have your phone and will handle anything important," Willa said. "Those reporters...you don't need to deal with them right now."

Fifteen minutes later, Josie heard the staccato march of two sets of heels, like fingers snapping. She smelled Beautiful. And Chanel No. 5. She lifted her head and it was as though someone punched her.

There stood Katherine, who was expected...tomorrow.

And Pauline, who was expected...never.

22

In the early morning of the second day at Grady, Josic startled, remembering where she was. She jumped from the reclining chair a nurse had brought the night before and rushed to Finley's side, same as she'd done during those newborn weeks when she'd rarely left his cradle, checking his breathing throughout the night so if SIDS tried to steal him, she'd be there for a fight.

If there'd been a change, she'd slept through it. But had she slept? The night had been punctured by the ins and outs of doctors and technicians, nurses checking vitals, and Josie dozing but never fully asleep. She stretched her cramped legs and yawned, her exhaustion bolstered with adrenaline. Wired and tired.

Part of the night and into the morning, she'd read to him from her journals. She stepped closer and lifted his hand, careful not to disturb the IV. She brought his warm wrist to her lips where she could feel his pulse, a slow bass drum, each beat with its dreadful pause before the next.

Finley's monster had entered on tiptoes back when he was young and drug-free with a sports future all but guaranteed. He never summoned this demon. Big Pharma pushed it, doctors prescribed it, and genetics pollinated it.

"Come on, sweet child," she said and gently returned his hand, fearing any movement on her part could affect an outcome. "Wake up and show them all how strong you are. I'm going to keep reading until they kick me out to do more tests. It's going to be fine, Finley. You've got this. You have it in you, so fight."

Josie grabbed an extra blanket from a small closet and placed it over her son. Who knew if he could feel discomfort, but after all this time worrying if he was cold or hungry, it seemed the right thing to do: these small acts of love she wasn't allowed for so long.

"I love you, Finley. I wish I could make this all better, but for now, I'm just going to keep reading to you. I'm going to start with what I wrote last night. It's the first entry I've made in this journal in nearly twenty years.

My darling son: The machines do the work. The breathing.

If they go, you go. This much they said. This much I'm struggling to believe.

In the weeks after you were born, I'd kneel at your cradle and watch you breathe. Every night after you fed from my body and lay dry and cocooned, I counted your breaths. I had to because sometimes you'd hesitate as if unsure what came next.

One, two, three. One, skip, two. One, skip, skip.

I'd nudge the cradle and startle you into another gasp of existence. I did this every night until my knees grew raw on the cold hardwood floor and my sleep-starved eyes shut down.

It seemed you were hesitant about this life outside of me, not sure you wanted the air that sustained, almost as if testing this world before it had a chance to do the same to you. Sometimes I never made it to my bed across the room. I'd awaken in a spill of moonlight, clumped and aching beneath your cradle. Mouth dry and hanging open, foot kicking that oak siding just to keep you going.

Now, more than twenty-three years later, I am doing it again. We're back to this two-step, this tango, this breathing game. I am counting the rise and falls of your chest and gently tapping the metal railings of your bed. The machine breathes and releases. It's a dance, a rhythm.

They tell me different things. One doctor says you're wanting to wake up, which is a good sign. Another says it's too early to assess the extent of the damage. That one uses words such as possible kidney failure or brain injury.

God only knows what else this monster's seduction has delivered.

Finley, I want you to know something so I'm going to lean over your bed and whisper it in your ear. I kept a diary for you from the moment of conception. It started that first day I knew life bloomed beneath my heart, until you were four, maybe five.

I should have kept it up. This journal. I should have written at least something each year but I didn't because I thought we'd have forever. I guess only the foolish can be so bold to think if you simply just answer the drumbeats of your body, that innate thrumming calling you to reproduce, the love you bear is yours forever.

So remember: if I could will you to breathe all those years ago, maybe I can will you to survive now. But you've got to help me. I'll be watching for your eyes to open. I'll be waiting for you to squeeze my hand.

For now, I'm going to tell you these stories. Stories of how much you are loved.

I'll be nudging you as I did all those years ago as the lights flicker and the machines beep and the air rushes through tubes, hissing and beating and sustaining all I hold dear in a single current.

She kept reading, but his eyes remained still. And closed. She read about the joy she'd experienced the first time she'd felt his tiny kicks, about the enormous love she had for his daddy, how talented Frank was and how proud she'd been of him.

I love feeling you poke and swish around. It's all so new to me. My heart feels as big as a full moon and I'm already experiencing that one-of-a-kind love mothers have when their babies enter the world. I only have five more months to wait, and then I can hold you. I love you, your mama.

Josie wiped away tears, and then she saw it. Movement behind his lids and a fluttering as if he were trying to open them. She waited, but nothing. The mind, especially a mother's, would always bend facts and details into hope.

"You're doing great, sweet boy. You just hang on and when

you wake up, we will get through this together. Your life is going to be better than it ever was. I promise. I love you so much, Finley." Josie rubbed her eyes, moist and yet gritty, and felt the enormous weight of her spent body. She held Finley's hand, touched his face and hair, and sang more lullabies from his childhood.

A nurse came in with hot coffee for Josie, and after checking Finley's machines and vitals, left with a nod Josie couldn't interpret. She blew into the paper cup and drank the bitter coffee in thirsty gulps despite its heat. It wasn't even eight o'clock, though it seemed like late afternoon. Time meant nothing. The hours were like a finger painting, muddling into shapeless forms that held no significance. It could be noon. Or sunset. And it wouldn't matter. All that mattered was now.

She sat back in the chair and picked up the diaries. People would be coming soon: her mother, Pog, Willa…flipping Pauline! She started to read but must have nodded off, falling from the chair. She scrambled up, unhurt, and returned to Finley's bedside to see if anything had changed in the what? Five minutes she'd been asleep? She scanned the clock, shocked she'd been asleep for nearly an hour. Her son's hair was damp around the ends and beginning to curl. His fingers had turned icy and she warmed them in her palms, blowing her hot, mournful breath into his skin.

Josie sat down again and rifled through the pages of the journal, skipping ahead to the parts she thought most important for her son to hear, and began reading aloud. She read about how she'd almost lost him, going into labor long before her due date. But doctors had saved him all those years ago, giving Josie medication to stop the contractions until he was almost full-term.

She read to him about the time he was seven months old and had his first set of studio photos taken. About how it wasn't planned but they'd seen a big sign at the store for cut-price photos and decided to participate.

You sat up on that carpeted platform, not caring a whit

that you were wearing a stained onesie and a wet diaper. You drew quite an audience with your beaming grin.

You have changed my life like everyone said a baby would, but only for the better. You have enriched my world and made every day special and worth coming home to. I hope one day when you read this, maybe as a grown man, you won't think I was too mushy or sentimental. I just can't help it. I want to always be a good mother.

As usual, my sweet little boy, I love you more each day.

Her throat grew hoarse from reading and Josie set aside the journal and watched her son as if she were waiting for a pot to boil. She wished that a doctor would hurry and get here. It had been too long since anyone had given her any new information—such as what the X-rays showed.

Looking at her comatose child, she thought of all the mothers whose kids had never opened their eyes, never smiled again. She couldn't imagine her child living like this, tethered to this world by technology, having no quality of life other than respirations and heartbeats.

"Come on, Finley. I'm begging you to wake up for Mama. Wiggle your finger if you can hear me talking to you."

Josie stared at her son's hands. Nothing. *God, please let my boy survive this. Please give me a sign that he's going to make it.*

And then it happened.

His blinking lids were unmistakable and not imagined. Her heart rate crescendoed as she squeezed his hand and he flicked his thumb against hers. Weakly, yes. But intentional.

"You're back. My baby's back." Tears poured and her heart flooded. She pressed a hand to her chest to slow her breathing. "I love you so much. I'm never letting you go." His mouth twitched and his eyes suddenly opened. He stared blankly at Josie. "I'm getting the doctor. Sweetheart, hang on. You're waking up. It's going to be fine. Oh, my God, thank you, thank you."

Josie flew to the nurses' station. "He's awake. He's waking up!" The nurse from the night before hurried with Josie to the room. "See? His arms are moving and he—"

"He may become agitated. I'll be right back. I'm getting the doctor on call."

"Wait, is this bad? What's going on?" Images of life or death flashed through her mind. She locked her hands together and willed herself to believe everything would be all right.

"The doctor's on his way," the nurse said when she returned. "Looks like Finley's responding to the treatments. It's a positive sign, but he's not out of the woods yet."

Finley kicked at the sheets; his hands jerked the tubes coiling through his body. "Honey, the doctor's coming. Here, hold my hands. Mama's here. I'm always going to be here." A doctor Josie had never seen arrived within minutes. He smiled and introduced himself and said he needed to do a few tests to evaluate and grade the level of coma.

"He's going to use the GCS, sorry, the Glasgow Coma Scale," the nurse explained. "It'll determine the next steps. You can stay in the room." She patted Josie's arm. The doctor, dressed in a coat and soccer-ball tie, stood over the bed.

"Mr. Chapman, can you open your eyes again?" Josie held her breath. Nothing. "If you understand me, I want you to open your eyes." Again, nothing. The doctor turned to Josie. "This may take longer. Responding to commands. Let's see if he responds to pain."

He lifted Finley's hand and pressed hard on his fingernail. Josie couldn't see her son's reaction so she pushed past the doctor and caught Finley's hazel eyes open and rolling. Her tense shoulders loosened, and she felt instantly lighter. A smile tugged at the corner of her mouth.

"He's registering pain. Mr. Chapman, can you follow this pen?" The doctor moved the pen slowly and Finley's watery eyes struggled but followed. "Good. Excellent. Now, I want you to tell me if you understand where you are. Can you do that?"

"He has a tube in his throat," Josie said, her voice sharper than she'd meant.

He ignored the comment. "I'm Dr. Harwood. You're in the hospital but we're taking good care of you."

Finley's eyes darted and he thrashed, knocking off the covers.

"It's okay. There's plenty of time for this," the doctor said and stepped away.

Josie moved to the other side of the bed. She took her son's hand and he struggled to hold on. His eyes moved side to side, finally focusing on her face. "We've got this. I love you." He grunted and mumbled.

"If you can hear me, please nod," Dr. Harwood said, seeing the patient responding to his mother. Finley's eyes never left Josie's face as he managed a weak nod. "Well done. Ms. Nickels, your son's status is improving. He's waking up. We need to monitor him for a couple of days. Check the kidneys and do more tests. Make sure he doesn't have another seizure. His blood pressure is still low. We'll wean him off the vent before he grows more agitated and tries to pull it out. Overdose patients can get angry and restless when the drugs flush out of their system."

"Is he in withdrawal?" She whispered this and forced her voice into steadiness. She couldn't risk upsetting Finley.

The doctor led Josie into the hallway, and said, "We're trying to prevent it and giving him Clonidine and benzodiazepines. We'll see how he responds to the Suboxone. His father said the Xanax abuse has been going on for years. He's adamant the young man is not a regular opioid user, but he had a high level of fentanyl in his system. Can't quit cold turkey without seizures and other complications. We'll wean him gradually and safely. We'll adjust the ventilator soon to evaluate his breathing. We should have a bed in the ICU in an hour or so. Meanwhile, we've given him something to ease the agitation."

The doctor excused himself, and Josie checked the wall clock. Nine-fifteen and yet it felt like late afternoon. She dug through her duffel bag for the diaries. She sipped tepid Dasani water and read to Finley from her journal while he drifted off to sleep.

23

Just as Josie closed her eyes, a gentle knock thumped at the door. Willa and Pog entered with coffee and bagels. Both hugged Josie tightly, and Pog moved toward Finley and quietly said, "He's got your face, that heart-shaped jawline. Same nose."

"Look at all that curly hair," Willa said in a chirpy voice. "Swirls of toffee. Last time I saw him it was straight and blond."

"He hasn't spent much time in the sun lately. Been in that basement, haven't you, Finley? Well, listen up. When you get better, I'm taking you into the brightest sun you've ever seen where you'll see the most colorful fish God ever made."

Finley stirred. "I think he's waking up again." Josie stood and stretched, her muscles stiff and her neck cramped. "The doctor this morning was very positive, right, sweet child?" she said in a baby voice. She couldn't stop herself from scooting onto the bed and lying next to him. Finley tried to turn toward her, and when he did so, like a baby rooting for its mother, she was reminded that this wasn't a child who hated her.

This was a young man who needed her.

He blinked a few times and nodded off again. Josie slipped from the bed. "I'm going to need to see about Frank soon. And deal with Mother and Pauline." Josie had been too exhausted last night to address that odd situation, but something was up for sure. She'd known it from that first day on the job when Pauline wouldn't stop with the creepy stares and her unrelenting nosiness. How strange that she'd been privy to private family matters that Josie had never made public.

"Let's all go outside and talk," Pog suggested. "Your mother and Pauline have checked in at a Hampton Inn and won't be here for a couple of hours at least."

Do they have to be here at all? Josie wanted to say. "I hardly remember them coming," Josie said as they sat in a small family waiting area. "It's like a dream. A nightmare." They'd stayed what? An hour or so? Her mother had hugged her, albeit stiffly. Pauline kept saying how "terribly sorry" she was.

"Let's get Finley on the mend," Willa said. "You can handle their *whatever* bullshit later."

Pog set down his coffee and clasped Josie's hand. "I want to start preparing for Finley's arrival at the center. It's where he belongs."

Those words infused Josie with a pearl of contentment. "I pray to God he won't turn this one down." She shook her head, remembering all the other failed attempts at treatment.

"He won't. This is a rock bottom. We're getting him excellent psychiatric and medical help at the center, and you're going to quit that makeup job and come work in marketing and PR with me." He smiled as he said this, and Josie knew it was far from a demand. He wanted her there. With him.

"What makes you so sure of that?" Josie didn't know whether to act cool and casual or to thank him. What she wanted to do was reach for his neck and kiss him.

"Because you'll be with Finley. You'll make more money and can work on all kinds of campaigns to tackle this epidemic. This is what you were meant for. Making a difference again." He paused and held Josie's gaze. "And you'll be near me."

She forced a poker face although her soul smiled. "Let me think on it. Right now, I'm going up to see Frank."

"Do you need me to go with you?" Willa asked.

"I think I'd better do it solo. You know how he is."

"When he's feeling up to it," Pog said, "we need to get him on board with Finley's rehab."

"Ha! It'll take PayPal promises to get that man to agree. Listen, if Mother and her little tagalong come, let them know I'll be down soon. And, guys, you don't have to stay here all day. I've got my phone and will call if something changes. I need to make time today to check on Dottie. When I called her last night, she seemed okay, but another night and...well...I also need to give the press a statement."

"I'm not going anywhere," Pog said.

Willa stood and gave Josie a warm hug and gentle shake. "Me either."

ॐ

Frank was sitting up in bed with his right arm wrapped in heavy bandages. Another dressing near his collarbone pushed through the thin hospital gown.

"Frank?" Josie had trouble finding her voice. He tried to get out of bed. "No. I'll come and sit over there."

"Josie. I…I had no idea he had a gun." Frank's voice broke apart and tears streaked his face. As he lay in a flimsy gown and seeping bandages, she nearly wept when seeing his vulnerability. Witnessing her adversary frail and mortal, human and fallible, dismantled the last of her grievances.

"I know," she said. "You were upset and trying to save our son's life. Don't think about it now. You and Finley need to heal physically first." Josie was shocked that she felt no anger. Those four and a half years of resenting and all but loathing this man had vanished. And while she didn't feel romantic love, she felt something. This man, this broken man, was once her husband, and a good one earlier in the marriage. He was also the father of her children.

"I need to be with him," Frank said. "The nurses told me he was improving. Have you seen him?"

"Yes. I spent the night in his room. He's getting better little by little. He can express some emotions and follow commands." She pointed to his wounds. "What about you? All this?"

"Son-of-a-bitch kid selling that fake crap and trying to kill people for a profit. Shot me three times. Nothing broken or life-threatening."

"What's that?" She looked at him and pointed to the bandage behind his ear.

"Shot me in the head. I have a concussion, but the bullet didn't crack my skull. Could have been so much worse. Oh, Josie, I know I've made so many mistakes and I—"

"It's okay."

"He needs help," Frank said, and she was taken aback by this sudden change of tune. "It's gotten bad. Every day it's something worse than the day before. I should have done it years ago when you wanted him—"

"I know. I'm here. I've found him the most amazing place, Frank. It's not a traditional rehab but more a fairyland for addicts. I'll show you all the details, and when you feel up to it, we can discuss—"

"There's nothing to discuss. Sign him up. Now."

Relief washed through her, and her muscles relaxed. "Thank you. I'm going with him. Not for rehab but to work. I've got a job there in PR." She surprised herself. She must have known for weeks that if Pog asked, she'd accept.

"Where is this place?" Frank asked and seemed genuinely interested.

"Near Asheville. Come with me for the first week or so. Heck, you may even like it up there. Get away from this city." She couldn't believe she was inviting Frank to her new town, especially when he'd decided years ago he wouldn't be part of Dottie's life.

"Josie," Frank said, his face falling. "I'm facing charges. Felony strangulation."

"That's ridiculous. The guy tried to kill you."

He shook his head. "I struck first. But to tell you the truth, I don't even remember putting my hands on his neck."

"Maybe you didn't. Let's just go slow and focus on you and Finley getting better and not going back to this lifestyle."

His face softened. "You were right, you know."

"Right?"

"I alienated him from you. I enabled. I wanted some kind of sick revenge for you leaving. I didn't give you much choice."

"I didn't handle things well either. And I'm sorry, truly, about what I said on TV. Listen, we've been given this second and probably only chance, Frank. We need to put our differences aside and work to help our son."

"I know. When can I see him?"

"They're moving him to a room in the ICU. I'll take you down there when we're allowed. Mother's due here any minute. Long story there. Anyway, I'll be back up later. You want anything from the outside world? Real food?"

"Just forgiveness."

"Me too." She turned to leave. She thought about Dottie and wondered if the two would ever be more than pen pals.

"Josie? Wait. I have something for you. My…well…my girlfriend brought it last night from the house. It's time you had this." He sifted through a plastic bag and pulled out a yellow legal pad. "I found it a few weeks ago. Finley had been sober for a week or so before all this. He was writing this to you. He loves you, Josie. You're his mother."

Josie's chest felt as if it were opening and liberating massive stones and long-held burdens. She reached for the legal pad as if it were life support. She was surprised by Frank's reactions and one-eighty change.

"I'm glad you're not alone," she said, realizing she meant it. "How long have you been seeing her?"

"A few months now. She'll be up later. You'll like her."

This was why Frank had changed his tune. Maybe the change was temporary, the way a near-death experience will alter a person until life returns to the status quo. Or maybe it took a man getting shot to inject a stream of sense into his head. Or maybe it was finding someone he loved. Frank had met someone. No longer was he pining for her or retaliating. A man is a simple creature. Give him love, give him security, give him a sense of mattering. Give him all that and the long-set sun in his heart dawns again. She smiled, thinking of Wilma Youngblood's lascivious recipe for a happy man. *Food, fucks,* and something about ball games.

She prayed this new woman stuck with him, knowing that some men need such attachments for stitching old wounds.

24

What caught Josie's eye first were the jeans. She'd seen her mother wear them only twice in her life. Katherine Nickels paired the creased and starched denim with a white square-neck, tailored three-quarter jacket. Pauline sat next to her, reading *What to Expect When You're Expecting* and eating a...what? A Big Mac and fries?

"Morning," Josie said without emotion. "Have you been here long?" She eyed the two up and down and decided she would find the strength to delve into exactly what was going on between them. It was time to settle this mystery for good.

"A few minutes," Katherine said. "How's Finley?" Her mother set down a copy of *The Language of Genes: Solving the Mysteries of Our Genetic Past, Present, and Future.* Good Lord.

"He's improving but still on the machine. I just came down from seeing Frank. He's going to be fine. Nothing major damaged, which is a miracle."

Pauline wiped ketchup from her mouth. "Can we bring you something to eat?"

"It's not even eleven," Josie said, stunned at the sight of Pauline gobbling fast food. "But thanks. Looks good."

"I forgot how scrumptious McDonald's is. Have a fry." She held up the large carton.

"Since when did you start eating real food?"

"Oh, since yesterday when I told Brigman's I was done. Right after finding out what happened with you, I gave my notice."

"You what?" This Mother-Pauline pairing, these words, nothing was making sense.

"I quit. That job made me someone I'm not. Turned me mean and vicious and brought out all my worst and hidden flaws." Since when were her flaws hidden? "With the baby coming and my other income, I should be fine." She patted her little bump.

"Other income?" Josie asked.

"Pauline wants to make amends and see if you two can start fresh," Katherine said with a tight smile. "This might be a one-off, but with your life in shambles, you girls are going to need to get along for everyone's sake."

"What do you mean, Mother? What does Pauline have to do with anything?"

"Let's get Finley up and running and we'll all have a nice dinner and chat," her mother said, and went back to reading her book as if all of this was as explainable as a weather change and not a big deal.

Josie thought of the times her mother had bought Estée Lauder from Pauline. She thought about Pauline's recruiting Josie from Atlanta and wondered if her mother had anything to do with that.

"I'm going to see if they've moved Finley to the ICU," she said, knowing it was pointless to ask her mother anything until the woman was ready to speak. "Once he's in there, there's limited visitation." She directed that comment at Pauline. Then she addressed her mother. "Have you seen Pog?"

"Who?" Katherine asked.

"The man with Willa."

"I thought his name was Paul. They were here a few minutes ago. He's a dapper chap. Probably a nutter, though, the way you attract them."

Josie ignored the insult. "I need to check on things and I'll be back. I appreciate you being here, Mother." To Pauline, she said, "You both have some explaining to do later."

Back in the ER, Josie stepped into Finley's room and saw a group working on transport. Finally. "We'll have him upstairs in a few minutes," someone said. "Bonnie's the nurse on duty and she'll let you know when you can come up."

Josie, not keen on rejoining Pauline and her mother, returned to the family waiting area and pulled out the legal pad

Frank had given her. She held her breath as she read her son's words.

Dear Mother:

It's true. I've been using Xanax and sometimes it's cut with fentanyl. As a college graduate with a minor in science, you'd think I'd know the difference between drug addiction, drug abuse, and using drugs. Turns out I can't distinguish between those things. Remember that time you found me with my eyes rolled back in my head? I can't imagine what your reaction must have been. I think about that every morning when I wake up and it saddens me how much I hurt you and the rest of my family with my addiction. Let me start by telling you how I got into it all.

Remember when I was fourteen and had my wisdom teeth out? That's how the drugs started. I did some research and learned dental surgery is the most common source of opioid prescriptions. Five days after having wisdom teeth removed, most patients have little or no pain but still have well over fifty percent of their opiate painkillers left. That's how the hard stuff started for me, Mom. Well, there'd already been pot and booze, but I'm talking about pills. Mom, there are so many drugs I've been using. I wanted to get off opiates, so I got hooked on kratom. You did a piece on that for the station and asked me if I had tried it and I lied and said no. Kratom acts on the same opioid receptors as painkillers and it's legal, at least in this country. It's poison, Mom. People are dying from it.

Mom, I used to blame you for my addictions. I thought that when you left it caused this hole I needed to fill with drugs. But really, the worst of it started way before Dottie was even born and before you left. Dad and I didn't tell you that we went to the hospital last month. I thought my kidneys had shut down. It was from kratom, Mom. Just like street drugs, kratom isn't regulated by the FDA. There's no way of knowing what the hell is in each batch and it's super addicting. Didn't the president declare a state of emergency with the opioid crisis? Kratom should also be part of this state of emergency.

Mom, I relapsed on crystal meth after that. I did it for a solid week or two and contemplated suicide. A friend brought me CBD oil to calm my nerves and took me to an NA meeting and then a meal at Waffle House. Looking back at the nine years of my life that I've been on drugs, I've done horrible things. Unimaginable things. Like the way I treated you. The unacceptable names I called you. It brings tears to my eyes as I'm writing this because I've relapsed yet again on pills and marijuana.

I've burned so many bridges. I don't know what else to burn besides this pot. Please know that I love you from the bottom of my heart and that nothing you did caused any of this. If something should happen to me, I want you to know this: I wish I'd gone to the rehab places you lined up for me. I guess it's too late at this point.

Josie released a rush of air and forced herself to breathe. Her tears fell on the pages. Kratom. He'd been abusing the psychotropic leaves from that tropical tree in Southeast Asia. She raced to the nurse's station, believing the doctors might have missed this. "It's kratom in his system. Kratom! Did you all find it in his blood?"

"I'll page them in the ICU," the nurse said in a monotone. "They took him up a few minutes ago and I'll let the physicians know immediately. Oh, and what's it called again?"

"Kratom. It's an herb, a dangerous one that can cause lots of serious illnesses and even death. Haven't you heard of it?" The nurse didn't answer. "You can buy it and drink it in teas or pill form. Please, hurry. Call them now and let them know." Josie wasn't leaving until the nurse made the call.

When she finally looked up, Josie shook her head. "I can't believe you don't know what kratom is."

"I just graduated nursing school two months ago," the nurse said, "and they never taught us anything about this. I'm sure the doctors are aware."

Josie knew then that she'd do everything she could to campaign for making this "supplement" illegal. "Please. Find out where my son is. I'm going up there now."

The nurse stopped typing and sighed.

"I can go in peace and with permission," Josie said, "or I'll march up there and find him myself. Your choice."

The nurse scrunched her nose and tucked her lips into a tight half-smile. "I'll call them now."

Fifteen minutes later Josie entered the room. Cloth restraints bound her son's wrists and ankles. The ventilator continued helping him breathe. She felt the bottom drop from her heart seeing him shackled like this. "Finley? Can you hear me? I'm right here." His body jerked and twisted against the sheets. His eyes flickered and opened, and he moaned, trying to speak. A doctor appeared. "Did the nurse in the ER tell you about the kratom?" Josie asked. "She didn't know what it is. Please, do something. He's clearly suffering."

"We're unfortunately seeing a rise in kratom poisoning. Our drug protocol and the measures we've taken will address kratom toxicity. Ms. Nickels, your son had multiple drugs and excessive alcohol in his system, so it's going to be a while before we can know the extent of the damage."

"But he's awake. He's in obvious pain and distress. He seemed to be getting so much better earlier. Why is he suffering now?" Her bone-deep fatigue wasn't helping her resolve to stay composed.

"His body is reacting to all those chemicals and his kidneys and liver aren't functioning the way we'd hoped," the doctor said. "He's begun retaining fluids and his potassium levels are extremely low. You can be with him, but we're going to give him medicine that will make him settle and sleep. If his renal function doesn't improve, we're scheduling dialysis today."

Josie stiffened and held back her emotions at the thought of lifelong damage. "Is this going to be permanent?"

"We hope not."

"I was googling breathing tubes and intubation. I read it's

not good to keep patients on them. I thought you were trying to wean him off."

The doctor shifted and looked at his phone where a call was coming in. "Once we address the psychomotor agitation and rule out other complications, we will begin monitoring his breathing," he said and declined the call. "We're trying to taper his sedating medications so we can assess his functioning, but with drug overdoses, you rarely get a compliant patient, so it's tricky. We need to do another chest X-ray and blood gas analysis, and a pulse ox—in other words, his oxygen saturation. We'll also measure his carbon dioxide and test his neuromuscular strength. Getting him mobile is a priority."

"May I stay with him for a while?"

"Of course. Talk to him and try to reassure him."

"His father wants to see him. And my mother and—"

"Two at a time. Also, anyone who might upset him needn't visit."

Josie dragged the chair as close to Finley's bed as possible. She rummaged through her bag and pulled out parts of her journal. "Are you tired of me reading this diary?" she asked, patting his leg. "I was just so happy when I found out I was pregnant that I couldn't stop writing down everything about it. About you."

Finley's limbs stilled. He opened his eyes and searched her face, nodding for her to read to him. A tear rolled from his eye and Josie wiped it away with her finger. An hour passed before the doctors and respiratory therapists returned and suggested she leave while they performed the tests. She leaned over and kissed her son. "I love you and I'll be back. Try to relax. Good things are right around the corner."

"He's stable," she said to Pog when she returned to the waiting area.

"And you?"

"Wiped out and on autopilot."

"How about we go to lunch? Poor Calvin's is not too far from here, and it's after one. Your mother suggested it. Willa's gone to check on Dottie and clean up before her shift. She'll be back around three."

Poor Calvin's had always been a favorite of Josie's. It was one of Atlanta's best-kept secrets, and it rarely disappointed. The menu, laden with Thai fusion and a Southern flair, was both exotic and comforting. She thought about their fried calamari and the lobster mac 'n' cheese and felt a deepening hunger.

Pog drove in silence but with a faint smile on his lips. In the car Josie caught everyone up on Finley. But she faced the front as she spoke, avoiding direct interaction with her mother and Pauline.

"I'm positively ravenous," Pauline announced, and Josie finally turned to see her smiling ear to ear and holding a polka-dotted gift bag stuffed with pink tissue paper.

"You just ate McDonald's."

"That was over two hours ago. Baby's gotta eat with a capital *E*. Won't be long now. Less than six months to go."

The restaurant was slammed, but Pog had called ahead. They nabbed a table and ordered right away. Josie skimmed the wine selection (old habits) but asked for a Diet Coke. Katherine ordered a seafood curry and tested the waitress's patience with her complicated request for a glass of water infused with lemon and cucumber with a dash of cayenne. Pog selected the crab-meat grilled cheese with wedge fries. Pauline, who'd morphed into someone Josie didn't recognize, ordered fried chicken and a side of fried green tomatoes.

Once the drinks, soups, and salads arrived, Katherine's face wore its closing-argument visage. Pog gripped Josie's elbow as if he knew what her mother was about to blather.

"I know this isn't ideal timing," she began, making eye contact with each member of her audience. "But with Finley's overdose and the family so fractured, I wanted to be right out in the open and discuss certain dynamics. Josie, you are well aware your twin sister died a few months after birth. You are also privy to the fact that I had a hard time getting over her passing, and your father told me more than once that you felt that I held you accountable. That I resented your survival, which is pure rubbish."

Josie dropped her spoon and gaped at Katherine, whose eyes flashed, daring her daughter to challenge this. No one ate. No one drank. Josie's senses blazed. She could smell the golden crust from chickens frying. The aromatic batter of shrimp sizzling. She heard voices speaking a melodic foreign language behind the kitchen doors. Forks clattered and spoons hit the sides of soup bowls. A chill shot through her like ice. Something was off. Something major, and although earlier she'd thought she was ready for explanations, now she wasn't. She needed all her energy focused on Finley. It took every fiber, every molecule, to keep from splitting wide open from everything that had happened to her son, his health uncertain.

"We really don't need to bring this up now," Josie said. "Let's all enjoy the food and then get back to the hospital."

"We are all here together, so I'd say this is the ideal time." Katherine dabbed her lips. A slash of coral streaked the white cloth napkin. "I'm not going to dally here, Josie. Maybe you should tell her." Her mother's eyes pleaded with Pauline.

Pauline seemed stricken. "It's not my place."

"For God's sake. Josie…Pauline is your—"

"We're sisters. Half-sisters." Pauline's eyes met Josie's. And her face exploded into a grin that showed every super-sized tooth.

Had Josie heard them correctly? "I'm sorry. What did you say?"

"We're sisters," Pauline said again, pride in her voice. "When your dad died, it all came out."

Josie's head throbbed and the room tilted. She had no space in her brain to process this bullshit. She pushed from the table and ran outside. Her heart battered against her ribcage. Her stomach seethed. The bagel and coffee from that morning, the few bites of tom yum soup, burbled in her throat. She crawled to the side of the restaurant where a few shrubs struggled for life; she curled into a ball, and then everything went hazy.

The last thing she saw was Pog's knees near her face. And the last thing she felt was his solid arms lifting her and placing her gently in the back seat of his car. Someone draped a cold cloth across her forehead. How much time passed, she didn't know. All she knew was that her body felt as drained as it ever had, as though all her organs had emptied.

The last thing she heard was Pog saying her name so softly she could have imagined it.

Three hours later, Josie awoke in a king-sized bed, her body buried beneath soft sheets and a thick down comforter. "Pog," she said, struggling to find her voice, trying to figure out where she was. It looked like a hotel room but she had no recollection of how she got there. "I need to get back. Finley is probably—"

"He's fine. You're not. Here, I made hot tea and got you crackers."

The news at lunch swam to the surface of her mind. "Is it true?"

"What's that?" Pog asked, fluffing a pillow and helping Josie prop up.

"That she's my sister. Half-sister."

"Let's not think about that right now."

"Pog?" Josie said.

"Yes?"

"Thank you. For taking care of me."

He moved closer and cupped her chin. "I plan to do more of this if you'll let me." He pulled her into a long, slow kiss she didn't resist.

When she finally broke away, breathless and tingling, she searched for the appropriate words. "This…this kiss. It needs to be a one-time thing." She hoped to God it wasn't.

"And why is that? You didn't seem to hate it." His thumb traced her jaw.

"My heart," Josie said. "It's been gutted. And it's currently being renovated and remodeled."

"Interesting," he said and smiled with his eyes. "I just so happen to be a carpenter."

25

Once Finley's condition had been upgraded, Josie felt strong enough to face her mother and sort through the unsettling family disclosures.

Pog had offered to sit in for support. Instead of going back to a restaurant or public venue, they met in her mother's suite at the Hampton, and when they arrived, Pauline was still gripping the same polka-dotted gift bag she'd carried into Poor Calvin's.

"I'm so glad you all could come today," Katherine said as if she were hosting a dinner party. She stood as erect as a heron and swept a thin arm to indicate everyone take a seat. "No one leaves this world without minor blips in their lives." She sat with perfect posture on the patterned love seat, Pauline next to her. She looked at Josie. "Everyone has skeletons. Everyone has pain. It's just with your father's DNA and—"

"I'm not going to sit here and listen to you blame my dad for everything that doesn't suit you," Josie said. *Round one of taking Pog's advice.* "My father is the reason I'm *not* crazy." From having you as a mother, she wanted to add.

Katherine closed her eyes and steepled her fingers. "Your father was a kind but weak man."

"My father was a genius beaten down by a woman with gravel in her chest where a heart should have been."

"Josie, just listen," Pog said, hand on her knee.

"He met a woman named Judith," Katherine said. "She got pregnant but refused his money or child support payments because he stayed married to your mom. She cut off all ties. He'd been putting that money away each month earning interest. It's almost a million dollars."

Josie should have figured this out. Pauline recruiting her from Atlanta, her mother uprooting and moving to Hendersonville out of the blue, Pauline's capital this and that, just like her father's conversations. That photo she'd found was of Pauline. It had to be.

"I really don't blame him for finding love and comfort with Pauline's mother when you ran off to England for what? Almost a year?" Josie said. Pog squeezed her knee as if to suggest she put the brakes on confrontation.

"If you'd calm down and let me finish," Katherine said, waiting what felt like a full minute before continuing. "It was only in the weeks following your father's passing that I learned the truth about his indiscretions."

Josie wanted to scream. Katherine couldn't stop beating the man down even in death. "So, everything is always his fault? You were this perfect little wife who—"

"Your father always wanted more children after Juliette died, but I had my tubes tied. It would have been completely irresponsible of me to bring another child into this world. Nothing short of playing genetic roulette."

Josie shook her head and tried to process her mother's words. Pog reached for her hand. "It's going to be all right," he said. "Look at it as an unexpected blessing."

"Blessing? This half-sister of mine has done everything in her power to see that I—"

"Josie, I have been a total bitch to you," Pauline interrupted. She searched Josie's face, eyes intense. "When your dad died and I learned you were my sister, I wanted you to come to Asheville. I wanted to be near you. Have a real family. Your mother and I are working toward having a relationship, and I'd like to see if we can put all this behind us and start over."

"Is this how *real* family treats each other?" Josie thought of the months of abuse at Brigman's. "Is this the way sisters, half or whole, behave?"

"Josie, I was jealous. You grew up with money and opportunity. I learned everything I could about you after he died, and I found out about all this. I didn't know Mr. Nickels was my dad until your mom and the lawyers got in touch with me about his will. My mother always told me my father died. I didn't push it."

"Will?" Josie had never heard mention of a will. She assumed her mother would inherit what her dad had left. Not his love child.

"Your father just had to have the last word," her mother said, throwing up her hands, sun catching that huge antique sapphire replacing her wedding rings. "He left a long letter spilling the details of Pauline and her mother. I'd had no clue about any of it. Gave her his Steinway. The rest he left to you after I'm gone. Except for a jolly nice sum of back child support."

That's the kind of man her father was. Providing for her mother, a woman who never treated him right. Leaving her comfortable. Giving Pauline years of money her late mother had never accepted. Josie thought about Pauline's similarities to her father. The weak chin, the capital this and that. But if Pauline had never met him, how would she have picked up on that?" Then it dawned on her. Pauline's mother probably used the phrase.

"I still don't get it," Josie said. "I didn't deserve all that... that...abuse you loaded on me for months. No decent person treats anyone like that."

Pauline's shoulders heaved. She let loose a piercing shriek followed by racking sobs whereby her lips got stuck on those tremendous teeth. Pog, uncomfortable seeing anyone in pain, hurried toward her. "I know it hurts," he said, patting her back. "I'm sure Josie will forgive you. Sounds like you need to forgive yourself first."

"Forgive her? Have you any idea the things that woman did to—"

"That woman is your sister, Josie," her mother said. "Sister! But you never even seemed to miss Juliette. Never talked about her. So I don't imagine *sister* means a hill of beans to you."

"That's ridiculous. And you never talked about anything *but* her." Josie stood to leave. How could she miss someone she'd never met? Pauline's crying intensified. Good grief, families were a messy thing. "I can't forgive and forget. But I'll certainly try to forget. Forget all of this hogwash."

Pauline quickly popped to her feet, still blubbering, and thrust the gift bag at Josie. "I hate myself for how I behaved. Here, take this. Open it before you leave. Please." Pog slid a handkerchief from his pockets and gave it to Pauline.

Josie reluctantly removed the tissue paper and braced herself when she saw a maroon velvet box. There, inside a large sterling silver heart on an antique chain, was a photo of Dottie and Finn. The same photo she looked at each night; Finn, nineteen and sober, holding Dottie with boundless love in his eyes.

"There's a card too," Pauline said, her face anticipatory, mascara like wet soot.

"Where did you find...it's my favorite photo."

"Your mother. I've had it for a month. I always wanted to have a relationship with you. I couldn't sort out my thoughts or feelings. Envy can be all-consuming. I was intimidated by you."

Josie walked to the window and stared into the parking lot. She tried to gather her thoughts but found them bouncing like the sun against the cars' chrome. Then she thought of the photo in her underwear drawer.

"I found a picture of a baby girl in Dad's car," Josie said, directly to her mother. "Do you know anything about that?"

Katherine shook her head. "I told you I didn't know any of this sordid business until your father died. It was probably of Pauline as a baby."

She turned to Pauline. "But having me come to Asheville? I don't understand why you wanted me there. To get me canned and berate me every day? I can't figure out—"

"It's messed up, I know." Pauline dropped her head in her hands. When she looked up, fresh tears fell. "I had so many conflicting feelings."

"The woman was in shock," Katherine said. "Have some compassion."

Oh, the nerve of Katherine Nickels. "Mother, why are you even having any sort of relationship with the love child of a cheating husband?" Josie walked from the window and sat next to Pog, who was the only composed person in the room.

"I was upset at first," Katherine said. "Purely gobsmacked. When we met for the first time to go over the will... I don't know... It was as if I had Juliette back. And she does favor your father a bit. Aren't you overjoyed you're going to be an aunt?" Katherine asked, beaming and trying, with her pleasantries, to sweep all this family dirt under the Hampton Inn bed. "I find it rather exciting."

It struck Josie that she had no idea who the father of Pauline's baby was, unless the rumors were true and she was in the family way with Mr. Hoven's child.

"I find it to be like a soap opera," Josie said. "Who's the father, Pauline?"

Pauline smiled. "Kyle."

Josie couldn't have heard that correctly. Kyle was married. And gay! "I thought Mr....well, how could Kyle...never mind."

"For God's sake, Josette," her mother said, voice rising. "Kyle was the donor. It's not like they actually shagged. Pauline has a fabulous partner who'll soon become her wife."

Wife? But Josie had seen Pauline leaving on Thursdays at three fifteen. With Mr. Hoven.

"I know what everyone thinks," Pauline said, reading Josie's thoughts. "Joel Hoven and I had a business relationship. I've been with Molly for almost two years."

Josie was surprised. "I never saw you with a woman."

"I keep my personal life private. She's been with Doctors Without Borders the past year or so. Molly's a midwife and will be back in time to deliver our child."

"Such an accomplished woman," Katherine chirped. "A real hero helping save all those poor babies and their mums."

"I'm sure she is," Josie said, but she was tired and had endured enough titanic revelations for a day. A lifetime. She was desperate to get back to Grady and read to Finley, give him the comfort she'd longed to provide for years. "Pog, you ready?"

"Josie, I know people talked about me and Mr. Hoven. But nothing ever happened between us. I teach his oldest son piano once a week," Pauline said. "I've been playing since I was six."

"Oh, my heavens, she plays brilliantly," Katherine gushed. "Just like your…anyhow, the talent she has is astonishing." Josie tried to take in all of this news, but by now it slid off like rain on a waxed car. The stress was too much. She couldn't listen to one more shocking revelation, so she changed the subject.

"So, Pog's getting Finn lined up for rehab," she said, as if the earlier conversation had never transpired. "I'm planning to live and work there so I'll be nearby until he stabilizes." She didn't dare allow herself to say *if* he stabilizes. *If* he doesn't leave after a few days. What was the saying she'd heard from her group? Feeling good with a short memory? Forgetting what lurks beneath. Always with a fully charged battery.

"What about your condo?" Katherine asked.

"She'll be working at the center," Pog said. "Your daughter can bring to light this drug epidemic and the ineffective way our country runs rehabs."

Katherine raised her eyebrows. "She needs to be back on the telly. Now, Josette, what about your little hovel in Asheville?"

"I guess I'll sell it. I don't know yet. The BMW sold fast, so I'm sure the condo will as well."

"For the life of me, I can't understand why you bought that hillbilly truck." Katherine's mouth rucked as if she'd swallowed vinegar.

Pog laughed and casually put an arm around Josie's shoulders. "She's going to need it. I'm going to have her pulling campers from all sorts of places."

Josie reflected on buying the truck and adding the hitch. It was as if some deep and dormant part of her knew she'd end up needing them. Sometimes life worked itself out long before she was conscious of its plans. "Mother, Pauline, if that's everything, we're going to see Finn."

Katherine rose in slow motion like a queen addressing her court. She placed her hands on Josie's shoulders. "It's not quite everything, dear. Since we're clearing the air, getting all our secrets out in the open, you need to know more about your other sister. Your twin."

"Mother, let's address Juliette another time. I need to go and—"

"You've probably wondered from time to time about that scar running up and down your torso," she said.

"Not really. I keep it covered and mostly forget about it."

"Well…our genes…rather, your father's were…well…for fuck's sake," she all but screamed. "You were ever-so-slightly… just a wee bit really…well…conjoined."

A wave of laughter built like a tsunami. The days of no sleep, turbulent emotions, and family revelations crashed into her. She collapsed on the king bed and laughed until she lost her breath.

"Josette. I'm not joking." Katherine stood at the bed and pushed her daughter's legs to rouse her. "It was nothing but a slight case. They called it omphalopagus twinning. You shared a liver. Nothing else."

Josie sprang from the bed. "Wait. Are you seriously saying this?"

"Just a smidge. Scant amount, in reality. So mild it was simply a few inches of connected tissue. Goodness, if you'd both sneezed, you'd have pulled apart. I wouldn't even let the doctors make public notes of it. Of course, with your father's genetics…"

"Mild? My sister died! I had a liver operation! Pog, it's long past time to go." She picked up her bags and marched to the door.

Katherine followed her, but not out of empathy. "Her body was weaker. You've always been so strong, Josie. Even with the televised—"

"I'm gone. Pauline, thank you for this lovely gift. Mother, I'm going on a sabbatical. Away from you for a while. Away from all of this craziness."

It would have to wait. Perhaps forever. Josie ran a hand down the front of her blouse and grazed her scar, the only link she had to her sister. Maybe this connection, this conjoining, was why she never felt they were apart. Because in some ways, they'd always be together.

26

Eight days after Finley's overdose, his doctors discharged him from the hospital. He was still fragile and unsteady as Josie helped him pack for detox and rehab. He looked like death. All bones and sunken eyes gone dark and dead.

As difficult as it was to watch her son rot from drugs, seeing him so beat down and remorseful was much harder than she'd thought. And the road ahead stretched as fragile as the one behind.

Physically, he'd dodged lasting damage. Mentally, the journey had just begun.

His moods alternated between crying and self-loathing. He constantly asked Josie for forgiveness. It was as if he'd hosted a demon for nearly a decade and a priest had successfully exorcised him. He didn't know how to process these new feelings. Or any feelings. And Josie's emotions shot all over the place, ranging from relief to crippling fear.

Pog had remained at her side for three days, before getting back to his work and young son. The admissions paperwork at Vintage Crazy had already been started. Her son would have a bed there. It was hard to believe. A dream come true.

In the back seat of the truck, Finley rested his head in Dottie's lap and allowed her to pet him like a kitten. "Bubby's good. Good boy, right, Mama?"

"You're both wonderful and precious to me." Tears pooled and she felt the muscles of her heart expanding. "We're going to get your brother all better, sweetpea. Pog, the nice man you met, is fixing us up a real caravan like in the movies. We might get to live for a little while in an old Airstream that's as silver as your princess crowns. Won't that be fun?"

Dottie squealed and Finley flinched. "Let's let Bubby sleep a little while and you play your movies. You're going to love it out in the country. There's a preschool close by and lots of fun stuff to do where we're going. Won't it be nice to be a hop away from Bubby?"

"What about Daddy? He still in sick place?"

Dottie had visited Frank in the hospital. She jumped on his hospital bed and he gave her his ice cream. They'd enjoyed a cuddle or two, and Josie wondered if that was all it would ever be. She hoped not.

"Daddy is all better and back home," she said. "I'm sure he'll come visit once we get settled."

Maybe that white lie wouldn't hurt. Maybe Dottie's questioning wouldn't last. Maybe Pog could step in and become a father figure to her little girl. Maybe Josie should loosen that tape around her heart and reopen the doors to possibilities. She couldn't help smiling as she thought of Paul Oscar Gavins. He'd shown them all honesty, integrity, caring, and compassion.

It was Pog who'd encouraged her to forgive Pauline. At least in words. And it was Pog encouraging her to accept her mother's failings but not tolerate any abuse from her.

Six hours after leaving Atlanta, stopping twice, for lunch and a break, Josie turned into Vintage Crazy's entrance, the truck crunching pea gravel. She had with her only the clothes she'd taken to Atlanta, but she planned to return to Asheville to get her affairs in order. She opened the car door to a blast of late summer heat just as Pog and a few of the staff rushed out with balloons and a cake. "WELCOME TO NEW BEGINNINGS" was written in blue frosting across the white cake featuring an aqua vintage camper.

Finley was sound asleep in the back seat. Josie unbuckled Dottie from the truck, leaving the AC running for Finn. She didn't want to wake him until it was necessary.

Within minutes, a registered nurse and heavyset male technician came out with a wheelchair and rolled her drowsy son toward the detox center.

"It's going to be okay," she said, kissing the top of his head which lolled to one side. He'd already fallen back to sleep.

Once they'd checked Finley's vitals and assigned him a room, Pog took Dottie to a play area, giving Josie privacy with her son, who was in and out of sedation from the seizure medication. "We'll meet back at four-thirty for a group session and have dinner an hour later. If Finley doesn't feel up to it, that's perfectly fine. We aren't too rough on our newcomers the first couple of days. Most of them sleep a day or so."

His room was nothing like Josie's at the state-run facility. There were two single beds, one of them empty. Pog advocated privacy during the first week of a patient's stay. Instead of papery hospital blankets, plump comforters printed with colorful vintage campers covered the beds. Murals lined the walls. On one side of the room, clouds seemed to drift against a powder-blue sky. Another painting displayed dozens of motivational quotes, and large whales and dolphins came to life on the wall behind the two beds. There were two desks and chairs and a bathroom with a toilet and shower, spa-grade toiletries lined on a shelf above plush towels.

"Nice, isn't it?" Josie said, her voice nervous. Here was the moment she'd spent years wishing for. Finley. In rehab. Not dead or in jail. But here. Safe. Still, she couldn't relax, fearing what the MAC mothers wrote about so frequently: their loved ones leaving treatment. But then again, this was different. This wasn't your standard run-of-the-mill rehab.

Finley slumped in the center of the bed, arms folded across his ravaged body. His skin had a gray pallor and a fresh crop of acne sprouted through a week's worth of facial hair. "I guess it's okay. Honestly, Mom, I feel much better. I want to go home."

And here it came. Even Pog said it would, that this was to be expected in the beginning. She had one shot at this and would do everything not to judge or scold. Not be *that* mom. Not pull *that* trigger. "I understand how you feel, son. It's normal. I was in rehab once and felt the same way."

"I need to get back to Dad. What if he goes to jail?" Finley fell against the bed and curled into a fetal position. "It's my fault all this happened. I should have—"

"Don't. He's fine. The kid isn't pressing charges. He has enough other stuff to worry about."

"Dad didn't choke him. He wouldn't do that."

"I know." But Josie didn't know. If she'd been down in the basement witnessing her son overdose under the nose of his dealer, she might have choked him herself. "Your dad said he's coming up next week. After you get into a routine here."

"I love you so much, Mom. But I want to leave." Finley cried and rubbed his bloodshot eyes.

She prayed for patience. With newly clean addicts, land mines simmered at every turn. "No one is forcing you to stay. But this place is different. I hope you'll give it a chance, sweetheart." She grew still for a few moments. When she turned toward her son, he was asleep.

Later that night, after "lights out," Pog led Josie and Dottie to one of the log cabins. "You can stay here. It's fully furnished. Even the kitchen."

"I don't mind staying in one of the bigger campers. It'd be like that guy on *Trapper John, M.D.,* Doctor Gonzo. Dottie's insisting we camp out in a silver Airstream. Once she makes up her mind, whoo." Dottie had fallen asleep and Josie tucked her into a queen bed covered with two handmade quilts. The cabin was perfect with its old-school logs on the outside and modern amenities and bright colors indoors. Art and pottery gave the place warmth and a homey feel. All created by the residents. Josie didn't want to call them patients.

There was an odd awkwardness without Dottie as a buffer. She and Pog faced each other in the living room, eyes locked and neither saying a word. Then he pulled her toward him and she relaxed for the first time in weeks. She felt safe and protected. She was surprised at her disappointment when he didn't kiss her.

"Look, I know we've barely discussed salary and your role here. And I'm not sure how to broach this."

She knew where this was going. "If Finley leaves. That's what you mean."

"Some do. It's the reality of addiction. When the doctors say, 'the next twenty-four, forty-eight hours are crucial,' it's pretty much the same thing in rehab. But at this place, if they make it through a week, the rest is where the transformation begins. After the detox protocol, we give them medications to help with cravings. Places that don't…it's like ripping a pup from his mother's teat and leaving him to flail on his own. Medication has proved as effective as therapy."

Josie sat on the sofa, trying to process everything.

"I'd still want you to stay. No pressure. It's a good job and I'm sure what we can pay is as well or better than selling promises at the counter." His eyes danced. "He's going to make it. Just remember to lie low the first few weeks. None of the other parents are here."

"I'm going to stay a few days, then head home to tie up loose ends before coming back. Is that good for you?"

He tucked a strand of her hair behind her ear. "You're good for me." He kissed her lightly on the lips and said his goodbyes. Whatever this was, he seemed in no hurry. And shouldn't that be how love is? Like a long country two-lane with double yellow lines? No passing. No speeding. No ramps for runaway trucks. Just a meandering trip at forty miles per hour. Taking in fresh air, sunshine, and a world through a different window. One tree, one field, one town at a time.

EPILOGUE

They darted past her. The fish.

Her favorites: the angels and parrots, colors impossibly bold, nature's tattoos on skins slick and shining. Josie slowly swam over the corals and sea fans, some torn and broken, a few reefs battered and ghostly.

It had been almost two years since Hurricane Irma whipped St. John into a war zone, the Category 5 storm one of the strongest on record, its savage lungs ripping up trees and swallowing, digesting, then spitting remains.

Josie's beloved island, at least half national park and all but leveled in the storm, now stretched lush and green, having mostly recovered. In some places blue tarps draped roofs and rubble remained from houses beyond repair. The island's beauty was profound, survivable. All around were sounds of construction, new businesses coming where others had perished in the storm. Houses going up. Roads repaired. And the grand hotels opening and flowing with tourists.

Recovery is a slow journey, a voyage you don't see until it's over. For the island. And for her son.

Josie kicked her legs and leisurely snorkeled her way back to the shallows of Salt Pond Bay. She lifted her mask, rubbed out the dents on her face, and shook the sea from the mouthpiece. The sun bit into her skin and climbed the sky, its heat both fierce and comforting. She pulled off her fins and walked a few yards down the crescent beach until she reached the portable cabana.

"It's not the same since Irma," she said. "I guess very few things ever are."

"No, and they shouldn't be." Pog smiled and wiped the sand from her chin. "Everything in life needs change. Growth can't happen in complacency."

"No. I guess not." Josie squeezed water from her hair, long and once again brown with caramel highlights. She'd lost twenty-five pounds in the past year while working at the rehab and resort and eating the nourishing foods from the farms. She wasn't worried about the other twenty-five and felt content. The extra weight suited her, and Pog loved her at any size. More importantly, she loved herself for the first time in years. While Finley worked on his amends during treatment, Josie worked on hers, sending the TV station a three-page apology for her actions. She also apologized to her former viewers in a two-minute-video message she'd recorded. The station aired it and job offers poured in. She politely thanked those recruiting her, but her life's work had taken a different path.

She spotted her son lying face down on a towel near the cabana, sun broiling his back, nose in a book. He looked good. Really good. He'd gained thirty pounds in the early months of treatment and the summer months had toasted his skin and lightened the curls at his neck. It's odd that what she'd expected her son to do, he hadn't done. Kids were more than an extension of a mother's thoughts. They bounced and pinged and never ended up quite as we'd imagined.

Josie had figured Finley would brood and prefer four walls and solitude, his face in screens. With all Vintage's residents required to work, she thought he'd choose computers or numbers or one of the white-collar offerings. But he hadn't. From the second month, he spent most of the daylight hours—when not in groups or therapies—outdoors, hoeing and planting. He took guests out on the river for fishing trips. He pounded a hammer and ran electric saws, transforming those dilapidated campers into sparkling showplaces. Driven to restore their souls, he ripped out the rot and blight until his pastel shirts turned dark with sweat.

After the first week at the treatment compound, she'd shared her dream of St. John and promised they'd go together after he'd completed his first year of sobriety. Except for a two-day relapse, he'd done well. Progress. Not perfection.

It had happened after the second week. She and Dottie awakened to a gentle tapping on the cabin door. Pog stood in the summer rain, fat drops rolling off his cap. "He's gone. Don't know how far he'll get without his cell. He must have arranged it last night before we locked up the phones."

Josie had let the words register. She'd motioned for Pog to come in and they sat on the sofa, Dottie heavy on her hip and thumb in her mouth, Mary-Mary in tatters near her cheek. "What's next?" she'd asked. Finley had shown no signs of wanting to leave. He'd participated in groups, seen the therapists and a psychiatrist who'd prescribed non-addictive meds for his anxiety and low-grade depression. "I don't know that I have it in me to keep this up, worrying night and day about another overdose. Another drug deal turned—"

"This is where you need to be tough. You know, Josie, as well as any of us, that relapse is part of recovery. A person can't rebuild without every wall coming down first."

Did she have the strength to go through this again? She thought of the mothers with nothing left but headstones or ashes. Every one of them had said they'd choose addiction's wreckage over laying out final clothes. They would rather live each day stewing in stress and heartache than never being able to wrap their sons and daughters in their arms.

Where there's breath, there's promise.

Late on the second night, Finley returned, dirty, shaking, and desperate. Stoned. "I'm scared," he said, looking at his feet.

"You should be." Josie pulled him into her.

"When will I beat this? Graduate or something?"

"You won't. It's not a race. There's no finish line. Each lap you get stronger. Each lap you go farther."

He hadn't left since.

Now, as she watched him reading, she marveled at the peace in his face, his body relaxed and not in the constant flight of chasing poison to plug his inner holes.

With the St. John sun showing no mercy this time of year, she saw his back rise and fall and was reminded again of when she first brought him home from the hospital and willed him to keep breathing.

"So, what do you think?" She unfurled her towel and placed it next to Finley's. "Pretty remarkable place, huh?"

He didn't seem to hear her, buried in a sci-fi novel, reading again after all those lost years. They'd been on the island a full day, staying in a Spanish-style four-bedroom villa in Coral Bay, aptly named "Ambrosia." It was a private, gated estate with a shimmering swimming pool and bathhouse and breathtaking views of the island. Pog had put Josie in charge of booking the villa, but she refused to let him pay her share of the expenses. She loved the man, God how she loved him, and the sex… She burned just thinking about it.

This trip, though, had been one she'd promised her son, and to have a man pay didn't seem right. He was paying her plenty to lobby legislators for drug reform, and she'd even worked some as a freelance on-air correspondent, selecting topics that revolved around addiction.

She'd sold the condo at 34 Could Be Worse Court for a small profit. And with her salary, plus free lodging in a spacious 1953 Airstream Cruiser she and Dottie had done up in a pink and black-and-white theme, she'd saved a small cushion.

Everyone she loved was with her: Dottie, Philly and Carmen, and Pog and his son, along with Willa and her youngest, who'd been clean for years. Pauline had also come, bringing Molly, who was now her wife, and their seven-month-old daughter, a gorgeous little thing with loads of dark curly hair who'd begun to crawl and constantly babbled. Pauline had named her Juliette as a way of honoring Josie's twin. Their sister.

Monica had taken Lowell back and couldn't make it. Kyle was coming with his husband for a couple of days at the end of the week to see the baby. Josie had wanted Ruby to join them, but the woman had sent a letter a week after Finley left the hospital.

"My work is done," she wrote. "I'll be leaving now for another little assignment, so to speak. Please, know this: I'll always be watching. So never stop hoping. Never stop praying." Inside the envelope was every bit of the babysitting money Josie had paid her. And a clipping of the newspaper article that had featured Vintage Crazy. The same article that had landed at her feet that morning last year.

Sometimes Josie wondered if Ruby had *actually* existed. People, she'd always been told, come into your life for a reason. And often just a season.

"Pretty cool little spot, right?" she said to Finley, squatting so he'd hear her.

He closed his paperback and sat up, both of them looking out over the sea, six shades of blue and green and smooth as a pebble. "I don't want to leave, Mom. It's unbelievable here. Dad would love it."

Josie put her hand on Finley's warm back. "He's going to Virgin Gorda and the BVIs for his honeymoon. He said he may sail over one afternoon."

"Cool. Hey, how 'bout we get a bite later and hit Waterlemon Cay for the awesome snorkeling you've told me about?" He was back, the Finley who'd existed before the madness of addiction. "Mom?"

"Yes, sweetheart?"

"You might want to fix your swimsuit before we go back out there."

Josie followed his eyes to a loop of elastic hanging from her bottoms. She laughed and was glad she'd brought extras. "I told you I plan to keep my face underwater at least seventy-five percent of the vacation. Waterlemon it is!"

"Don't forget those two days we're volunteering," he said. They'd signed up with the Friends of the Virgin Islands National Park to help with what remained of the beach and island cleanup. It seemed her son couldn't satiate his appetite for physical labor.

It would be years before this island fully recovered. Many of its landmarks, such as Josie's beloved Concordia Eco-Resort, might never rebuild. The island would change. A thing destroyed and rebuilt is never the same. Maybe that's a good thing.

Instead of seeing her island as a victim, Josie was in awe of its spirit not just to survive, but to become better. Like Finley. That evening, as everyone gathered on the covered terrace and enjoyed fat boiled shrimp, fried crab cakes, corn, and red potatoes, Josie stood at the edge of the balcony. She squinted as the sun sank on another day, stirring the water into pools of topaz and turquoise and revealing the island's amber heart.

As the others lingered over dinner, Finn nudged her from her trance. "Mom? You okay?"

"I used to chase happiness," Josie said, watching the water, the pelicans, and sailboats drifting past. "I thought that if I did everything right, exactly by the book, the way everyone expected...I don't know. It's not that way. It's like the women rushing into the store thinking that buying a new outfit or makeup will make them happy. It's fun, maybe it feels good, but once it's worn or used a time or two it loses its power. Joy, though, is different. Joy is rich and calming. A sense of complete contentment for what's going on in the moment. "

"Deep, Mom," he said and slipped his arm around her as they viewed the day melting to dusk.

"Ruby must've worn off on me."

Josie would join the others soon. They would all chip in and do the dishes, sit around the long dining table, or sprawl out on the sofas and chairs. They might play charades or board games or spend the evening talking and laughing. She would listen as Pauline chattered and had fits over Juliette, Josie's own heart enamored with the child, her niece. She would try to find the good in her half-sister, who'd become much nicer with Molly in her life. She might even think about her mother and wonder if she was enjoying England this time of year.

Later, with the full Sturgeon Moon like a watchful eye above them, she would crawl into bed, foot reaching for Dottie's, and go over the day in her mind. Once her daughter had begun her purring, she'd ease out, tiptoe downstairs, and gently knock on the door where Finley slept on the bottom bunk.

And just like when he was a boy, with *Power Rangers* posters on his wall, *Star Wars* figures guarding his nightstand, she'd whisper the stories of their lives. Or maybe, she'd just listen to him breathe.

Thanks to the women who've allowed me in their book club, "The Not Quite Write Book Club," for the past couple of decades. Cheers to our leader and founder, Laurie Pappas, and to Stephanie Beach, Joan D'entremont, Maite Harte, Gray Looper, Louise McCauley, Nancy Twigg, Sandy Waldrop and Diane Knoebber.

I'd also like to thank the amazing Women's Fiction Writers Association for all their contributions to authors who write in this versatile genre. And to my high school friends from La-Grange, Georgia, who agreed to be part of my street team. Go Grangers!

Finally, a nod to those in the medical field who helped with the hospital scenes: Dr. Will Jones, a debonair Southern doc and fitness guru; Sherry Rambin, a fantastic nurse, photographer, and family friend; and my "brand-new" cousin, Joanna Brabham, a nurse anesthetist and Clemson fan who has been known to pull for my team, the Georgia Bulldogs.

But most of all I want to thank every person on the frontlines of addiction. Whether you're in the trenches, in treatment, or in recovery, or are family members and friends of those brave souls seeking freedom from addiction's bonds, I honor you all.

I couldn't have made it without the support group The Addict's Mom™ for the mothers of those who suffer from Substance Use Disorder (SUD) and whose mission is dedicated to giving members a place to "Share Without Shame" their personal journeys relating to substance use in their family.

May your loved ones find the path to grace and healing. May you never lose hope.

Acknowledgments

While this is a work of fiction, I couldn't have done it without the love and support from my son Niles Reinhardt. His own experiences overcoming drugs, his research, and introducing me to others suffering from addiction made this more real. More accurate. And more human.

Thank you, Niles, for the inspiration behind the diaries. When I was pregnant with you, my firstborn, I kept similar journals from your conception through those first years.

God gave you life. And you gave mine meaning.

I'd also like to thank my daughter, Lindsey Reinhardt, whose compassion and work with those in active addiction also contributed to the storylines of this novel. I'm sorry, Lindsey. You are an equal and beautiful occupant of my heart, but life was busier when you came along, and my diaries weren't as detailed.

The luxury to spend much of my time writing wouldn't have been possible without the support of my husband, Donny Laws.

I'd also like to thank my editor Pam Van Dyk, whose talents made this novel shine with her excellent skills. And to Jaynie Royal and the Regal House Publishing team who believed in this story, and from the moment I signed the contract have been a dream to work with.

Thanks to my Facebook and Twitter friends, including my main critique partners and others who were early readers.

I'd also like to thank my parents, Sam and Peggy Gambrell, who've been behind me in this writing journey since I was twelve and penning angst-filled poetry about unrequited love. You both made this dream possible. And you're brave enough to "hawk" my saucy material to family members and church friends. As our little joke goes, "Y'all can always go to altar call if this novel offends you."